Prais
WALLB

"An instant classic, with plenty of laugh-out-loud moments and riveting characters."

—Jennifer Probst, *New York Times* bestselling author of *Searching for Perfect*

"Sultry, seXXXy, super-awesome . . . we LOVE it!"

—Perez Hilton

"Fun and frothy, with a bawdy undercurrent and a hero guaranteed to make your knees wobbly . . . *Wallbanger* delivers the perfect blend of sex, romance, and baked goods."

—Ruthie Knox, bestselling author of *About Last Night*

"Alice Clayton strikes again, seducing me with her real woman sex appeal, unparalleled wit and addicting snark; leaving me laughing, blushing, and craving knock all the paintings off the wall sex of my very own."

—Humor blogger Brittany Gibbons

"Finally a woman who knows her way around a man *and* a Kitchen-Aid Mixer. She had us at zucchini bread!"

—*Curvy Girl Guide*

"A funny, madcap, smexy romantic contemporary. . . . Fast pacing and a smooth flowing story line will keep you in stitches. . . ."

—*Smexy Books*

THE REDHEAD PLAYS HER HAND

"This zany and smoking-hot romance will keep readers in stitches as two strong, well-defined protagonists struggle to navigate their relationship while fame, jealousy, and snarky fans attack from all sides. Fast pacing, witty dialogue, and a cast of well-meaning friends provide the script for an Oscar-worthy story about a couple whose journey has delighted readers since the beginning."

—*RT Book Reviews*

"Completely sigh worthy . . . a must-read for contemporary romance lovers."

—*Fiction Vixen*

"As fresh and sassy as ever. . . . Alice Clayton makes me laugh, cringe, yell at the characters and cry."

—*Harlequin Junkie*

"I adore Grace and Jack. They have such amazing chemistry. The love that flows between them scorches the pages. These two are soul mates who are destined to be together and you believe that with all your heart."

—*Smexy Books*

"Great humor and sex . . . Alice continues to make me laugh out loud, and then writes a scene so hot I swear the windows steam up in the room I'm reading it in."

—*Bookish Temptations*

THE REDHEAD REVEALED

"The love that flows between Jack and Grace scorches the pages. Witty commentary and playful hilarious sexual banter adds laughter and realism to this story. It's unusual when an author can find a healthy sexual balance that translates well to paper without sounding raunchy. . . . Hilarious, snarky, smexy, [and] romantic. . . ."

—*Smexy Books*

"Steamy romance, witty characters and a barrel full of laughs. . . ."

—*The Book Vixen*

"The serious parts of the story (Grace's self-doubts, the long distance between Grace and Jack and dealing with the paparazzi) together with the fun scenes full of witty remarks and the very hot sex scenes make this book so special and great. *The Redhead Revealed* will make you laugh, smile, cry and might also get you thinking about some serious issues."

—*About Happy Books*

"Where has this series been all my life? It's just the right touch of everything that makes a book a good read. It had romance (and some steamy sex), funny parts, things that make you cry."

—*One Book at a Time*

"Another wonderful addition to this series. I laughed out loud on the airplane reading this baby. It's funny, sexy, and has an addictive ongoing story line."

—*Penelope's Romance Reviews*

THE UNIDENTIFIED REDHEAD

"Laugh out loud funny."

—*Smokin Hot Books*

"If you like your contemporaries sexy, funny, and made of pure fun then get Alice Clayton's *The Unidentified Redhead* and get ready for a wild laughter filled read about Hollywood, cougars, and poo heads."

—*Smexy Books*

"Reading this was the equivalent of going out for martinis with Ms. Clayton and swapping lengthy pop diatribes and chortling our way through witty repartee."

—*Alpha Reader*

"Not only was Grace and Jack's chemistry off the roof, but their romance was an utterly captivating and engaging one that I couldn't help but gobble up as fast as I could."

—*Larissa's Bookish Life*

also by alice clayton

Wallbanger

The Unidentified Redhead

The Redhead Revealed

The Redhead Plays Her Hand

RUSTY NAILED

alice clayton

G

GALLERY BOOKS

NEW YORK   LONDON   TORONTO   SYDNEY   NEW DELHI

Gallery Books
A Division of Simon & Schuster, Inc.
1230 Avenue of the Americas
New York, NY 10020

First Gallery Books trade paperback edition June 2014

GALLERY BOOKS and colophon are registered trademarks of Simon & Schuster, Inc.

For information about special discounts for bulk purchases, please contact
Simon & Schuster Special Sales at 1-866-506-1949 or business@simonandschuster.com.

The Simon & Schuster Speakers Bureau can bring authors to your live event. For more
information or to book an event contact the Simon & Schuster Speakers Bureau at
1-866-248-3049 or visit our website at www.simonspeakers.com.

Manufactured in the United States of America

10 9 8 7 6 5 4 3 2 1

Library of Congress Cataloging-in-Publication Data

Clayton, Alice
  Rusty nailed / Alice Clayton.
     pages cm — (The Cocktail series)
  Gallery Original fiction trade.
     I. Title.
  PS3603.L3968R87 2014
  813'.6—dc23   2014008624

ISBN 978-1-4767-6666-9
ISBN 978-1-4767-6673-7 (ebook)

To Peter
For being there before, during,
and always ever after.
Thanks for keeping me sane.
Which is a relative term.
XOXO

acknowledgments

This book is 100 percent the result of wanting Banger Nation to have a little more time with their Simon and Caroline. It is because of you, you perfect reader you, that this book is even on the page. Thank you for being patient as you waited for it, for being mouthy when you told all your girlfriends to read it, for being steadfast in your devotion that sexy and silly *can* exist in the same space. Banger Nation, you get me. So this is for you. Thank you from the bottom of my tiny Grinch heart.

Thank you to my editor, Micki Nuding, and the entire team at Gallery Books for taking such an enormous chance on a new author. Most days I have to pinch myself to make sure I'm not dreaming.

Thank you to my San Francisco/Sausalito detail police, the one and only Staci Reilly. And yes, the Hillevator is real and she could tell you some stories . . .

Thank you to my family, who is incredibly patient with me when I have to say no to things because I'm on a deadline, and for remembering that even though I work in my pajamas some days, it's still work.

Thank you to the bloggers who bang this drum day in and day out, promoting all of us authors and putting our books into the hands of your readers. At the end of the day, I am a reader first and a writer second. I appreciate your love of storytelling and your eagerness to share your new favorite book more than you know.

Thank you to some of my favorite authors on the planet, whose words I not only love but who I can now call friends: Kristen Proby, Tiffany Reisz, Jennifer Probst, Ruthie Knox, Kresley Cole, Samantha Young, Sylvia Day, Helena Hunting, Debra Anastasia, Mina Vaughn, Leisa Rayven, EL James, Katy Evans, Jasinda Wilder. Thanks, ladies.

Thank you to Christina Hogrebe, my agent and friend and guide to this crazy world of Get Alice on the Shelves. You're a brave woman, and I appreciate you a thousand ways. Looking forward to the next meal at Mohonk when we are celebrating something big!

Thank you to one of my oldest and dearest friends, Jessica Royer-Ocken, who has literally gone through the fires of hell to help get this book ready. The fires of hell being my lack of punctuation skillz and my shitty formatting capabilities. Not to mention, she's a helluva sounding board. And not a bad baker . . .

Thank you to the Captain Hookers, my partners in crime, PQ and Lo (you'd know them as Christina Lauren). For the podcasting, for the texting, for the Tower of Terror. For the love of the mouse.

Thank you to Nina, the best taco a girl could ever ask for. Thank you for the endless motivation, the RPatz pics, and the Gummi Bears when I get fussy. Which, let's face it, is almost always. Can't wait for your book!

And a big fat thank you, thank you, and thank you again to you Fantastically Loyal Readers. To those of you who've been here from the beginning, to those of you who are just jumping on the Crazy train, thank you. It's been the ride of a lifetime, and it's just the beginning. So hold on tight, chickens; here we go!

Alice
XOXO

prologue

It was the best of times, it was the nakedest of times . . .

December

I'd never spent a Christmas away from my family. Christmas to me *is* family: immediate, extended, and later, created. My family and friends gather, trees are trimmed, presents are wrapped, nog is made and most certainly consumed. It's Norman Rockwell, with a drunk uncle. I wouldn't change it for the world.

Except this year. This Christmas was entirely different. This was Rockwellian with a Wallbanger twist.

As a freelance photographer, Simon had a seriously cool job. He traveled the world on assignment for *National Geographic* and Discovery Channel, or whoever needed a photographer to go to the farthest-flung places on earth. This Christmas he was photographing European cities in their holiday best, and he'd be gone nearly the entire month of December.

Since officially becoming a *we*, we'd settled into our own normal. He'd continued to travel for work, booking trips all over the world: Peru, Chile, England, even a long weekend in LA to do a study at the Playboy Mansion . . . Hardship.

But when my globe-trotting Wallbanger's home, he's *home*. Home with me, either in my apartment or in his. Home with me for the dinners out with Jillian and Benjamin, or playing poker with the other two couples that make up our best friends. Home with me, in my bed or his, my kitchen or his, *on my counter or his*—home.

Yet apparently Simon was *always* away on Christmas. He'd taken jobs in Rome, covering the mass in St. Peter's Square. The Vanuatu Islands in the South Pacific, the first time zone to celebrate the holiday. He'd even traveled to the North Pole one year and made a snow angel at midnight.

Strange, you say? Not really. His parents were killed in a car accident when he was a senior in high school. Eighteen years old, and his entire world was turned upside down. With no other family, he left Philadelphia a few months later when he enrolled at Stanford, and never looked back.

So yeah, Christmas was hard on him. I was beginning to understand my Wallbanger, beyond the man, the myth, the legend. Holidays were sticky in general. And as such a new couple, Christmas with *my* parents would be a Very Big Deal. He hadn't even met them yet, and a Reynolds Family Christmas was perhaps not the best time to take that major *we* step.

So I wasn't surprised when he started planning to be away for the entire month. The surprise was all on him when I brazenly invited myself along.

"From Prague I'm heading to Vienna, then Salzburg, and I'll probably be there on Christmas. They have this festival where they—"

"I'm coming."

"Still? Damn, I'm good. We finished an hour ago . . ." He covered the area between my legs with one of his beautiful hands. We were lying in bed, well into the late-November night. He was home for a few days between trips, and we were nooking after nookie.

"No, sir, I mean I'm coming with you to Europe. I'd like to spend our first Christmas together actually *together*. It'll be fun!"

"But what about your parents? Won't they be disappointed?"

"Sure, but they'll get over it. Will there be snow?"

"Snow? Yes, of course there'll be snow! Are you sure about this? I've been alone most Christmases the last few years. It's not a big deal. I don't mind being alone," he said, not meeting my eyes.

I smiled and lifted his chin. "I mind it, okay? Besides, I have the week off between Christmas and New Year's, so I'm coming. It's settled."

"You're bossy, Ms. Reynolds," he noted, moving his hand decidedly south of my hip.

"Yes, I am, Mr. Parker. Don't stop doing what you're doing there . . . mmm . . ."

And that's how I found myself in a holiday fairy tale. I flew into Salzburg, Austria, where we stayed in a wonderful little inn in the old city center—snow falling, trees lit with thousands of little white lights, and Simon looking ridiculously adorable in a ski cap with a pouf at the end. Being supremely touristy, he'd arranged for a horse-drawn sleigh with actual jingle bells. On Christmas Eve, underneath a warm blanket and wrapped entirely in Simon, I gazed out at the city and the moonlight on the river.

"I'm so glad you're here," he whispered, followed by a light nip to my ear.

"I knew you would be." I chuckled as he snuck a hand underneath my sweater.

"Love you," he murmured, his voice laced with honey.

"Love you more," I answered, my eyes sparkling with tears.

New tradition? We'll see . . .

• • •

February 14

Text from Simon to Caroline:

> Just pulled up, you ready
> to go?

> > Almost. Still need to get
> > dressed. Just come on in.

> I'm on my way up the stairs.
> We're going to be late.

> > No, we won't. Just keep
> > your pants on.

> Never heard that before.

> > Quit kicking my door and
> > get in here!

I pressed send, then settled back against the kitchen counter. I could hear his key in the lock, and I muffled a grin. We were due to meet the gang for a romantic dinner in twenty minutes. With traffic, we'd be very lucky to make it in forty. If I was even luckier, we wouldn't make it at all.

"Babe! What're you doing? We gotta go!" he called. I could hear him dump his bag in the entryway.

As he came down the hall, I sighed dramatically and called back, "I decided against going out tonight. I'm not feeling so good." I heard him stop dead in his tracks, and I would've bet my Le Creuset double boiler he was running his hands through his hair and swallowing a sigh.

I'd been pestering him for weeks to take me out for Valentine's Day, and I'd insisted we make it a night out with our friends. But he was only home for a week, and I knew that he wanted nothing more than to stay in, veg out on the couch, and sleep with his girlfriend.

Girlfriend.

I still get goose bumps when I ponder this. I'm Simon's girl-friend. He was once the Harem Master, and now I'm his *girlfriend*.

So, after dropping hints to him since mid-January about making sure he'd be home for Valentine's Day, and then spending hours on the phone with Sophia and Mimi planning the perfect romantic evening out, my deciding at the last minute to stay in had to be making him question exactly why he'd decided a girlfriend was something he wanted.

"You sure about that? I thought you had your heart set on—"

He stopped as he rounded the corner to the kitchen. Perched on the counter, wearing an apron, a grin, and six-inch heels, was *moi*. Holding an apple pie on my lap.

"I have my heart set on something," I told him. "But it isn't a crowded restaurant. How could I get away with wearing only this?" I hopped down from the counter and turned around. Oh yeah, I was wearing the apron, and only the apron. And the shoes—don't forget the shoes.

"Caroline. Wow," he managed.

I grinned bigger. "I have pie."

"You sure do."

"Silly boy, I *baked* for you. Your very own hot apple pie. All you have to do is come over here and get it." I broke off a piece of the crust and dragged it through the cinnamon sugar goo dripping down the side. Would he want pie or me first?

Turns out, he wanted both.

April

"See, now, I thought we were making progress. We watch baseball together, I sneak you peanut butter every now and again, and you go and do this? Why? *Why* do you continue to do this? And furthermore, why do I continue to allow this to happen?"

As I reached the top of the stairs, I overheard the conversation inside my apartment. Simon was home alone—maybe he was on the phone. Once inside, however, I peeked around the corner and found him sitting across the table from my cat, Clive, his Stanford sweatshirt between them. Clive had "marked his territory" on this very sweatshirt several times early on in our relationship, but it had been a while since he'd deemed it necessary to remind Simon who was the actual man of the house. We both thought Clive was over this particular peccadillo. Apparently not . . .

I stifled a laugh at how seriously Simon was staring at Clive, and how unseriously Clive seemed to be taking all this, batting at his tail as though it were unattached from his body. I backed down the hall silently, and then made a big show of rattling the doorknob to let them know I was home.

When I came into the dining room again, I found Simon reading the newspaper nonchalantly. He made no mention of the conversation he'd been having with my cat.

I allowed him that dignity, and pretended not to notice when I found the sweatshirt in the trash a few hours later.

May

A noise filled the bedroom, rending the night and pounding my eardrums. A great sawing, a loudness of indeterminate origin dragged me from my dreams of Clooney. I was sweltering, with a very warm body wrapped around me from the back and horrible noises pouring forth from his mouth, directly into my brain. I grappled for a cool spot on my pillow, his heat billowing toward me in waves as the snoring—oh my sweet Lord, the snoring—rattled my insides.

Even Clive had retreated to a safe perch on top of the dresser.

In a completely shit move reminiscent of schoolyard playgrounds, I drew back my legs and kicked the mass of sweaty, snoring boy that was filling my bed and ruining my sleep.

"Oof!" He woke with a start, inadvertently pressing more of his hot skin against mine. I peeled myself off the bed to stand over him, brandishing my pillow, which no longer contained even an ounce of coolness.

"Babe, what're you doing? Did you kick me?" He curled back in on himself like a roly-poly.

"You have to stop!" I yelled.

"Stop? Stop what? Come on . . . come back to bed," he mumbled, already slipping back into his dreams, where he seemed to be a lumberjack.

"Don't you dare go back to sleep! No! More! Snoring!" I yelled, wild inside and out now. Being deprived of my sacred sleep turned me into a woman possessed.

"Snoring? Come on, it can't be that bad—what the hell!"

I'd snatched his pillow away, dropping his head to the mattress.

"If I can't sleep, *no* one will sleep! You are *loud,* and you are *hot!*" I shrieked.

"Well, the hot we knew, right?"

"Aaarrgghh!"

"Wait, are you PMS-ing?" he asked, almost immediately looking fearful as he realized his mistake.

Simon finished the night across the hall in his own apartment. I needed my sleep.

July

"Goddamn, Caroline, that was amazing."

"Yes, yes it was," I purred, stretching my legs around him, clutching him closer to me, feeling him still inside me. His breathing synched with mine, relaxing into me as I scratched at his scalp and made little patterns on his back with my fingertips. After a few minutes he raised up on one elbow, and I smoothed his hair back.

"You didn't come, did you?"

"No, sweetie, but it was fantastic anyway."

"Let me make it up to you," he insisted, moving his hand in between us, surprised when I stopped him. "Babe?"

"It's not always about that. It can still be amazing, you know? Some nights, being here, being close with you, is all I need," I said, bringing him down for another kiss, slow and sweet. "I love you so much," I whispered in his ear, his answering grin making my heart swell.

After the Great Orgasm Hiatus, which in my head is how it was officially known across the land, was she always there for me? Of course not, not every time. But mostly she was there, and mostly she was there for multiple Os, and sometimes she brought G with her. Those were the nights I damn near passed out.

But while I loved the countertop sex, and the shower sex, and the kitchen floor sex, and the stairway sex—well, one night of stairway sex—the quiet sex was still my favorite. When it was Simon on top of me, letting me feel his good weight and his good love pressing down on me, inside me, all around me. And if on occasion the O stayed away, it was okay.

I knew she would always return.

Simon shuffled back toward the bed, bringing a bottle of water with him, Clive close at his heels. Clive wisely stayed away during the relations; he'd attacked once and was almost punted. So now he took cover away from the action. Simon getting water was the signal that he could come back in to snuggle.

As Simon passed me the bottle, I turned on the news to check the weather for the next day to see if I'd need an umbrella. Each on our own side, with Clive in between us, we watched the forecast. Our hands were clasped on the pillow in between.

Pretty fucking great.

• • •

August

"Go ahead, I know you're dying to say it."

"I don't think I have to, Caroline. Your moaning is saying it all."

"No, no, I know you want to. Go ahead."

"Fine. I told you so."

"Feel better?"

"Yes."

"Good. Now shut up and let me get back to my noodles."

Simon laughed as I slurped up my pho, a delicious Vietnamese noodle soup. For years, I thought I didn't like Vietnamese food. I suppose eating it in Vietnam made all the difference.

Once again, being Simon's girlfriend had proved to be a windfall. He'd invited me along on a trip in Southeast Asia: Laos, Cambodia, and ending in Vietnam. I couldn't join him for the entire journey, but I was able to meet him in Hanoi and spend a week with him as he photographed for *National Geographic*. We toured cities and villages, sandy beaches and quiet mountaintops. We ate amazing food every day, and loved our way through every night.

Our current state of amazing found us floating in Ha Long Bay, eating a wonderful meal that had been cooked on the houseboat we were staying on. I gazed at the tiny islands, which broke the surface of the water like the backs of dragons swooping up from underneath. The sun was setting, and to cool off from the sweltering heat, Simon had taken a dive off the back of the boat. Water trickled off his skin, his cargo shorts stuck to his legs, and his shirtless torso made my mouth water even more than the pho, so life was good.

Of all the trips I'd taken with him—the quick weekend getaways or the weeklong journeys to exotic places—this was the one that had taken me truly outside myself. Vietnam was magical, intoxicating, and magnificent. I already wanted to come back. I wanted *him* to *bring* me back.

I continued to slurp my noodles while he popped open a Tiger beer, and we grinned at each other. Our months together had created a shorthand where no words were necessary. As I turned to watch the sunset, he pulled me back into his lap. We were warm and sticky, salty from the water and our sweat. I had lived in my green bikini top and sarong for almost two days now, and his hands spanned my hips, thumbs dipping just under the fabric.

"It's good, right?" he asked.

"It's so good." I watched the sun dive into the bay, then I turned back to kiss him, feeling the butterflies that had never gone away. I hope they never do.

September

"Hey."

"Hey, you."

"You awake?"

"Not really. Wait, what're you doing here?"

"I caught an earlier flight back. I missed you."

"Mmm, I missed you too."

"My, my, Caroline. What are you wearing . . . or not?"

"It's too hot for clothes."

"That's a very good thing," he whispered.

Lying behind me, his warmth felt welcome in spite of the heat. Hands moved across my ribs toward my hips, angling me backward as I moaned at the feel of him, my body always ready to respond to his hands on my skin. He stopped momentarily to join me in my nakedness, and I arched into him when I felt him again, anxious and ready to love me.

He stroked my breasts, his movements deliberate and teasing.

He knew the instant reaction he'd receive. Nudging between my thighs, he brought one of my legs over his, opening me to him.

"Yes?" he asked, his breath warm in my ear.

"Yes." I nodded, reaching behind me and tangling my fingers in his hair. With a groan, he thrust inside me. I sighed as I felt him, insistent and tangible, where he belonged.

chapter one

"Oh, God."

Thump

"Oh, God."

Thump thump

"Caroline, don't say those things to me when I'm so far away." Simon chuckled, his voice low. And still as thrilling as it ever was.

"Silly Simon, I'm simply reacting to the banging on the other side of the wall."

"Who's on the other side of the wall?"

"The guy with the hammer. You should see it. It's huge."

"I'm going to have to ask you not to talk about some other guy's hammer."

"Then get home and wow me with yours." I laughed, closing the door to my office to reduce the noise. It wouldn't be my office much longer, though. I was moving up in the world—or at least down the hall. That was the cause of the banging: renovating my new space. Bigger office, corner office, thank you very much, right next to Jillian's, my boss and owner of. Better view of the bay and almost twice the size of my old office, with a small anteroom for a possible future intern.

I might one day have an intern. How was this my life?

"I'll be home tomorrow. Think you can keep your thoughts on *my* hammer until then?" he asked. I glanced at the calendar on my desk, Simon's arrival home circled.

"I'm gonna do my best, babe, but you should see how thick that tool belt is. No promises." Simon groaned and I laughed harder. I loved torturing him across multiple time zones. "And don't forget my present."

"Do I ever?"

"No, you're a thoughtful one, aren't you?"

"Don't forget my present either," he said, his voice going low again.

"Pink nightie is ready to go; I'll be in it when you get home."

"And then I'll be in it, on it, under it, I'll—oops, gotta go, taxi's here."

"We'll continue the nightie talk in person. Love you," I said.

"Love you too, babe," he said, and hung up.

I stared at the phone for a moment, imagining him half-way across the world in Tokyo. This year alone he'd logged more frequent-flier miles than most people accrued in a lifetime, and he was booked solid for the rest of the year.

I was still smiling at the phone when Jillian knocked and breezed in, then sat on the corner of my desk.

"Something on your mind, Jillian?" I asked, pulling a browned petal from the vase of coral tinged roses next to where she was resting her cashmere-clad bum.

"I can see something is on *your* mind. Was that Simon on the phone?" she asked as I grinned. "Only he can make your face light up like that."

"I say again—something on your mind, Jillian?" I repeated, poking her ever so slightly with my pencil.

"I have something on my mind that might make your face light up even brighter—although it is an interesting tomato-soup color right now," she teased.

"Does your fiancé find you as annoying as everyone who works for you does?"

"Way more, way way more. You ready to hear the big news, or did you want to keep sassing me?"

"Hit me," I said with a sigh.

I love my boss, but she does have a flair for the dramatic. Like when she played matchmaker last year for Simon and me, playing dumb the entire time. But her heart was in the right place. It also belonged 100 percent totally and completely to Benjamin, a venture capitalist. They'd been together for years and were finally tying the knot in a few weeks, in a wedding that all of San Francisco was talking about. Benjamin was a certifiable dreamboat who made my best friends and me giddy and word-trippy whenever he was around. Jillian knew we all had a not-so-secret crush on her man, and teasingly used it against us as often as possible. Now she was finally marrying our dream man, and heading off for a dream honeymoon all over Europe.

"So remember the job we did last spring for Max Camden? The waterfront Victorian we did, before his daughter got married?"

"Yeah, he gave it to her as a wedding present. Who does that?"

"Max Camden, that's who. Anyway, he owns the old Claremont Hotel in Sausalito, and he's looking for a new design firm to update it and give it a modern twist."

"Fantastic! Did you do your proposal already?" I asked, picturing the property. Right off the main drag in Sausalito, the Claremont had been there since the turn of the last century, one of the few to survive the Big Quake.

"No, because *you're* doing the proposal. You'll be the lead designer on this project if you get it," she clarified. "You think I can take something like this on? Right before my wedding? I'm not giving up my honeymoon for work—I've given up too many vacations over the years as it is."

"Me? No no no, I'm not ready for that, *you're* not ready for that, what are you thinking?" I stammered, my heart leaping into my throat. This was big-time, baby.

"Please, you got this." She kicked me gently. "Feel that? That's my foot, kicking you out of the nest."

"Um, yeah, I've been out of the nest awhile now, but this is different," I protested, chewing on my pencil.

Which she plucked out of my mouth. "You really think I'd give this to you if you weren't ready? And tell me the truth, aren't you even the slightest bit intrigued?"

She had me there. I'd always wanted to do a project this big. But to actually *be* the lead designer on an entire hotel redesign?

"I realize I'm asking a lot—you're already going to be running the show around here while I'm on my honeymoon. Do you truly think this is too much to bite off at one time?"

"Wow—I just—wow," I answered, taking a deep breath. When she'd initially asked me if I'd keep things running while she was on her honeymoon, it was things like making sure the alarm was set each night and that Ashley made sure to order coffee creamer. The list had steadily grown larger as projects stacked up, but still very much manageable. Now this?

I let the idea sit for a moment. *Could* I do this? Jillian seemed to think so.

"Hmm . . ."

I pictured the hotel: great light, great location, but needed a major overhaul. I was already thinking about potential palettes when she tapped me on the head with her pencil.

"Come in, Caroline. Hello," she said, waving her hand in front of my face.

I grinned at her. "I'm in, let's go for it," I said, my head already full of ideas.

She grinned back and offered me a fist bump. "I'll let the team know you'll be presenting."

"Presenting my vomit, most likely," I said, only half kidding.

"Just make sure it matches the drapes and we're in the clear. Now, let's celebrate by choosing a song to walk down the aisle to." She pulled her iPod out of her pocket and started scrolling through.

"Is that in my job description?"

"That you indulge me? Yes, check your contract. So when I walk down the aisle, which song should I . . ."

There was no stopping her once she'd put on her Wedding Hat, so I relaxed a bit, even though my mind was spinning. This *was* big-time baby, but I had this.

Right?

I spent the afternoon framing out the beginnings of a pitch to Max Camden. As I pulled archival photos of the hotel and the surrounding area, ideas were beginning to present themselves. Not fully formed yet, but hinting at what might be an approach interesting enough to take a chance on a young designer. I knew that the strength of my ideas would be bolstered by Jillian's reputation; anyone who was good enough to work for her was usually granted wider berth. However, it still came down to whose ideas were best—and I wanted this concept to be epic.

Still musing over the project as I turned my key in my front door, I heard a distinct thump, followed by a *click click click* padding toward me.

Clive.

Pushing through the door, I was greeted by my wonder cat, my own little piece of feline heaven. In a burst of gray fur, my ankles were surrounded by purrs and insistent nudges.

"Hi there, sweet boy, were you a good boy today?" I asked, leaning down to scratch his silky fur.

Arching up into my hand, he assured me that yes, he was in fact a sweet boy, and also a good boy. Berating me for leaving him alone for a thousand years, he cooed and chirped, herding me toward the kitchen.

We talked as I readied his dinner for him, which of course I'd been put on earth expressly to do, and our conversation covered the normal subjects. What birds he'd seen from the window today, whether any dust bunnies had emerged from under the bed, and whether I'd find any toys buried in the toe of my slippers. He was noncommittal on this last question.

Once his kibble was in his bowl he ignored me completely, and I headed back to the bedroom to put on some comfy clothes. Untucking my turtleneck, I went to the mirrored dresser to grab some yoga pants. While pulling my arms out of my shirt, my heart leapt into my throat when I saw the reflection of someone sitting on my bed. Instinct kicked in and I whirled, fists clenched, a scream ready to let loose.

My brain only processed that it was Simon after my fist was flung.

"Whoa, whoa, whoa! What the *hell,* Caroline!" he yelled as he grabbed his jaw.

"What the hell, Caroline? What the hell, *Simon*! What the hell are you doing here?" I yelled back. Good to know if I was ever actually attacked, I wouldn't freeze.

"I came home early to surprise you," he managed, rubbing his jaw and grimacing.

My heart was still racing in my chest, and as I tried to calm down, I noticed the suitcase in the corner. The one I'd missed when I'd come into the room. I looked down and saw the turtleneck still hanging around my neck like a scarf.

"I could just kill you!" I yelled again, charging him and pushing him back onto the bed. "You scared me to death, you idiot!"

"I was planning on calling out to let you know I was here, but then I would've missed that entire conversation with Clive. I didn't want to interrupt." He grinned underneath me, threading his hands around my waist and in and out of my belt loops.

I blushed. "Traitor!" I yelled down the hallway. "You could have let me know someone was here—you're a terrible watch-cat!"

A disinterested meow floated back.

"I'm hardly just *someone*. I think I rate a little higher than that," he told the side of my neck, which he was now feathering with the tiniest of kisses. "So, are you going to say hi to your boyfriend who flew all the way across the globe just to show you his hammer, or are you going to punch me again?"

"Not sure yet; I'm still a little freaked out. My heart is literally racing, can you feel that?" I asked, pressing his hand over the left side of my chest.

Only so he could feel my heart. Yep. That's the only reason. Heart was in fact delighted to have Simon home early; she loved a good romantic reunion. Other areas were delighted as well.

"See now, I thought it was racing because of *me*," he said with a low chuckle, dipping his nose along my collarbone as he "felt my heart."

"Dream on, Wallbanger," I said, feigning indifference. The truth? My heart was now in Simon mode, and it *was* pounding for him. And speaking of pounding.

"So you came home early just to see little ol' me?" I breathed into his ear, sneaking a wet kiss just underneath it. His hands dug a little deeper into my hips as he shifted on the bed.

"I did."

"Think you can help me with this turtleneck?"

"I do."

"And then after that, you wanna show me your hammer?" I asked the front of his T-shirt, nuzzling at him, positioning my legs on either side of him. In answer, he thrust up and let me feel that very hammer. I chuckled. "Mmm, am I gonna get nailed?"

He lifted my turtleneck off, then unsnapped my bra and my

breasts tumbled out, causing his eyes to flare, then focus with precision. "No more questions," he directed, sitting up underneath me as he pulled me closer.

I mimed zipping my lips just before he flipped me over onto my back. God, I loved this man.

His lips danced along my collarbone, nipping occasionally with his teeth in a way he always knew got me warm, *fast*. I got it; I'd missed him too. Arching my back, I pressed my breasts against him, twisting and turning to bring me into contact with him as much as I could be, my skin needing to feel his. After a year, he could still bring me to my knees in seconds with one touch, one kiss, one look.

I pushed back against him, flipping us once more and pulling at his jeans. "Off, now," I instructed.

When his belt was gone, his buttons unbuttoned, I pulled apart his jeans to find that once more my man had gone commando.

It's like he was put on earth just to make me come out of my skin.

I snuck one hand inside, grasping him firmly, feeling how warm he was; ready to take me on my own trip around the world.

"Fuck, I missed you," he breathed, his body lean and taut. I slid down the bed, kissing and licking at his skin hungrily. His hands came up to my face, fingers fluttering along my cheekbones, sweeping my hair back. So he could watch.

I took him into my mouth, entirely. His hands clutched at my hair, freezing me in place, holding me exactly how he wanted me. "Mmm, Caroline," he moaned, thrusting ever so slightly. Slightly, my ass—that wasn't how this show was going down.

I pulled back then took him in again, hard. Using my hands I caressed him, alternating my touch so he never knew quite where I was coming from, using my tongue and mouth to tease and tempt him, coaxing the sweetest dirty words out of that sent-from-heaven-mouth of his. That mouth that I knew would exact the sweetest dirty revenge all over my body.

I loved him this way, loved that I could make him this insane. But just before he got too far gone, he pulled me up his body and took my panties off before I could say, hey, those are my panties.

Then he pushed up my skirt, nudging my knees apart with his own. Gazing down at me with those piercing sapphire eyes, he ran his fingers over me, through me, making me groan and moan and shake and shimmy. "So gorgeous like this," he breathed as I cried out.

"Need you, Simon—need you, please!" I was ready to tear my hair off my head and throw it at him, if I thought that would get him inside any faster.

Any further thoughts vanished as he slid home. Thick, hard, and ten kinds of fantastic were all I knew the second Simon pressed inside me. "God, that's amazing," I moaned, the feeling of him filling me overwhelming me.

And when he rolled us so I was on top, and he thrust up hard inside me, it was perfection.

Until afterward, when we lay in a heap of sweaty limbs, and he asked me how I liked his hammer.

Then it was beyond perfection.

chapter two

The next morning, I crawled out from under a sleeping Simon. After a second round of hammer time, when he collapsed on me, spent and . . . Wait a second. You know in romance novels, when they say the guy collapses on top of the girl, spent and exhausted? Take that, add a transatlantic flight, and then you have what happened to Simon. He literally collapsed onto me, sated and jet-lagged. I barely had time to set my alarm before 190 pounds of warm boy collapsed on me and wasn't letting me up.

But when you go weeks without that same 190 pounds in your bed, the truth is, it felt kind of nice to sleep underneath that. Or at least, off to the side just a little bit. I loved him, but I loved my kidneys too.

After attending to Clive, I quickly showered. By the time I was dressed, he was at his post in the front window, making sure the neighborhood was still out there. Pulling my damp hair into a ponytail, I took a moment to admire Simon, sawing logs in lumberjack land. Dark messy hair, made messy by my own hands, fell across his brow. Strong nose, killer cheekbones, a few days' worth of sinful scruff and full lips that had chanted my name several times just before he . . . Mmmm.

I took another moment to appreciate the still life in front of me: stretched out, arms above his head, torso long and lean, and nothing between him and that sheet but a promise.

I shook my head to clear it, then crossed the room and sat next to him. In his sleep, he mumbled and reached for me. Smiling, I let myself be caught into a sleepy bear hug, kissing him on the forehead until those gorgeous blues opened into mine.

"Morning, babe." I grinned as he pressed against me more fully. I knew this game. I didn't have time for this game. "No, no, I gotta go. The girls are waiting for me." Breakfast with my two best friends, Mimi and Sophia, was something I always made time for, Wallbanger or no Wallbanger.

"Girls? Where do you think you're going? I just got back," he complained, still half asleep.

"I'm having breakfast with the girls. You weren't supposed to be home until tomorrow, remember?"

"But I'm here now," he mumbled, his eyes struggling to stay open.

"You stay here and get some more sleep. I know how tired you are," I whispered, kissing his forehead once more and tucking him back under the covers. Which really was a shame, because, come on, Simon on a bed? It seemed a sin to cover any of that up.

But as he scrunched up his pillow and settled back in, he sure seemed cozy. With a deep sigh, he said, "I'll stay here and get some more sleep."

I bit back a laugh as he slipped back to dreamland.

I made my way toward the front door, nodding at Clive as I put on a jacket. "Everything look good out there today?" He looked back out the window, then back at me again. He blinked, then I'm pretty sure he shrugged.

I grinned and left my boys to go have breakfast with my girls.

• • •

"I'll have two eggs scrambled dry, whole wheat toast with peanut butter, a cup of berries, and a coffee, please."

"I'll do the egg-white omelet with spinach, tomatoes, and feta, no toast, and the strawberry smoothie, please."

"I'll take the large waffle platter with blueberry syrup *and* whipped cream, please, side of bacon, side of sausage, and a chocolate milk. And could I please get a side of rice pudding also?"

I'd been having breakfast with Mimi and Sophia ever since our freshman year at Berkeley. The three of us knew each other exceedingly well, so much so that we could tell what kind of a mood each was in based on our orders at the diner.

Mimi and I looked at each other with raised eyebrows as Sophia ordered and then went back to making a town out of the jelly containers. It was quite elaborate, with several buildings already. I shrugged as Mimi inclined her head toward Sophia, trying to get me to broach the subject.

"Stop talking about me and get me the jellies from the table behind you," Sophia snapped, looking up from her Jelly Town. I rolled my eyes but grabbed the jellies.

"Here you go. Make sure you put a roof on City Hall there." I nodded toward the recent addition.

"No, Caroline, that's City Hall down *there*. Right now I'm working on the fire station," she huffed.

Mimi's eyebrows disappeared into her hairline. "Okay, that's it. I'm staging an intervention," she cried, reaching over to sweep the town off the table.

"You touch that jelly and I'll punch you in the throat," Sophia warned, her mouth set in a grim line.

"Ladies, let's not get violent so early in the morning, shall we? I haven't even had my coffee yet," I said, just as the waiter brought my coffee. "Okay, never mind—fight it out, you two." I laughed, leaning back in my chair.

Sophia stuck her tongue out at Mimi, which carved a small smile into her tiny face. Mimi was darling as always this morning, clad in a plaid miniskirt, kneesocks, and a turtleneck sweater. Give her some pigtails and a backpack and she'd look like a Filipino schoolgirl—an outfit I'm sure her fiancé, Ryan, would love.

Yep, Mimi and Ryan were engaged. Like a scene from a romantic comedy with a twist, Mimi and Sophia had met their knights in shining sweaters on the same night. Best buddies to my Simon, Ryan and Neil had fallen head over feet for my ladies. After a little switcheroo, mind you. So between Jillian and Benjamin, and now Mimi and Ryan, wedding fever had hit my little circle in San Francisco.

But part of my circle was broken. Broken up, rather.

As Sophia and Mimi bickered, I noticed again how tired Sophia looked. She wasn't sleeping well—not that I could blame her.

When she first told us that Neil had cheated on her, we didn't know what to do. Our first instinct was to set fire to his car, something Simon wisely talked us out of. Arson charges are a hard thing to have following you the rest of your life.

For a brief and crazy moment we considered breaking into the studio during one of his broadcasts and telling his viewers that they got their sports news from a cheating dick, but again, wiser heads prevailed.

So Mimi and I simply stood by our friend as she fell apart.

It started when I got a call from Sophia late one night, after midnight. She was swearing nonstop; sailors all over the world would have been proud. I could only catch occasional phrases like "asshole cheater" and "the nerve of that fuck" and "balls are in my pocket." By the time she walked over to my apartment and came up the stairs, the swearing was beginning to calm down and the tears were falling fiercely. She pushed away my offer of tea, sucked back some scotch, and told me what had happened. By the time Mimi made it over, it was all out on the table.

Neil had had dinner with an old girlfriend; dinner turned into after-dinner drinks; after-dinner drinks turned into kissing. Or *a* kiss, depending on who was telling the story. Regardless, that's what caused her to flush his car keys down the toilet.

We were all stunned. They'd seemed so happy; perfectly matched and twisted in the best of ways. Neil was the local sportscaster for NBC, great looking, sweet, lovable, an all-around great guy. Who was a cheater, something no one saw coming.

She broke up with him immediately, livid. She refused to see him, refused to take his calls, refused any attempt through Simon or Ryan to have any contact with him at all. She was mad, then got really sad, and now she was . . .

Well, it was weeks later and she was sitting in a diner in her pajamas with her gorgeous red hair in straggles around her puffy face, wearing no makeup and fifteen extra pounds, and was making a town out of jelly. A musical child prodigy, she was a cellist for the San Francisco Symphony. One of the most beautiful and accomplished women in all of San Francisco was now making it snow in Jelly Town. God, no—not with dandruff, but with sugar packets.

"Sophia stop, stop—stop!" I yelled, grabbing her hand and spraying sugar snow everywhere. "This is enough. No more pouting, no more hiding. This is ridiculous!"

"Yeah!" Mimi chimed in.

"Seriously, this has gone on long enough. I don't want to go all Afterschool Special here, but my God, woman, wash your hair!"

"Yeah!" Mimi added.

"You're fucking hot, and you're fucking great, you're a fucking catch. And if fucking Neil doesn't get to have you anymore, who cares, because you're fucking awesome," I finished.

"Fuck, yeah!" was Mimi's contribution.

The table fell silent. Sophia played with one last sugar packet, running it along her fingernails, then stopped to really look at them. Bitten down to the quick, jagged, polish peeling. She sighed, and then looked up at us, two big tears rolling down her cheeks.

"I hate him," she whispered, drawing a shuddering breath. "And I miss him."

"We know, sweetie," Mimi said, drawing Sophia's hand into hers.

I leaned over and gave Sophia my napkin, which she used to wipe her eyes. She looked down at her sweatshirt, rumpled and stained.

"I kind of stink," she said with a grimace.

"We know, sweetie," Mimi said again, which cracked a smile out of Sophia for the first time in a while.

A little pink crept back into her cheeks. She pulled a ponytail holder out of her purse and wrapped her messy hair back into a bun, out of her face. She glanced up as the waiter came to bring our food, her eyes growing huge when she realized the mounds of food she'd ordered. Once he had left, she unfolded her napkin and tucked it in her lap.

"Okay, no more wallowing. I ordered it, so I'll eat it. But starting this afternoon, no more wallowing includes no more eating like a thirteen-year-old boy."

"Boys that age have to eat like that. They have to keep up their strength for their many boners a day," Mimi said matter-of-factly, separating her blueberries from her raspberries, then lining them up on the side of her plate like tiny cannonballs. Sophia and I stared at her as she went on to explain the extreme impact of boners on the social lives of junior high boys. As related to her by her fiancé, apparently an expert.

"Ryan really told you all this?" I asked as I sipped my smoothie.

"Yep, he said when he was that age, he couldn't keep his hands out of his pants for the life of him," she prattled, oblivious to the attention the table behind us was now giving her.

"You and Ryan sure seem to share a lot," Sophia said, shaking her head incredulously as Mimi demonstrated a particular "technique" that had been employed by the teenage Ryan.

"Okay, okay, no more!" I protested, waving my hands. "It's enough that I won't be able to look him in the eye next time I see him; no more yanky-wanky details. Let's change the subject—Who has news?"

The gossip section of breakfast had officially begun.

"Okay, I'll start. I found out the Palace of Fine Arts *is* available; looks like that's where my reception will be!" Mimi sang.

"Jillian asked me to head up the team bidding on the Claremont Hotel redesign in Sausalito," I offered.

"I've spent the last three weeks in a dark cloud, so I got nothing. But did you know that my hair is long enough that if I lean back far enough I can sit on it?" Sophia volunteered.

We chewed.

"I had a client ask me if I'd mind organizing her porn collection," Mimi said.

"I might have ordered a porn collection at three in the morning a few days ago," Sophia told the inside of her sweatshirt.

"Simon came home early last night and surprised me. So I had some live-action porn."

"He came home early? Wow, that's impressive. Seems like lately he's been traveling more than usual," Mimi commented, eating the cannonballs in alternating order. Blueberry. Raspberry.

"Yeah, he has been busier than normal. What can I say? My boyfriend is the darling of the photography world." I grinned, flushing when I thought about how sexy he looked when he was working.

"I don't know how you guys do that, be apart so much. I'd die if I didn't see Ryan every day—I'd just die!" Mimi exclaimed. Blueberry. Raspberry. "I don't know how you don't miss him like crazy!"

"Of course I miss him—some weeks it's really hard. But this

is who he is, this is how he's always been, and we make it work. Honestly? Sometimes it's kind of great: I have my time, he has his time, and then when he's home, it's our time." I swiped my finger through a little bit of Sophia's whipped cream, barely evading the tines of her fork. "Anyway, I like the idea that we're not a couple who has to sleep together every night. Admit it. Don't you sometimes miss having the bed all to yourself?"

Mimi instantly began shaking her head, while Sophia just avoided eye contact.

"Okay, change of subject again. Let's talk about the wedding. *The* wedding of the century"—I started, then backpedaled as soon as I saw Mimi's look—"at least until Mimi here takes that mantle. Until she does, though, Jillian is going for it! And wait until you see Benjamin's tux. Good lord, the man can wear tails like nobody's business."

At the mention of Benjamin everyone perked up, even Sophia. The category of sexy older man had been created specifically with him in mind, and we all sighed together.

"Anyway, we gotta start thinking about dates for you, young lady. Who are you thinking about taking?" I asked, looking at Sophia. She turned white.

"Ah shit, I didn't even think about that! Neil's going, isn't he?" she asked, her expression panicked. She looked down at herself, then back up at us. "Ack, I can't let him see me looking like this! What's he going to think? He's gonna think I'm, like, on the floor in a puddle over him!"

Mimi started to interject, but I placed a hand on her arm and shook my head as Sophia went on.

"And what if he brings someone? Shit, he's totally bringing someone, isn't he? Isn't he? That's it—that asshole; he thinks he can show *me*? He thinks he's gonna get the better of *me*? Hell no, not on my watch. Stupid overgrown boy-looking sportscaster motherfucker."

This entire conversation was had by Sophia alone as she grabbed her purse and headed back toward the bathroom.

Once she was gone, I grabbed the rest of her waffles and divided them between my plate and Mimi's. We clinked forks and tucked in for a few minutes.

"Do you think he's bringing someone?" I asked.

"I'm sure he is. I've tried asking Ryan about it, but he's claiming guy code, or bros before hos, or something ridiculous like that."

"Same with Simon. I wonder if they—" I stopped as Sophia exited the bathroom.

The sweatshirt was now tied around her waist, the revealed tank top tight. Her hair was braided, bangs swept back revealing a clean, shining face. Lip gloss had been added; a little blush too. The girl was stunning once more; you just can't keep that kind of beauty buried for too long. But what made every man and more than a few women do a double take were her double D's. Accentuated more than ever by the purposeful rip she'd given her tank top, perfectly highlighting each D to its full potential.

"Can you believe I was ever worried about gaining a little weight? Look how great my tits look!" she announced as she came back to the table. "Let's head over to the park and pick up hot boys. Let's see how many I can get to stop jogging with these," she said, pulling a wad of cash from her purse and throwing it on the table.

I couldn't help but laugh as she dragged a protesting Mimi away from her food. Sophia was back on the prowl, and she took out two busboys on her way out of the diner.

I went to the park just long enough to see that Sophia was indeed back out of her coma. I doubted she was actually over the situation with Neil, but sometimes you have to pretend to be feeling better to actually feel better. It's why new workout clothes make you feel like you want to work out.

I was still waiting for that one to turn out to be true . . .

I begged off staying the whole afternoon on the grounds that I had a Wallbanger in my bed, which needed no further explanation. As I turned the corner onto my street after hopping off the trolley, I thought about what Mimi had said earlier, about needing to see Ryan every day. They could easily do that: Both had jobs in the city and rarely traveled for work. Mimi was a professional organizer, helping families declutter and clean up, while Ryan headed up a nonprofit that helped put computers into schools in low-income areas.

Would I like to see Simon every day? Of course I would—the speed bump abs alone are worth the price of admission. But more than that, we just . . . worked well together. There was an ease to our relationship that I had never had with anyone else, maybe because we became friends first. And while we had our share of raised eyebrows like every couple, we rarely fought. Maybe because we spent less time together than regular couples.

I shook my head as I walked up my stairs. It didn't matter why we worked, we just did. And since Simon would continue to be in demand professionally, we'd continue to make it work long-distance. I liked the idea of an unconventional romance, especially since the beginning of ours was so much so.

I'd been on a dating freeze after a one-night stand with He Who Shall Not Be Named (read Cory Weinstein) scared my orgasm into hiding, disappearing from the earth entirely. Going, going, gone it was; no good-bye, no nice knowing you. Just gone. I'd attempted to recover the O by bringing back a few tried-and-true partners, but no go. And of course I'd tried to reconnect by using the Holy Trinity of Fantasy Lovers (the Leto, the Damon, and the Holy Clooney), but even by my own hand, the O had left the building. Finally Simon and I were able to conjure her again in a poof of flour on the floor of my kitchen, surrounded by raisins and honey.

And speaking of unconventional, Simon had never dated anyone in the traditional sense. When I met him he was king of the Friends with Benefits scenario, with an actual harem. As Simon and I were becoming friends in those early days, he'd confided that all the women he'd ever dated seemed to want the same thing: a white picket fence. I convinced him that in fact not all women want that, especially this woman in particular. I'd told him, "The right woman for you wouldn't want you to change anything about your life. She wouldn't rock your boat, she'd jump right in and sail it with you."

I used to date someone who wanted me to be his picket fencer, his own personal Mrs. Stepford. Or Mrs. James Brown, in this scenario. Lawyer, not Godfather of Soul, to be clear.

Picket fences? Thanks, but no thanks. I liked my life, I liked *our* life—it was pretty great.

A perfect example was our living situation. As I put the key in my lock, I looked across the landing to his apartment door. When he was home we tended to spend most of our time at my place, but I liked that we still had our own apartments. I'd lived with room-mates most of my adult life, and even though I was technically subletting from Jillian (no way would I ever be able to afford this amazing apartment without her rent control), it was still my own space.

Which I shared with a very particular feline. I let myself in, looking around for Clive but not seeing him. I had an idea where he might be, though. Kicking off my shoes, I padded quietly back to the bedroom, peeking my head around the door.

Tucked into the one corner of the bed I typically allowed him was Simon, still sleeping off his long trip home. Curled into a ball behind Simon's knees, Clive opened one eye and registered that I was home. He flicked one ear and stretched his back out, tucking himself tighter into his favorite spot.

I whispered, "Hiya, Clive, how's my sweet—"

He cut me off with a quiet but very curt meow.

And he gave me a very specific look, letting me know that my boys needed their sleep and I should leave well enough alone. I chuckled to myself as Simon let out a loud snore, then backed away. Clive remained behind Simon's knees.

Simon's Knees . . . What a great name for a band.

While the boys slept I did some laundry, I worked on some sketches for the new hotel project, and I baked. Baking centered me, helped me focus and see my way around corners, especially when I was working on something new. Two loaves of zucchini bread later, I was perched on the kitchen island with a colored pencil in my mouth when I heard shuffling.

Simon came into the kitchen, nose first. I caught my breath, almost inhaling my pencil when I saw him in his loose pajama bottoms, rumpled hair, and sleepy expression. I knew if I pressed my face into the exact center of his chest, he'd smell like Downy and warm boy. Heart, as always, skipped a beat.

"Zucchini?" he asked while sniffing the air, his eyes still at half-mast but scanning for bread. His eyes weren't the only thing at half-mast . . .

"Zucchini," I affirmed, nodding my head.

A slow grin crept across his face; nothing could make him happier than homemade bread. Well, almost nothing.

"You want some?" I asked.

He walked toward me, and the bread behind me, with a determined look on his face. "You're kidding, right?" he asked, uncrossing my legs so he could stand between them. "I always want some."

"Are we still talking about zucchini bread?" I asked, as his hands dug into my hips. Sliding me closer to the edge suddenly, he pressed a wet kiss below my ear.

"I'm hungry, yes," he whispered, in a voice that instantly told my thighs to part. "And the zucchini bread can wait."

I moaned. I mean, of *course* I moaned.

Gone in sixty seconds was everything under my apron, which

was flipped up and out of his way. To his knees he went, pulling my hips exactly to the edge of the counter, my legs roughly thrown over his shoulders.

"Christ Simon, what brought this—oh!"

I lost my train of thought as his open mouth pressed against me, his tongue strong and searching. With one lick, I was close. With a second lick, I was close to stupid.

With the third . . . Here's the funny thing about my orgasm. Once I got out of my own way, she was happy to come. Ahem.

"Oh God, you . . . that's . . . so . . . wow . . . mmm," I moaned. He moved, I moved. He pulsed, I twitched. He plunged, I . . . Oh, hell. I flailed.

"Responsive, aren't you?" he murmured, raising his head and wickedly licking his lips. I threaded my hands through his hair and not so gently pushed him back down.

"If you stop now I'll kill you with this egg timer," I managed, grabbing for the only thing that was nearby. Which I dropped as soon as he returned to me, my breathing fast and impossible to control. I dug my heels into his back, shamelessly flexing my hips to bring him closer to where I needed him. Giving a long lick to the inside of each of my thighs, he splayed his hands under and around my hips, holding me still as best he could and opening me further to him.

"Like I could stop? Don't you know I dream about this when I'm away?" he asked, nudging me with his nose, exactly where I needed his mouth to be.

"You . . . dream about . . . this?" I asked, arching my back. I was so close, so very close.

"Fuck, yes, are you kidding?" He flattened his tongue and dragged it across my entire sex, dipping inside and continuing up, closing his mouth now and encircling me with his lips. Releasing me with a groan of his own, he brought one hand down, using his fingers to press into me. "I think about this, and the sounds you make when you come, the way you taste. Mmm . . . sweet Caroline, you drive me crazy."

His words swirled my thoughts. I leaned up on my elbows, skin on fire, my fuzzy gaze on this gorgeous man, this shockingly gorgeous man, with his mouth on me. Riding his hand, my hips undulated as his tongue and lips consumed me. His eyes burning into mine, I gasped when my orgasm hit me like a freight train. Shaking, I fell back onto the counter.

He stood, one hand continuing to caress my skin as I shuddered, the other pushing his pajama bottoms down. He ran his fist up and down his length, then pressed inside me, but just barely. His head dropped back as he wrapped his hands around my hips, using my weight as leverage as he slowly . . . sank . . . inside.

He was perfectly still.

I was perfectly not.

I simply couldn't be. It was too much; he was too much. I would never get used to the feeling of him inside me, stretching me and filling me and being perfectly there. I thrashed, I shimmied, I arched and I flexed. And he stayed perfectly still. The muscles in his arms bunched, his neck corded, his torso gleamed with the sweet strain of not moving. He was like a naughty work of art.

Then he lifted his head and opened his eyes. Singularly focused, dark, and of one mind-set.

Simon was about to fuck.

Pulling out almost entirely, he thrust low. And hard. And serious.

And I came out of my skin.

He rode me, rode my body and my sex, and when he leaned heavy over me and chanted the dirtiest words imaginable in my ear, I came again. Right as he came. Low. And hard. And so serious.

Wrapping my arms around him, I kept him inside as long as I could. Even when he lifted me off the counter I fought that loss, keeping my legs around his waist as he laughed. He unraveled me, threw me over his shoulder in a fireman's carry, and slapped my bottom.

He then ate an entire loaf of zucchini bread with his pants around his ankles while he leaned on the counter, resting his head on my bottom.

"**S**o remind me to never stop baking for you," I said fifteen minutes later, when I was finally allowed to put my pants back on and start cleaning up the kitchen.

"Would that ever happen?" Simon looked stricken. At the thought that I might stop baking, or perhaps because he'd just eaten an entire loaf of bread?

"Doubtful. It's a mutually beneficial kind of thing, obviously."

"I should say." He smirked as I poured him some coffee and marched him over to the sofa. "Why am I on the couch?"

"Because I'm cleaning and you're in the way. Plus you just got back, so let me fawn over you a little."

"But mainly because I was in the way, right?"

"Right." I grabbed a broom and swept up some raisins. Clive had spirited a few away already; I imagined I'd find those in bed later tonight. He loved to hide them one by one. I'd stopped asking questions.

Simon relaxed on the couch, watching me sweep and commenting when my backside looked particularly fetching. Looking over the rim of his coffee cup, he asked, "Hey, what were you doing sketching on a Saturday? You gotta work today?"

"Kinda sorta."

"Kinda sorta?"

"Yeah, a big job that Jillian put me on. We're bidding on it next week, and if I get this job it'll mean . . . Well, it'd be a big deal." I hesitated, not even wanting to say it out loud. This would be big giant balls big.

"That's great! What kind of job?"

"A hotel in Sausalito. Jillian's given me the lead on it, due to the wedding and her honeymoon. So yeah, big week at work." I finished the sweeping and threw the raisins into the trash. Grabbing my sketchbook, I headed into the living room and sat next to him, propping my feet in his lap.

"Sounds big. That's good, babe."

"Plus, I'm kind of taking over while they're on their honeymoon. I'm gonna be swamped."

"You can handle it. I'm proud of you."

"Well, be proud of me if I get the job. Till then it's just a bid. But fingers crossed, right?" I laughed, lying back against the cushions as he rubbed my heel.

"I have a good feeling about this. Maybe we'll have something to celebrate next week," he said, wiggling my big toe. "Speaking of celebrations, how'd you like to come to Rio with me this December?"

Whuh?

I say again, whuh?

"I love when you drop your consonants," he murmured, scooting closer and leaning over me.

"I said that out loud?"

"You sure did."

"Okay. Well, then, answer my whuh."

"No one on the planet has ever said that exact sentence before." He chuckled, drawing a line with his fingertip down my nose and pressing it against my mouth.

"Rio? In December?" I mumbled.

"For Christmas."

"Whuh?"

As he laughed, I scrambled up from beneath him. "Explain, please."

"Nothing to explain. I booked a job in Brazil—I'll be working in Rio on Christmas. I want my best girl with me."

Christmas in Brazil. Sultry warm ocean breeze. Sipping caipirinhas under festival lanterns. Coconut oil. Bikini. Simon.

Second Christmas away from home in a row?

I flashed back to Christmases past, growing up. I had a favorite aunt and uncle— doesn't everyone? Technically my *great*-aunt and -uncle, Liz and Lou were legends in our family. They never had kids, and whether that was by design or nature, I never knew; no one ever talked about that. But they led a life that I had always dreamed of.

They traveled every year, and I mean they *traveled*. Uncle Lou made good money, invested wisely, and when he retired at sixty-five they hit the road. They owned a home in San Diego, but they just used it as a base. They had friends all over the world and spent time in places like Madrid, Athens, Rome, Lisbon, Amsterdam, Caracas, and São Paulo. *Rio de Janeiro*. They took off whenever they wanted, and went wherever the wind told them to go. They were only occasionally around for Christmas, and I was always excited to see where my present would come from each year, what faraway place the postage would be from.

Did they love their family less because they chose to travel across the globe for Christmas? I never thought so, although some of the more traditional members of the family felt it was strange and a little selfish that they didn't want to be singing carols at my grandmother's and eating turkey with everyone else.

I thought it was romantic, exciting, and a little wonderful.

They passed away a few years ago, within three months of each other. After they died I was helping to go through some of their things and I came across their passports. They were battered, worn, and stamped with cities all across the globe, some of which I had never heard of.

And when I went to Salzburg last year to keep Simon company on Christmas, I didn't feel selfish or strange. I thought it was romantic, exciting, and more than a little wonderful. Furthest thing from traditional, but maybe a Simon and Caroline tradition?

I mentally calculated whether my additional work responsibilities would allow me to take time off. The holidays were a busy period for us, but the week between Christmas and New Year's was pretty manageable. This invite was out of the blue, but not out of the world of the possible.

I began to hum "The Girl from Ipanema," a grin slowly spreading across my face.

"Is that a yes to Rio?" he asked.

"It's a *hell* yes, Wallbanger—hell yes to Rio!" I squealed, wrapping my legs around his waist and seeing the look of excitement on his face before I brought him down for a big, wet kiss. Last year, I invited myself along. This year, *he* wanted me with him. Fuck, I loved this man.

We kissed for a moment, then he went back to his side of the couch and resumed my foot rub and I went back to my sketching.

A few minutes later, I got a text. I snorted, then told Simon, "Hey, this just in from Wedding Central. You need to get measured for your tux, pronto. Jillian said you and Benjamin are supposed to go together; she's freaking out."

"I know—best man and all; I need to look good." He rolled his eyes.

When Benjamin asked Simon to stand up for him at the wedding, it was kind of perfect. Since I was one of Jillian's bridesmaids.

"You'll look good, no one is worried about that." I laughed as he tickled the bottoms of my feet. "The one that I'm worried about is Sophia. She's out of her funk as of this morning, and ready to buy the sexiest dress she can find for this shindig."

"Mmm-hmm," he replied, concentrating on my instep.

"I think she really just wants to make sure that she'll look good if Neil comes, you know? I mean, *is* he coming? For sure?"

"Mmm-hmm," he replied again, the tiniest of crinkles appearing on his forehead. I let him rub my feet for another minute.

"So, is he bringing anyone to the wedding?" I asked in the most nonchalant tone possible.

"Caroline," he warned.

"What? If he's bringing someone, that's something that would be good to know ahead of time, don't you think? It's not like you're betraying the guy code just by telling me if he's bringing anyone, right?" I asked, poking him in the belly with my big toe, eliciting a smile.

"Yes, he's bringing someone," he allowed, watching my face carefully. I breathed out just as carefully.

"Okay, see, that wasn't so bad, was it?" I asked, pushing my foot under his hand again. He resumed his kneading. I let one minute go by.

"So, is she pretty?"

"Not gonna do this," he said, lifting my feet off his lap and standing up.

"What? I'm just asking if she's pretty," I insisted as he turned back toward me.

"I've told you, this is not something we can talk about. You get too worked up to be rational, and I—"

"I get worked *up*? Of *course* I get worked up! My best friend had her heart ripped out because your best friend was an idiot who cheated on her, and—"

"For the last time, he didn't cheat!" he snapped.

"Kissing *is* cheating! Of course it's cheating!" I snapped back, standing up to face him.

"He kissed an ex-girlfriend once—it happened *once*. And he told her. He didn't have to tell her about it at all! He could've kept it from her, but he told her!"

"Oh, now he's supposed to get points for that? For telling her after he cheats on her?" I cried.

When I said Simon and I didn't fight, we really didn't. Except for this one thing.

So here's the full story. When Neil's ex-girlfriend came to town and their dinner ended with the kiss, Neil told Sophia about it, and she left. And since then, she's refused to talk to him, refused to see him, refused to have anything to do with him. Erased e-mails and deleted texts. She didn't want him to try and explain anything, because in her mind there was nothing to explain.

The problem is that all of the guys agreed that what Neil did, wrong as it was, wasn't enough to break up over. Of course, the girls all agreed that kissing was cheating: dicks didn't need to be inserted for it to be cheating. Sophia had every right to end things with Neil, and as the cheater, he didn't get much say in how it went down.

Hence the arguments.

Mimi and Ryan had fought over this as well; it was something that everyone had an opinion on. Opinions that Simon and I had agreed weren't worth sharing, since it made us argue every time we talked about it, yet the subject kept bubbling up.

What *was* cheating? Where was that line that, if crossed, you couldn't come back from? Was it different for every couple, or was it black and white?

"He doesn't get points for it. That's not what I meant, and you know that—"

"That kind of thing doesn't just happen, Simon. He made a choice—"

"A kiss! And that had to end everything? What about Sophia? She won't even give the guy a chance to explain, she—"

"There's nothing to explain, don't you get that?" I yelled, throwing my sketchbook across the room.

Quiet.

"I don't want to talk about this anymore," I mumbled, crossing the room to pick up my book. He caught my hand as I walked by.

"This is exactly why I didn't want to talk about this from the beginning. There's no right or wrong here"—he raised his fingers to my lips when I started to explain that yes, in fact there is—"or at least it's a gray area. But no matter what it is, it's not worth us getting in a fight over, right?"

I sighed, letting him pull me into his chest. I pressed my face into the exact center. The scent of Downy calmed me.

"Right."

He held me tight.

"I love you," he told the top of my head.

"Love you too."

Being half of a "we" is sometimes hard.

chapter three

"It's melon."

"It's marigold."

"Marigold! It's pumpkin way before it's marigold, but that doesn't matter—because it's melon."

"If you think that's melon then you need your eyes examined, because it's obviously—"

"Mimi, what do you think? This is totally melon, isn't it?"

"Yes, Mimi, look at this and tell me how in the world *this* is melon."

"Goldfish," Mimi said.

"What?" I asked, looking at Jillian.

We were standing in the ladies' bridal salon at Neiman Marcus. Wait, strike that. *I* was standing in the ladies' bridal salon, in my bra and underwear, while Jillian and Mimi sat on giant tufted chairs sipping champagne.

"Goldfish. Your dress is the color of those cheddar Goldfish crackers. And it's kind of perfect for your skin tone, actually," Mimi said, pouring another glass and drinking it down. "Now both of you shut up. Honestly, listening to two designers argue about the color of your bridesmaid dress is boring."

Jillian and I looked at each other in the mirror and we each raised our eyebrows.

"Okay, fine. It's goldfish. Now can you please try it on?" she said, handing it to me. I agreed, stepping into the dress. As I twisted to zip it up, I distinctly heard her mutter "melon" under her breath.

I let it go.

I turned into the mirror and looked at my reflection, and had to admit, I looked good in goldfish.

Full skirt, scooped neck, thin straps, bare arms. With a tan, it would work just fine. Better than fine. I twirled in the mirror, then stopped midtwirl when I saw Mimi going for the champagne again.

"Jillian, stop her, she's cut off," I said. Mimi was barely bigger than a champagne bottle herself, and more than two glasses knocked her on her tiny ass.

"You're no fun, Caroline," she huffed as Jillian snagged the last glass for herself.

Jillian looked triumphant as she approached me in the mirror, standing behind me. "It looks great," she murmured, smoothing the skirt.

"Thanks again for asking me to be a bridesmaid," I replied, meeting her eyes.

We both smiled, and then smiled bigger when we heard Mimi making retching noises. "Ugh, you two are so sweet, I'm gonna puke."

"Okay, moment's over. Outta that dress and let's go get Mimi something to eat," Jillian said.

Mimi cheered. We finished up, headed out, and grabbed a table at a favorite bistro in North Beach.

Once we were settled and got started on some appetizers for Mimi to soak up the champagne, we talked about the honeymoon.

"Wait, wait, when did France get put on the table? I thought you were going to Italy," I said, buttering a piece of bread.

"Well, Benjamin and I talked about it and we realized it's been ages since we had a real vacation, not just a weekend away. So we wanted to extend the trip a bit."

"Wow, that's going to be some honeymoon! Italy and France—sounds amazing," I replied.

"And Switzerland. We added Switzerland too," Jillian added, a guilty look on her face.

Mimi sighed romantically, clutching her roll close to her chest. "That sounds heavenly—a European honeymoon! I can't wait to start planning my honeymoon. Ryan said we can go wherever I want, provided I wear lots of string bikinis for him to enjoy. And remove." She giggled, then hiccupped. Champagne was still lingering.

"Wait, wait, wait—you're going to Switzerland too?" I asked incredulously. "Anywhere else you're planning that I should know about?"

"Well, I was planning on talking about this at the office, but—"

"Whoa, what's going on?" I asked.

"Actually, we're taking an open-ended trip," she said matter-of-factly. " We just want to wander freely, and this seems like a good time to do it."

I sat back in my chair, my head spinning. "How long are you planning on being gone?"

"Long enough to know that you're gonna need an intern."

"Wait a minute, just wait a minute. An intern? Seriously Jillian, *how long* are you going to be gone?" I asked, thinking of all the projects that were coming up on the calendar, to say nothing of the Claremont Hotel, if I was lucky enough to land it.

"Let's talk about it at the office, okay? The food is here," she said, nodding at our waiter with our dinner.

As he set plates down in front of us, I met her eyes across the table. "We'll talk about it at the office," she said again. "It'll be fine, I promise."

It was a quiet dinner. Except for Mimi's hiccupping.

. . .

Text from Simon to Caroline:

Hey, babe, you free for lunch today?

I wish. I'm slammed.

I can come down there; I'll even bring my hammer.

As much as I do love your hammer, I'm literally buried under a pile of colored pencils at the moment.

Hmm, how about dinner?

Negative, Ghost Rider, I'm heading out to Sausalito tonight as soon as I leave work.

For the hotel? And did you just Top Gun me?

Yup, tonight is the first chance I've had to get out there to actually see the place. And yes, I totally Top Gunned you. You want to meet me out there? We could grab a quick dinner afterward.

We could grab a quick
something . . .

Babe.

Sorry. OK, text me the
address and I'll meet you
out there. 7?

Perfect.

Dammit Simon, now all I
can think about is a quick
something.

Aaand we're back. See you
at 7.

I walked around the property, checking sight lines and viewpoints, noticing where the late afternoon light hit the buildings. I saw windows where they weren't, walls where they could be moved to exploit the natural landscape, and pocket gardens that could be renovated to bring a sense of green to a modern shell.

I was getting excited to bid on this job.

A Range Rover's honk broke me from my reverie. I turned from the front walkway to see Simon pulling up in front. Not quite done with what I was doing, I lifted a finger to indicate that I needed another minute. He parked and walked to where I was.

"So this is the place, huh?" he asked, wrapping his arms around me as I gazed up at the structure.

"Yep, what do you think?"

"I think my girl's gonna kick some ass on this project," he replied, resting his chin on the top of my head.

"It's a beautiful location, isn't it?"

"What, Sausalito? Yeah, I suppose."

"Are you kidding? Look at that view!" I pointed back over the bay at the city. San Francisco twinkled in the twilight, the cars going back and forth over the bridge. Coit Tower. Transamerica building. Lovely.

Then I did a 180 and looked back at Sausalito. It wasn't just a great place to gaze at San Francisco. The houses were glowing against the mountain, streetlights just coming on, sailboats dotting the marina, people walking along the waterfront on their way to dinner or shopping or going home.

"The restaurant isn't far from here. Let's walk," I said, tugging him toward the main drag.

He twined his fingers through mine and as we walked, we talked. About my design ideas, about the upcoming wedding, about his next trip. He was leaving again in two days, this time for South Africa. He was going out on a shark boat, getting shots of the great whites feeding. I couldn't really think about it without shuddering.

Shudder.

"So Jillian told me today they added France and Switzerland to their honeymoon. Looks like they're going to be gone awhile," I said as we headed toward the pier with the restaurant.

"Oh, yeah? Good for them. I know Benjamin has always wanted to travel more."

"Jillian too, but she was building a business. Hard to leave a business like that—unless you have Super Caroline back home, running the show." I laughed, making a show of my muscles, which he squeezed appreciatively. "But I admit, I'm surprised they don't seem to have more of a plan."

"Sounds like they just want to wander around."

"Sure, sure. Except wandering without a plan is not like Jillian."

Simon shrugged. "It's their honeymoon, babe. And it's not like they can't afford it."

"Yes, I'm well aware of Benjamin's giant assets," I replied, getting a swat on the bum for that one. Simon indulged my crush on Benjamin, but he still reminded me whose assets I needed to be concerned with. "I'm just . . . a bit nervous, I guess. This is a lot to take on."

"Did you talk to Jillian about it?"

"Not since this hotel proposal came up. She's so busy with the wedding right now and everything else she's got going on, I've barely seen her."

"I'm sure she knows what she's doing. She wouldn't leave if she didn't know you could handle it, right?"

"That's what she said," I told him, thinking of how much I was really biting off here. "And she did say she'd bring in an intern for me, so that'll help."

"Nice! Moving on up," he exclaimed, humming the tune from *The Jeffersons*.

"Yeah, the president of the design firm is bopping around Europe for who knows how long, but I've got a twenty-year-old intern to help me make copies, so it'll be fine," I snapped, reaching for the door to the restaurant. A strong hand reached over mine, stalling the door.

"Hey, it'll work out. Don't worry so much," he said, gently nudging my chin up with his fingers to meet his eyes. My frustration that had flared so suddenly melted away when those sapphire eyes starting spinning their voodoo.

"You're probably right." I sighed, letting him open the door for me and guide me inside, one hand on the small of my back.

"Of course I'm right," he teased.

Once we were seated, I pulled out my calendar.

"Okay, you get back two days before the wedding, right? I want to make sure you have time to settle in before the festivities start."

"Yep, I'll be back in time and ready for all best-man duties."

"Cutting it pretty close, aren't you?"

"I don't know what I was thinking when I said I'd do this shoot, but it'll be fine. I can sleep during the vows, right? They don't need me for that," he joked.

I turned his palm up on the table, tracing the lines with my fingertips. I glanced up at him, noticing his gaze had turned dark under his lashes. "You can't sleep during the ceremony, babe. Besides, there'll be a bridesmaid across from you thinking the dirtiest thoughts imaginable."

"Dirty, huh?"

"Oh my, yes; I'm not sure I'll be able to control myself. You? In a tux? Deadly," I purred, raising his hand to press a quick kiss to his fingers.

As the waiter came over to get our drink order I winked, dropped his hand, and mouthed "later."

While Simon looked over the wine list, I looked out the large picture window at San Francisco. The sun had finally set, and the light from the city bounced back across the water. I smiled, considering myself one of the very lucky to call my favorite city home.

chapter four

I sat across from Max Camden, my designs tacked up on boards around the room and my formal presentation in my hand. On a disk. And in a folder. And backed up to a thumb drive in my purse. And a thumb drive in Jillian's purse. And after a midnight run to Sophia's apartment, a thumb drive in her jewelry box.

I had thumbs all over town. But would I get the thumbs-up from Camden?

Nerves gave Backbone a high five for punning in the face of life-changing moments.

I had circled the room for an hour, laying out my ideas, bolstered by pictures, charts, and more graphs than high school geometry. Jillian had interjected occasionally, but she let me take the lead. The vision I had conceptualized for the Claremont was clean and simple, with a nod to the boutique hotels that used to line the California coast.

While Camden's hotels were known for their modernistic design, there was a reason that he wasn't going with his usual design team. He was looking for something new, whether he knew it or not. Would he be swayed by what I had to say?

His gray eyes flickered back to me, his gaze narrow and sharp. This guy was intimidating, and he knew it.

As I had presented, he had stopped me only a few times, asking very clear and concise questions that were exactly the right ones. I was ready, though. I was as prepared as I could be with the limited time I'd been given, and I thought I held my own. Now it came down to whom else he was seeing, and whether their vision matched his own.

It was time for me to bring it home.

I slid one more picture across the table toward him, a photocopy from an old *San Francisco Chronicle* article about the town of Sausalito. It was old, nearly eighty years, and the picture showed that the town was much the same as it was now. Picturesque but bustling, quaint but proud. Next to its much grander neighbor of San Francisco, it could have lived for years in its shadow. But Sausalito had a heartbeat that was all its own; its own DNA. It was *family,* in whatever way the modern times defined it.

"So you can see, Mr. Camden, that while other towns around the Bay Area have grown up and out, Sausalito is content to remain in its own little oyster shell, enclosed by the bay that makes it such a unique community. For a new hotel to succeed here, it needs to be unique as well. The existing hotel fails to do that.

"This hotel needs to be appealing to both young and old clientele at the same time, environmentally conscious without appearing to be so, green without being granola, with a design that harkens back to the town's beginnings but nods toward the future," I said, then took a breath. Jesus, I hated speaking in motivational.

"A modern hotel will be out of place here, Mr. Camden. This needs to melt into the landscape, but leave such a strong memory that once you stay here, you'll never think of booking anywhere else."

I sat back in my seat, putting the cap on my pen.

"And that's exactly what you'll get with Jillian Designs," I finished. Hoping that no one noticed that I'd been struggling under the table to get back into my left shoe. I'd lost it somewhere between harkening back and nodding toward the future. When I was nervous, my feet tended to go pigeon-toed.

The room was quiet.

Camden looked at me for another moment, his eyes indecipherable.

We all sat, waiting for him to say something. Finally, he sighed.

My heart sank. And there went my right shoe.

"Well, Max," Jillian said, breaking the silence. "I'm sure you've got a lot to think about, so we'll make sure you and your people have everything you need to—"

"You can bring this project in on time, young lady?" he asked me directly as everyone on his side of the table had started to get up.

"Yes, sir."

"And you think you can get this done with the budget you've set out here?"

"Yes, sir," I answered, toes frozen in their quest for my shoe. Everyone else hovered in their half-standing poses.

He smiled at me, then stood up . . .

" . . . and then he said, '*Okay, you've got the job,*' and walked out! Just like that!" I squealed. "I got the *job!*"

I was recounting the story to Simon, who had called me as soon as his plane landed in Cape Town. The biggest news of my professional career, and I had to share it with him over the phone. Ah, well.

"That's great! Oh, babe, that's fantastic! Damn, I wish I was there to take you out to celebrate."

"I know, I wish you were here too. But you can kiss on me when you get back—we'll celebrate then."

"I'll for sure kiss on you, plus other things."

"Right now I'd settle for the kissing. Let me fantasize about the other things." I sighed into the phone. I could hear him exhaling. That was his tell, right before things got out of hand . . .

"Anyway, before things get out of hand—"

"You mean before I *take* things in hand?" he replied in a husky tone.

"Simon, control yourself. Pretty sure you're still in the airport, aren't you?" I asked, my face blushing when I thought of him walking through customs with a bone diddy.

"You're getting off on a technicality. So talk me down. You got the job, what's next?" he asked, his voice taking on a businesslike tone. I could tell he was struggling to maintain, so I went easy on him.

"What's next is I won't come back up for air until the wedding, then go right back into the thick of it. Seriously, I can't even *begin* to tell you how busy I'm going to be. It's a good thing this is your busy season, because I will be swamped for the foreseeable future. I'm interviewing final candidates for the new intern tomorrow, I'm simultaneously putting the final touches on several projects that I'd normally deal with one at a time—it's insane."

"Insane good, though, right?" he asked, and I grinned broadly.

"Insane good, yes. I'm so glad you understand what it's like to be wrapped up in your work. You're kind of the best, Wallbanger."

"I aim to please."

"You *do* please; often," I whispered, my voice taking on a husky tone.

"Getting ready to go through customs now, Caroline."

"Do you have any idea how much you please me, Simon? Over and over again. Just the thought of you almost makes me want to please myself," I murmured, and heard him groan.

"Business or pleasure, Mr. Parker?" I could hear an official-sounding voice say.

"Pleasure, please," I answered naughtily, and Simon hissed.

"Hanging up on you now." And he did just that.

I fell back into the pillows, flushed and giggly. The things that Wallbanger made me do.

Text from Simon to Caroline fifteen minutes later:

Someone's in trouble when I
get home.

> Promise?

Woman, you give me ideas.

> Do I, now?

Seriously though, all sexting
aside, congratulations. I'm
proud of you.

> I'm proud of me too.
> Thanks.

Now then, what are you
wearing?

> Go chum the water,
> Wallbanger.

That's what we're calling it
now?

> Sigh. You remember the
> first time you texted me?
> From Ireland?

I do.

And you remember when
I went across the hall and
kicked your door?

There was a short pause. Then:

You just did, didn't you?

Maybe.

Love you.

Love you more. Be careful
with Jaws.

"**Y**ou got a minute?" I asked, standing in Jillian's doorway. I'd been trying to pin her down all week to make a final decision about the intern I wanted to bring on board, but she was booked solid with clients and last-minute wedding appointments.

"I've got my last dress fitting in twenty minutes; what's up?" she asked, looking frazzled.

"Well, I've interviewed all the interns and narrowed it down to three that I think you'll want to meet with, and one is actually—"

"You pick, Caroline. This is going to be mainly your intern, so you pick." She smiled, turning off her computer and grabbing her jacket off the coatrack.

"Um, okay, I can do that, but—wait! Are you leaving now? I thought I had twenty minutes!"

"I have to *be* there in twenty minutes, which means with traffic, I'll actually be late. Walk me out?" She gestured for me to follow her.

"Jillian, I need to talk to you about some stuff. There's a few things that need to be taken care of before you—"

"Caroline. You've got this. I trust you. Hire the intern you think is best and I'll sign off on it, okay?" she called out, walking past me and out into the hallway.

She's getting married, she's getting married, be happy, be happy, I chanted in my head.

"Okay, but we need to have a serious powwow about some things before you leave. I don't know if—"

"Make a list of everything we need to go through, then e-mail it to me, okay? I'll read it tonight and we'll talk first thing tomorrow morning, I promise," she replied, sailing down the stairs and out the front door, calling back over her shoulder, "And congratulations on your first intern!"

I smiled in spite of myself, watching her get into a waiting car. Hair perfectly done, killer heels, off to try on the wedding gown she was going to marry her Prince Charming in.

Spinning on my own slightly less expensive but still somewhat lethal heels, I caught the eye of our receptionist. "Hey, Ashley, can you call that last one, Monica, from Berkeley? Let her know she's our new intern," I said. One task down, I headed back to my office to tackle the next thousand.

chapter five

The next morning I was waiting in Jillian's office when she arrived. As asked, I'd sent her my list of questions and tasks that needed her approval or input before the wedding. We had lots to discuss, but foremost was getting a better idea of when she was coming back.

"Wow, you're here early," she exclaimed, shrugging out of her coat and unwrapping her scarf.

I arched an eyebrow at her. "Hey, my boss is all over the map—she's getting married this weekend, you know. Figured I better nab her while I could."

She sighed, sinking down into her chair. "Have I been a bridezilla?"

"Nah, I'd characterize you more like the phantom boss," I joked.

"Watch it, Reynolds; I'd hate to have to write up my maid of honor for insubordination," she warned, a twinkle in her eye but enough steel to tell me I was pushing it. "So I read your list. It's long."

"It is. And I can handle practically everything on there. I just need to know what your plans are, and what your expectations are of me so I can manage things."

"I know, kiddo; sorry I've been a little absent lately. Who knew weddings had so many arms and legs?" She grinned. "I can't wait to watch when *you* go through all this. It's a lot to have on your plate." She picked up the list and grabbed a pen.

"When *I* go through this?" I asked, my breathing going a little, well, breathy.

"Sure. Don't you think you and Simon are heading that way eventually?" she asked, putting on her glasses and positioning them so she could look down at me. Cheeky.

"Um, I don't, well, I mean, how can I, Jillian!" I stuttered, blood rushing to my face at the thought. Picket fence territory.

"Whoa, strike a nerve there?" she asked, a twinkle growing in her eye. "Don't you think Simon's the marrying kind?"

"I don't . . . I mean . . . he's never had a relationship longer than the one he's currently in, I don't think we need to push the issue, and besides, it's good the way it is now and—I don't know that I, I mean, what if I don't want—"

"Easy there, Trigger, settle down." She grinned, pleased that she'd rattled me off course.

"Okay, this isn't what we're here to talk about this morning. We need to go through this list and put out some fires, and I need to know when you're coming back from your honeymoon, woman!" Simon and me getting married. Pffft.

"Not sure," she said calmly.

"Wait, *what*?"

"We're not sure when we're coming back. Wanna house-sit too?"

"House-sit too?" I asked, my eyes crossing.

She sighed, sitting back in her chair.

"The thing is, Caroline, I need a break. I love my job, you know how much this business means to me, and I'm so very proud that I've been able to carve out a niche for myself. But I need a break, and Benjamin and I just want to go wherever we feel like for a while. Does that make any sense?"

It made perfect sense. A gorgeous man and his gorgeous new bride, with all that money burning a hole in their bonds or funds or whatever really wealthy people had their money in. They wanted to see the world while they were young enough and sexy enough to do it right.

Hell, I'd do it if I had the chance. A never-ending vacation with Simon? Gondola rides in Venice? Yodeling in Saint Moritz? Fucking in Frankfurt?

But I couldn't afford to think like that. I had to think about the person left behind, the person left behind holding the design bag. How could Jillian Designs function without Jillian?

"I've already talked to my accountant, who can walk you through any weird payroll issues that might come up. And it's not like I'll be in a cave somewhere. We'll do weekly conference calls; I can assist with whatever you need. You'll see, it'll be fine," she assured me, her face filled with a confidence in me that I didn't share.

Could I do this? Jillian seemed to think so. Plus I'd have a new intern. I didn't want to say no, not when I knew she was counting on me.

This is too much.

This is also an opportunity. One that would likely never come along again.

Shit yes, I could do this.

"So tell me about this house-sitting gig. Does it come with the Mercedes in the garage?"

"It sure does."

"I'm in!"

"That's great! Now, back to you and Simon. So no marriage just yet, but have you talked about living together?"

I bit through my colored pencil.

• • •

"How's the sexiest interior designer on the West Coast?"

"You flatter me. Have you been keeping your bits and pieces tucked into your wet suit and away from shark week?"

"Best as I can. How're things going at work? You ever pin Jillian down about how long they're going to be away on their honeymoon?" Simon asked, calling in for his nightly chat. Which was really breakfast, his time. It's amazing how fast you learn all the time zones when your boyfriend was usually running across all of them in any given month.

I sank back against the bed pillows. "I got a vague idea. Somewhere between indefinite and sabbatical."

"Wow, really? What does that mean for you?"

"In a word? Fucking busy."

"That's two words, nightie girl."

"I'm so busy it can't possibly be contained to just one word. The good news is, I scored us a house with a killer view of the bay."

"Huh?"

"Jillian asked if I wanted to house-sit for them while they're gone."

"And you said yes?"

"I did; how could I turn that down? Why, do you not want to stay there? It'll be fun."

"It'll be boring." He groaned.

I rolled my eyes. Simon loved his city living. "Oh please, it'll be great. Besides, I don't think we need to stay out there every night. I think they just don't want the place sitting empty for all that time."

"Humph," was his response.

"We can go hot tubbing."

"Humph?" was his more interested response.

"As you recall, I tend to lose all control when bubbles are involved," I said, thinking back to the first time we hot tubbed in Tahoe.

"True. Will there be skinny-dipping?"

"You bet your sweet bippy."

"Mmm, you're killing me." He groaned, but this time in a very different way.

"Anyway, as busy as I'm going to be, it'll be nice to have a change of pace. It'll feel a little like a vacation just across the bridge. I'm barely going to be able to come up for air in the next few months."

"Speaking of vacation, I just booked a job in Bora Bora. Wanna go?"

"What?"

"Yep, after the wedding. What do you say? Thatched hut over the water? Coconut bikinis? Actual sex on the beach?"

I clenched my hands in frustration.

"Have you been listening to anything I've said? I'm *swamped,* and about to get even swampier. I can't go to Bora Bora. I couldn't even go to *Napa* if I wanted—" I stopped myself from going on a full tirade and took a deep breath. "Simon, that's very sweet of you, and you know there's nothing I'd like more than to run off to the South Pacific with you. But I just can't. I literally can't even think about that right now, okay?"

He was silent for a minute. The line was a bit crackly, and I imagined how far he truly was from me that night. How far that phone connection was, stretching halfway around the world to reach me. I sighed into my half of that connection.

"You're right, babe, I wasn't thinking. I do know how important this is to you. You know that."

"I do know that."

"Maybe this isn't a good year for Rio?" he asked, his voice quiet, but with an underlying tone.

"Don't you dare—I'm looking forward to that trip more than I can say! Things will have settled down by then. But in the meantime, I just can't drop everything and island hop."

He was silent.

"I love you," I whispered, wishing he was here to hug and hold.

"I love you too. I'm glad I'll be home soon." His voice had mellowed some.

"We'll have fun at the wedding," I said, changing the subject. "You gonna dance with me?"

"You bet your sweet bippy. I'll even get them to play us some Glen Miller."

"That always works." I giggled.

"Caroline?"

"Yes, Simon?"

"I *know* it works." He chuckled.

We said good night, then I went across the hall and let myself into his apartment. Putting the phonograph needle down, I slipped back to my apartment and into bed. Glen Miller played me to sleep through the walls, and I dreamed I was dancing on a beach in Brazil with my photographer.

T hree nights before the wedding, I was still at work at eight thirty and I'd just canceled dinner with Sophia and Mimi.

Bring a grown-up sucked sometimes.

I'd been in meetings all day with Camden's people, finalizing details on the construction that was beginning next week. We weren't doing a complete teardown, just a gut rehab, using the existing lines of the hotel but reworking the layout of nearly everything.

Monica, the new intern, was enjoying a first week of trial by fire. She'd been thrown into the deep end headfirst, but she was swimming. She'd run errands, she'd delivered paperwork, she'd filed for permits; she'd really taken a lot off my plate. And speaking of plate . . .

My tummy was grumbling. I padded into the kitchenette,

pretty sure I had a burrito stashed somewhere in the freezer, when my phone rang. Sophia.

"Still can't believe you ditched us, Reynolds," she sniped in my ear, and I bit back a snipe of my own. Seriously, did no one understand how busy I was?

"You'll get over it, I promise. Where'd you guys end up going?"

"Your favorite restaurant in Chinatown. You missed out, sister. We got that shrimp thingie with the noodles, what's it called? The one you love more than anything?"

My stomach rumbled even louder, and I gritted my teeth. "Mei Fun."

"We *did* have fun, thanks for asking!" She laughed in my ear. "Now let us in the front door—it's freezing out here."

"I'm still at work; I told you I was working late. Why are you at my apartment?"

"We're not at your apartment, you idiot, we're outside your work. Let us in," she said. I could hear Mimi grumbling in the background.

"You're outside my—oh, for God's sake." I walked down the stairs to the front door, and there on the other side of the glass were Mimi and Sophia. With Chinese take-out containers.

"I'm hanging up on you now." I grinned into the phone, unlocking the door and throwing it wide. "What in the world are you two up to?"

"It's dinner, silly, and we promise we'll only stay a little while," Mimi answered, walking inside and heading straight up for my office. With arms full of the most heavenly scented food on earth.

Sophia posed in the doorway, a vision. No more sad sacking for her, she was dressed to the nines and looking lethal. Red hair piled high on her head, makeup flawless, just the barest hint of leg peeking out from under her trench coat. "You're not gonna, like, flash me, are you?" I asked.

"Hell, no. Mama's got a date after we feed you." She grinned, handing me a bag.

"Mei Fun?"

"Someone's gonna have some fun tonight, that's for sure." She winked, sauntering past me. "Don't eat all the wontons, you little shit!"

Mimi yelled something back to her, but it was muffled by something in her mouth. My money was on the wonton. I locked the front door, shaking my head as I followed my two friends into my office.

Ten minutes later we were all sprawled across the floor cross-legged, with plates piled high with delicious food. Noodles, pan-fried shrimp, crispy pot stickers, spicy sautéed vegetables; it was a feast. Chopsticks were passed and we dug in.

"This sure as hell beats the burrito I was going to eat." I sighed, my mouth full of delicately seasoned noodles.

"Since we knew you were gonna be here late, we thought the least we could do is bring you dinner," Mimi responded, offering me an egg roll.

Sophia intercepted it, wielding it like a megaphone. "Oh, please, it was so I could tell you all about my new boy toy. You're impossible to get ahold of, lady, and I needed to dish!"

I grabbed my own egg roll and spoke directly into the mega-phone end of it. "So dish."

Sophia told us all about the new guy she'd met at the gym. Once she decided she was officially moving on and looking for love (read, a date to Jillian's wedding), she left no stone unturned. And this stone happened to be an insurance salesman. Car, life, you name it, he sold it. Hmmm.

"And let me just tell you, he is F-I-N-E fine. Tall, dark, and handsome, he is seriously sinful," she gloated. "I'm gonna have the hottest date there."

"Did she just quote a line from *Grease*?" Mimi asked me.

"Pretty sure she did. Let's just hope this guy's name isn't Cha Cha," I replied.

"His name is Barry, and he's great," Sophia insisted.

"As in Gibb?" I asked.

"As in White?" Mimi chimed in.

"As in Derry," Sophia said through clenched teeth.

"Wait a minute, hold up. Stop everything. His name is Barry—" I started.

"—Derry?" Mimi finished.

We collapsed on the floor howling amid chopsticks and soy packets.

"Silence, whores, silence. Besides, Reynolds, you dated a guy named James motherfucking Brown," Sophia snapped back.

"I sure did. That's fantastic compared to Barry Derry," I cried, wiping tears from my eyes. Which was a terrible idea, as I still had hot mustard on my fingertips. "Shit!"

"Serves you right," Sophia said, handing me a stack of napkins.

Mimi was still chortling, muttering something about him being hairy, and I gave her an elbow to the ribs.

Through my mustard haze I saw that Sophia was putting on a brave face, but this wedding wasn't going to be easy for her. I wasn't looking forward to seeing Neil either. I had a recurring fantasy where I accosted him by the cake stand and make him choke on fondant. I smiled encouragingly. "I'm sure he's great, sweetie. We can't wait to meet him."

We were all quiet for a moment.

Mimi cleared her throat, ready to change the subject. "When is Simon getting back?"

"Thursday night," I answered, then remembered my news. "Hey, I forgot to tell you! Guess who's house-sitting over in Sausalito?"

They both shrieked; we all loved Jillian's house. Especially the hillevator.

"That's gonna be so much fun. What did Simon say?" Mimi asked.

"Simon says it'll be boring out there, but Caroline says too bad. That house is a fucking rock star—who wouldn't want to stay out there? Plus it's so close to the Claremont, it'll be nice to have a home base over there. And I don't think we're going to spend every night there, just some."

"Look at you two, playing house. Isn't that sweet," Sophia remarked, earning a glare from Mimi. "All I'm saying is what you guys have now is great. Together but not. Separate but equal. It gets all fucked up when you start buying furniture together."

"Says the girl who moved in with Neil not even six months into the relationship," Mimi pointed out.

"Says the girl who is no longer with Neil," Sophia responded, waving her chopsticks in the air.

"But that's not why you broke up. Living together had nothing to do with it. You two had the best time living together—don't try and tell me you didn't."

"Sure, we had a great time. But it was too soon. Separate but equal—all I'm saying," she said, picking a bamboo shoot from her cleavage.

This was getting into sticky territory. And I don't just mean the cleavage.

"Okay, well, thanks for the advice, kids, but Simon and I aren't moving in together. We're house-sitting. And taking advantage of a killer house in which we will have the sexy times. So there," I finished.

The stack of paperwork on my desk was calling my name and I sighed, nabbed one more shrimp, then started closing up containers. The girls followed suit, making me keep the leftovers so I'd have something for lunch tomorrow. "You guys didn't have to do this, but I'm glad you did."

"I know how hard you've been working; just thought you might need a break," Mimi said as we walked toward the front door.

"Don't make it seem like this was your idea. *I'm* the one who suggested we bring her dinner," Sophia said. "*You* wanted to go get street tacos when she canceled."

"No way! I'm the one who said that we should—" Mimi started, but I beat her to the punch.

I knew where this was going and I shoved them out the door, laughing. "Ladies, I love you both. Now get the hell out of here."

They tossed back good-byes as they went on their way. I headed back up to my office, rolling my shoulders a bit and fighting the egg roll sleeps that were now threatening to take over. Then I flipped on every light in the place and turned on Pearl Jam. Loud.

Simon and I weren't moving in together. Pffft.

Twenty minutes later I got a text from Mimi:

Did Simon tell you Neil's
bringing someone?

> He did. What did Ryan say?

He won't say anything, just
that he's bringing a date.

> That's all that Simon will
> say too. She better not be
> pretty.

Of course she'll be pretty.

> I know. This could be bad,
> you know . . .

Count on it. Besides, it's
already bad—the guy's
name is Barry Derry, for
God's sake.

                              Scary . . .

Quiet.

Simon should have been back Thursday night, but his flight into
New York was delayed, making him miss his connection to San
Francisco. He was rebooked on a flight Friday morning, but he'd
be cutting the wedding rehearsal close indeed. He'd texted me to
let me know he was on his way to the airport, and then he'd texted
me for the address of the church. Then another text needing the
address of the restaurant the rehearsal dinner was being held in.

Jillian was stopping by the office this morning to finish up a
few things. I'd tried to talk her out of working the day before her
wedding, but she'd insisted she only needed a few minutes to tie up
a few loose ends. Then she'd leave for the bridal luncheon, which
I was missing to head a last-minute meeting with Mr. Camden.

I was in my office frantically printing out the reports I needed
for my meeting when Jillian breezed by. "I'm out of here, Caroline.
See you tonight?"

"I'll be there."

"Think Simon will make it back in time? Benjamin can have
someone else stand in tonight, if we need to."

"He'll be here. Last I heard from him, he was sitting on the
plane waiting to take off."

At that, my phone beeped again. Simon, wanting to know if
he was supposed to make some kind of speech tonight. Boys. I
typed back no, said good-bye to Jillian, and grabbed the last of the

reports off the printer, just as the receptionist called over the intercom to let me know that the Camden team was here and being shown into the conference room.

As Monica came to help me take everything in, my phone beeped again.

I handed it to her. "Can you take this while I'm in the meeting? And if Simon needs his shoes tied or his shirt buttoned or anything else, please tell him to— Never mind. Just tell him I'm busy, and I'll see him when he gets in tonight." I tried to smile, smoothing my shirt so I didn't appear frazzled. Sometimes it really was perception equals reality.

I am calm.

I am calm.

I am calm.

"No problem, I'll take care of it. Everything else you need is already in the conference room; just let me know if you need anything else."

As we walked toward the meeting, my phone beeped again. Stifling a growl, I looked over at her. She looked at the text and frowned.

"Shoes tied? Shirt buttoned?" I asked, nodding a greeting to Camden's team through the window in the conference room door.

"Um, not exactly. He wants to know if you can pick up his tux at lunch today?"

I am calm.

I am calm.

I am calm.

chapter six

I sat in the back of the cab, drumming my knee and trying not to look at my watch again. I'd make the rehearsal, but I hated cutting it so close. By the time I'd finished up everything I needed to at work to make sure I could truly take the weekend off, it was only an hour before the rehearsal began and I still hadn't changed. Luckily I'd brought my dress to the office and quickly changed there.

Could I pick up his tux at lunch, ha! I didn't even *eat* lunch, but no matter. Monica the wonder intern was nice enough to run the errand, bringing the tux back to the office with a smile. She was the best. Simon, I'd deal with later.

I made it to the rehearsal with a few moments to spare, and as I made my way in I got a text from Simon. He was on the way. I cringed when I thought about how exhausted he was going to be after flying halfway around the world. But it wasn't his fault his flight was delayed, and I made a mental note to go easy on him about the tux.

Greeting some of the other bridesmaids and mingling with Jillian's family, I made my way inside the church to where she and Benjamin were chatting with the minister. Damn, that man was stunning.

Dark suit, tanned skin, that little bit of salt starting to edge out the pepper at his temples, and those eyes that were full of fun. This was the guy you wanted *your* guy to become one day. He winked as he greeted me, knowing full well that when he went full charm we all turned to mush.

"Hi, Benjamin," I said, already on my way to Mushtown.

"Caroline, you're looking lovely tonight." He tucked me into his side with a grin, and I could feel the blood rise to my cheeks. Now I was a blushing mush. "So where is that idiot best man of mine?"

"Here! Idiot is here!" I heard, and in rushed Simon. Hair still damp from the shower, clad in his own dark suit and tie, he hurried to my side. "Hey, old man, let go of my girl."

Shaking Benjamin's hand, he dropped a kiss on Jillian's cheek, then turned to me, taking me in. He reached out, hands spanning my waist, and pulled me into him. His gaze met mine, my hands resting on his chest. His face was sun kissed from the days spent on the ocean, with the tiniest of freckles here and there. Fucking gorgeous man. And the best part? The way he looked at *me*. Like I was the prettiest girl in the room.

"Hey, babe."

The man was a poet.

"Hey."

I was too.

He leaned down, eyes staying with mine until a second after his lips touched mine. His kiss was soft, featherlight. His mouth brushed against mine once, then twice, then by the third time, more than his lips got involved. His tongue darted out to gently nudge at the seam of my lips, and when they parted for him, it flicked out to taste me.

Were we in a church? I was clueless, because in that moment all I felt, all I knew was Simon. His hands restless on my waist, the planes of his strong body anywhere it was pressed against mine, the scent of his shampoo and the ever-loving Downy filling my nostrils, and his mouth bearing down on mine.

I heard coughing, and as he broke our kiss to rest his forehead against mine, I saw Jillian arching her eyebrow at us.

"Simon," I whispered, within our bubble.

"Yes?"

"I missed you too," I said, giving him one more quick kiss.

Grinning, he spun me so I was next to him, and we turned back to Jillian and Benjamin. And the small crowd that was watching us.

"What? I missed my girl." He tucked me farther into his side and I smiled up at him. "Now, what are we rehearsing?" he asked.

The rehearsal went well, the dinner even better. Jillian and Benjamin had picked a beautiful restaurant, renting a private room with a rooftop terrace. Wine and champagne flowed, families mixed and mingled; it was a festive mood. Serving heavy appetizers instead of a formal sit-down encouraged everyone to get to know each other as they moved from table to table.

Simon and I stuck close to each other most of the evening, when I wasn't assisting Jillian with last-minute details. While there were several other bridesmaids and a maid of honor, Jillian trusted me implicitly to be her eyes and ears on All Things Wedding. Which is why I was the one with the sewing kit and the hemorrhoid cream in my purse.

For puffy eyes.

In between meeting second cousins and business partners on both sides, Simon managed to steal me away for secret kisses and whispered dirty talk in every nook and cranny of that restaurant.

"What's got into you?" I asked, breathless after a fevered kiss on the terrace. I'd come out to get some air when I was cornered against the glass railing by a handsy Wallbanger.

"*Into you*, now that's sounds like a wonderful idea," he murmured, turning me so I was facing the city. Caging me in with his arms, he pressed his body into mine. I leaned my head back onto his shoulder as he teased me with wet kisses up and down my neck.

I sighed, letting my hands reach back and tangle into his hair. "Behave yourself, mister."

"Not a chance." He thrust gently but insistently into my backside. My eyes popped open, as my insides went on instant clench. "I missed you. How long do we need to stay here?"

"Um, I don't think we should leave until Jillian and Benjamin are ready. I think that'd be—wow!" My head dropped back farther as he swept one hand up from my waist to just below my breasts.

"Shouldn't or can't?"

I struggled to think, to stay focused.

"Uh, well, maybe we could, mmm—" I was powerless, his hands getting more sure as they began to nudge my skirt higher on my thighs. "Okay, now I think we *should* leave. This is crazy."

"Atta girl." He had me saying good-byes in less than a minute, into the elevator in three minutes, and had me in the back of a cab five minutes after that.

And when I say had me, boy, did he try.

After successfully fending off Simon's attempts to get under my skirt in the cab, and then under my skirt while walking up our apartment stairs in front of him, I gave up all ownership of what was below my belly button when he bent me over the back of the sofa inside my apartment and removed my panties. With his teeth.

With his mother-loving teeth! I can't even!

I'd read this particular scene in many romance novels; I'd never experienced it in real life. I always wondered how exactly that would happen. Did he take a big bite of the part over your hip?

Use one canine to peel it off from the front? Sexy novels only mentioned teeth, so would lips be cheating? And speaking of cheating, if he used his hands to assist, but the teeth were the primary method for panty removal, would that be legal?

Romance novels, schmomance novels, here's how Wallbanger does it.

Hands went inside my skirt from either side as soon as we cleared the front door. As he guided me backward through the darkened apartment, his mouth was on my neck and his hands inside my bra, when the back of my thighs met the sofa.

Which I then had the honor of feeling with my eyeballs when I hit the pillows face-first, after he'd spun me and pushed me over the arm with my bum in the air. Think I even noticed that I had a forehead full of sofa? Hell no, I had a Wallbanger kneeling between my legs.

Wet kisses were smacked along the back of my legs as my skirt was lifted and placed out of his way. I felt his hands nudging my knees apart, felt his warm breath on the inside of my thighs as his fingers dipped inside the lace of my panties. Had I dressed up for my man? Oh hell, yes.

White. Lacey. Sweet. Guaranteed to make him pant. Which he was doing now, heavily. He kissed me through the silk, his tongue pointed and strong even through the barrier. I cried out, having been ready for that mouth ever since he pushed me up against the railing in the restaurant.

With his hands wrapped around my waist, he pressed down on the small of my back, angling me toward his face. Growling—and I swear that's the only way I can describe the guttural noises coming from the back of his throat—he grasped the top of my panties in his teeth and tugged. Down my thighs and toward my knees, and that's as far as they went, because: Simon. Was. Impatient.

With my ass in the air and my panties at my knees, he groaned.

"Mmm, there's that sweet pussy."

Not all men can handle the P-word. And boy, is that a mouthful. Ahem. Some say it all the time, some use it in common conversation. But a good P-word is all about placement: when to say it, where to say, how to say it. Dirty talk is an art. Do it too often, it becomes routine. Never do it, and you're missing something. Simon did it just right. He was like a perfect bowl of smutty porridge: just right. Let's get back to that mouthful . . .

I was done for even before his lips hit mine. And I meant that exactly how I said it.

There are nights when I need it slow. And there are nights when I need it sweet. And then there are nights when I need it fast and filthy.

Guess which night this was?

I came twice on his mouth. And twice more when he stood, unzipped, and plunged into me with one swift stroke. With one hand flat on my back and the other pulling my hair to angle me exactly how he needed it? Hell, yes.

It was deep and hard and intense. And so very fast and filthy.

Was I still wearing my heels when he finally brought it on home and shouted my name? Good gracious, yes.

Later on, piled into a pile on the couch with Simon using my hip as a pillow, I heard my phone ringing. Which was in my purse, barely inside the door. I lifted my head, looking over my shoulder and reaching with my hand. Knowing it was still ten feet away.

"I can't reach my phone."

"You don't need your phone."

"But it's ringing."

"Pretty sure it's not," he insisted, twisting around behind me.

The phone stopped ringing and I sank back against the cushions. Then it promptly starting ringing again.

"I can't reach my phone," I repeated dumbly. Being plowed like that will make you a little thick in the head. "Hey, did you just bite me?"

"You don't need your phone. And yes, I did. I've got two scoops of delicious staring me right in the face."

He had indeed bitten one of the two scoops. I rolled my eyes, and tried to actually go for the phone.

"Don't take away my scoops, Caroline, I'm warning you."

"Oh, scoop this," I teased, managing to sneak out from under him and hobble over to my purse, pulling my skirt down as I went. As I dug for my phone, I looked back at Simon, prone on the couch still with his pants around his ankles.

"You look charming, babe."

"Charm this," he mimicked, gesturing to a very specific part of his body.

With a laugh, I looked at my phone, seeing that it was Sophia. It was after midnight. I frowned and called her back.

"Hey, what's wrong?"

"Why does there have to be something wrong?" Her voice was low.

"How long have I known you? What's wrong?"

She didn't say anything, but I could hear her. Sniffling.

"Is it the wedding?"

Sniff.

"You don't think you want to go?"

Sniff sniff.

"Because you're gonna see Neil?"

Honk. Kleenex, not car.

"Sweetie, you know you have to go, right?"

Sniff.

"Not just because Jillian's expecting you, but because you have to see him eventually and—"

Angry honk!

"Do you want to come over? I made chocolate chip cookies last night."

Jingle jangle. This was the sound of Simon's pants being buckled as he blazed a trail into the kitchen.

"No, I'll be okay. God, this just sucks, though!" she finally said, blowing her nose again loudly.

"It totally sucks, sweetie, but you're going to be fine. You're a badass—I'm actually scared of you," I said.

"That's because you know I could kick your ass." She snorted. "Is he bringing someone?"

"Yes."

"Shit. I totally need to go, don't I?"

"You totally do," I responded, biting down on my lip. Did I dare? "Besides, think how disappointed Barry Derry would be."

Silence.

Then peals of laughter broke across the line. In between, she told me she loved me and would see me tomorrow. Then she hung up, still laughing.

I made my way into the kitchen to see Simon with his hands in the cookie jar. I shook my head, then poured him a glass of milk.

"It's criminal how much I love you right now," he said, his mouth full of cookie and smile.

I stood next to him while he finished his midnight snack, and as soon as he was done, I opened his arms and wrapped them around me. Cuddling me into his chest, he kissed the top of my head as I held on as tightly as I could.

The next day would bring all sorts of excitement, but tonight I had my Wallbanger in my bed. And that was all I needed.

Text from Caroline to Mimi:

> You gotta watch our girl
> today—she'll tell you she's
> fine, but she's not.

> Oh boy, what happened?

Just watch her.

Done. How's Jillian?

Radiant.

Naturally.

We're heading over to the church in a few hours.

I'll watch our girl, you go be a bridesmaid.

Text from Mimi to Sophia:

Hey, pretty girl, you still want to ride with us to the wedding?

Yep, just pick us up on your way.

You're still bringing Barry, right?

Yep, just pick us up on your way.

How're you feeling?

Mimi.

Yes?

Just pick us up on your way.

Ooookaaaaay.

• • •

Text from Simon to Neil:

You still down for windsurfing
tomorrow?

> Dude! It's gonna be
> freezing, no way.

Pussy.

> Dude. It's gonna be
> freezing.

Pussy. See you at the
wedding.

> Hey, about that, should I
> bring my gift there or what?

We have to get them a gift?
Hang on . . .

Text from Simon to Caroline:

Did we get them a gift?

> Of course we got them a
> gift. I signed your name.

Are we bringing it to the
wedding?

> No, it's already been
> sent. I always send them
> ahead; last thing a bride
> needs to worry about
> is making sure her gifts

are wrangled during her wedding.

So if someone didn't send it ahead of time, he shouldn't bring it?

From an etiquette standpoint, it's fine to bring it. People always do; I just like to take care of it ahead of time—wait, why are you asking?

Text from Simon to Neil:

Dude, you're fine, you can bring it with you.

Cool. See you there.

Text from Caroline to Simon:

Hey, mister. Why were you asking me about bringing a gift?

No reason.

Seriously, what's up?

Neil wanted to know if he should bring his gift with him or not, that's all.

Tell him to call me, I'll tell him where his gift can go.

Did I tell you how
pretty you look in your
bridesmaid dress?

You haven't even seen me
yet . . .

Safe to assume.

You're good, Wallbanger.

Text from Neil to Sophia:

Hey. Just wanted to say hey.
You're going today, right?

Ah. Still not talking to me,
I see.

So anyway, I just wanted to
tell you that I'll be glad to
see you. I think it's time we
talked. Still can't believe you
hang up every time I call,
but I don't want to get into
that today. I'll just be glad to
see you; I'd like a chance to
explain.

Sophia?

Soph?

Eat me.

chapter seven

The anteroom at the Swedenborgian Church in Pacific Heights was full to bursting with shades of maple, copper, champagne gold, and cheddar goldfish. Crinolines crackled and swished, nervous giggles spilled from delicately painted lips, and a proud father stood straight and tall.

A bride stepped forward to take his arm as her ladies gathered before her, their hands full of peaches-and-cream dahlias. She was tall and regal, blushing and not at all bashful. Draped in ivory silk and century-old Italian lace, the solitary spot of color was a four-karat canary diamond on the fourth finger of her left hand.

The oaken doors opened.

Her eyes danced.

As a string quartet played, her bridesmaids glided down the aisle, one after another. The church was full, but not overly so. The small chapel, earthy and charming, had a coffered ceiling made of ancient wood accented by the thousands of softly lit cream-colored candles. In the hearth, uncommon in most churches but perfectly suited to this rustic setting, a fire crackled merrily, casting its own fairy-tale light.

Guests smiled, their faces aglow with quiet expectation,

turned toward the center aisle. And as I walked down that very aisle before the bride, I saw Benjamin at the end, beaming.

And next to him? My own piece of heaven. I smiled when I saw him, resplendent in a tuxedo that was cut to accentuate his tall and strong frame. His eyes glowed azure in the firelight, his face extraordinary. His grin burst across his face as I neared him. He winked, and I swooned.

As did most of the ladies in the chapel.

Taking my place in line, I watched as Jillian's maid of honor joined us, the music changing as the bride was about to appear. I turned to see not Jillian, but Benjamin.

Have you ever watched a groom when his bride appears for the first time? All eyes are on her, yes, but the true magic is wherever that groom is. To witness his eyes light up, to see the emotions fall across his face. To be there as he fights to retain control of his feelings, as all men are supposed to do in that situation. But those first few seconds, you see the truth. You can see everything he feels when he sees her that first time.

I didn't need to actually observe Jillian turn that corner to know when she had entered that chapel. Because I saw it all on Benjamin's face, the second he saw her.

Surprise.

Longing.

Relief.

Need.

Pure, naked joy.

Tears sprang to my eyes, as I knew they would. I could feel my grin take over my face, threatening to split it in two. As my gaze swept across to where Jillian was walking toward us, I caught Simon's eye.

And I'll be damned if there wasn't a tear in his eye too.

· · ·

The ceremony was short and sweet. Vows were exchanged, tears were shed by most, and under a shower of petals, the newlyweds exited the church into a perfect autumn afternoon.

And who did I see throwing those petals? Mimi and Ryan, of course, Sophia and Barry Derry (who was admittedly hot), and Neil and . . . no one.

He didn't bring a date after all.

Something that was noticed by Sophia, even though she pretended not to notice him at all.

Although I was required by wedding party law to accompany Jillian everywhere she went (and yes, this included the ladies' room, where I can now say I've helped my boss pee), I managed to sneak in a little time with my friends before getting onto the very inelegant but very necessary party bus.

Simon and I were separated by our "bridal order," since the best man was always photographed officially with the maid of honor, but once the photographer was done I was able to sneak a kiss or two.

"I knew you'd look pretty in your bridesmaid dress." He spun me to take in the full skirt, his eyes widening when he saw it flare up and reveal a little extra leg.

"You cleaned up very nicely yourself," I answered, taking a moment to admire the treat that was Wallbanger in a tux.

"So now what happens?"

"Now we get on the bus and drink champagne with the rest of the wedding party, take pictures over at Baker Beach with the bridge in the background, then off to the reception. Where you can get me drunk, if you like."

"I like. I also liked that ceremony back there. They seemed really happy, didn't they?"

"They did." I smiled, gazing up into those sapphire eyes, which looked over my shoulder and clouded over.

"What? What's wrong?"

"Nothing. Maybe nothing." He grimaced, and I turned. Sophia and Barry Derry talking with Mimi and Ryan, with Neil walking toward them.

"Oh boy," I muttered, and we headed in.

"So I said, no way, Barry—not here; anyone could see us!" Sophia cried, grasping the guy who had no idea what he was in for. I looked over at Mimi, who was struggling to keep a straight face, while Ryan just frowned.

"Hey everyone, wasn't it a beautiful ceremony?" I asked, pulling Simon into the ring just as Neil reached the group.

Mimi took the cue, responding loudly, "It really was! Sophia, did you get a look at those roses by the altar? We should go get some pictures before they—"

"Hi, Sophia," Neil said from behind Sophia, and her eyes blazed.

I looked at Simon, Simon looked at Ryan, Ryan looked at Neil. Neil looked at the back of Sophia's hair, while Barry Derry looked at his fingernails.

Finally Simon walked over to Neil and clapped him on the back in that man-clappy way.

"Hey, man, did you see Benjamin yet? I think he's still doing that receival line or whatever it's called. I'll walk you over." Simon nodded at Ryan, who crossed over as well. That left Mimi, Sophia, and me on one side of the circle, and the boys on the other. Mr. Derry was still in the middle, clueless. But still way hot.

"Sophia, come on, baby, are you going to ignore me all night?" Neil asked, and her spine stiffened.

"Baby? You're gonna call me *baby*?" she hissed, spinning on her heel. A Come Fuck Me heel, I might add; the girl was fierce. Her hair was waved back in perfect curls, makeup was flawless, body with its newly added breakup pounds was poured into a slinky black dress. And her boobs? Shit. *I* was even a little curious.

But Neil? He was astonished. Dumbstruck. Clotheslined. The linebacker stared at the cellist, eyes like saucers. Hungry saucers—this boy was still stupid in love.

But she was so very angry. And I couldn't blame her. Because no one can hurt you quite like someone who says he loves you.

"You don't *get* to call me baby," she snapped, hands on her hips, chest thrust forward; she knew how to use what she had. Grabbing Barry by the tie, she led him toward the parking lot.

Our circle closed in, my hand going into Simon's and Mimi's arm going around Ryan's waist.

"She's not gonna talk to me, is she?" he asked, his face sad.

I rolled my eyes. "I doubt it." Our bus pulled up and I tugged on Simon. "Come on, we've got to go. We'll see you at the reception." I nodded to Mimi, and shot one more look back at Neil over my shoulder as we left.

"Go easy, okay?" Simon said as we walked across the parking lot.

"You're kidding, right?"

"I'm not kidding. She's your friend, and I get that, but that's *my* friend." His eyes were warm, but warning.

I saw Sophia walking with Hot Barry, her laughter deliberately loud. "Let's just enjoy the night?" I whispered to Simon as he guided me onto the bus.

We settled into our seats with the rest of the bridal party, celebrating with the happy couple. And as we maneuvered through the streets of San Francisco toward the bay, watching Jillian and Benjamin kiss every minute or so, I felt very happy that I had my Simon at my side. And very sad for Sophia that she did not have her Neil.

But it was a happy day, and after a few glasses of champagne I was ready for a fancy night on the town.

And with the reception at the Fairmont Hotel? It was guaranteed.

• • •

If the ceremony was simple, the reception was anything but. *Elegant* was the best word to describe the Fairmont's Venetian Room, and the reception overall.

If I thought every candle in San Francisco was at the chapel, then every candle in the rest of the entire Bay Area was lit inside this ballroom. Add to that the golden chandeliers, the crystals dripping from every sconce, the mirrors reflecting and dancing back every flicker and twinkle, and the effect was not of this world.

It was of the planet Money. Which was within the galaxy Ridiculous.

But it was still Jillian and Benjamin. Were there floral arrangements taller than I was? Yes, but there were also copies of their high school senior pictures at each place setting. Was there a full orchestra? Yes, but it was playing instrumental versions of Def Leppard, Journey, and U2. And a band called Rush, which every guy was going bananas over.

When we'd arrived with the bride and groom in tow, we made our grand entrance to an applauding crowd. Once seated at the head table, I saw that Jillian had designed the seating so that even though Simon was the best man, he was still seated next to me. As I looked around at all the pomp and sparkle, I saw that Jillian had seated Sophia and Neil at separate tables (hastily adjusted when the breakup went down), but their tables were next to each other. And there was an empty seat next to Neil.

"I don't get it, I thought you said he was bringing someone?" I whispered to Simon.

"He was, but he changed his mind. He wanted to talk to her tonight, and he decided he'd have a better shot if he was alone," he whispered back, a told-you-so look on his face.

"Hmm," I said.

And as I watched their story unfold from up on the dais, their communications were very clear.

First Sophia realized that while they were technically at different tables, her place card put her directly behind Neil's chair. And when she approached the round table and pulled her chair out herself (way to go, Barry Derry), she made sure to accidentally-on-purpose bump his chair.

Then when Neil rose to shake hands with someone and accidentally (but maybe not on purpose) bumped *her* chair, I saw Sophia pick up her salad fork and begin to turn, before Mimi removed it from her hand.

By the time the entrees were served, they were both jostling so much it looked like they had ants in their pants. Except that Sophia's dress was so tight I was pretty sure she wasn't wearing any. Panties, that is.

"Are you seeing this?" I asked Simon, nodding toward the chair bumpers.

"How could I miss it?"

Just then, Neil turned around and tapped Sophia on the shoulder. Her response was to scoot her chair back as far as she could, stand, and conveniently stomp on his foot with her stiletto as she dragged an unwilling Mimi off to the ladies' room, leaving Neil to swear quietly into his napkin. When she reached the edge of the ballroom, she whirled, spied me spying on her, and curled her finger at me.

Damn. Powwow in the toilet.

"I'll be back; don't let them cut the cake without me."

"Yes, I'll be sure to explain to the bride and groom, as well as all these good people here, that they have to wait on cake because of chitchat in the henhouse," Simon responded drily.

I dropped a kiss on his forehead and headed in.

As I neared the ladies' lounge, I noticed the women coming out were looking a little shell-shocked. I hurried my pace.

Once inside, I understood. The extremely imaginative blue streak of cursing that was falling out of Sophia's mouth was enough to make my hair curl. Mimi just sat on the settee, helpless.

I came in on the tail end of "—lousy-no good-motherfucking-dickface-asshole-sonofawhore-fucking fuckhead fuck!"

"Who're we talking about?" I asked brightly. Mimi stifled a snort.

"How much trouble would I get in for stealing the cake knife and castrating him?" she asked, two more women hustling by to get away.

"Lots. Can we talk about this without mentioning castration?"

"Doubtful; right now I want his dick in a hot dog bun."

Oh, boy.

"If I may interject just the tiniest bit of normal here, you need to settle down, missy," I began, putting up my finger when she started to interrupt, "because you love Jillian. And no one wants their wedding to be known as the dick-in-a-hot-dog-bun wedding, right?"

"It would make the newspaper."

I sighed. "No more chair bumping, no more attempted forking. Just go be a polite guest at a wedding, okay?"

"I hate you," she huffed, smoothing out her dress and checking her lip gloss in the mirror.

"No, you don't," I huffed back, then turned to Mimi. "And you, I thought you were going to watch her," I muttered while Sophia adjusted her boobs.

"I was, but then Ryan had his hand on my leg under the table, and—"

"Save it—we don't want to miss their first dance," I replied, glancing in the mirror myself. Damn, I *do* look good in goldfish.

"Okay, ladies, knockers up: We're going in. No more drama," I instructed, and we headed back into the ballroom.

To find that the chair to Neil's left was no longer unoccupied.

A chairful of hot blonde had taken up residence, and over her giggles and squeals, Neil made sure to catch Sophia's eye. And wink.

Message delivered: Two can play at this game.

Shit.

The rest of the wedding passed by in a flurry of images. Jillian and Benjamin sharing a spotlit first dance. A five-tier wedding cake being cut and unceremoniously shoved into the groom's gorgeous face. Simon toasting Benjamin with raised glasses and laughter, and more than one throat clearing.

Neil parading around a preening Blonde in front of Sophia and Hot Barry. Sophia clocking Hot Barry when he had the nerve to look at Blonde himself. Neil's stone face as he watched Sophia and Hot Barry dancing in a very, very close way. A bemused Benjamin as Hot Barry tried to sell him additional life insurance.

And sharing my own dance with Simon, swaying under the disco ball. Which always seems like a terrible idea, but in reality bathed everything in the coolest sparkles ever. He held me close, his hand fitted into the small of my back, the other holding my hand. Weddings are romantic by nature, and I wasn't the only one who had sparkles in her eyes tonight. The sapphires were off the chart.

"What are you thinking about?" I asked him, my voice dreamy. Simon looked dreamy too. What was on his mind? Me in this dress? Me out of this dress?

"Fishing poles."

"What?" Not at all what I was expecting.

"Fishing poles. You asked." He chuckled, twirling me.

"I see. And what about fishing poles?" I asked, my nose wrinkling.

"Where I grew up, there was a state park not ten minutes from the house. River, rocks, old mill spillway, and walking trails everywhere." His face grew peaceful, describing it. He so rarely talked about his past, I wondered what it was about this night that made him think about it. "Anyway, the last time me, my dad, and Benjamin were all together was one Sunday afternoon, fishing. And Benjamin sat on my dad's favorite fishing pole, almost broke the damn thing!" He laughed, his hand holding mine just a tiny bit tighter.

"It's funny how you remember certain things. Someone was burning leaves that day, so everything smelled like smoke—you know that smoky smell that you only get in the fall? I remember that, and how cold the water was. Nobody caught anything that day, not even a nibble," he finished, his eyes faraway.

I let my hand tangle in the back of his hair, slipping down to smooth over his brow, feathering my fingers there. "Sounds like a good day."

"It was a good day." He smiled down at me, pulling me closer still. The band began to play Duke Ellington, and I was twirled and whirled and dipped by my Wallbanger.

This was a good day too.

Made even more so by nary a dick ending up in a hot dog bun.

chapter eight

"Okay, all your extra linens and towels are in closet down the hall, extra blankets in the cedar chest, hmm . . . what else? Oh, the window next to the bed tends to stick a little when it's raining, but not too bad. I left notes on all the remotes with instructions on how to use everything—it took me forever to learn how to just turn the damn thing on . . . let's see, oh! Let's go back into the kitchen and talk about the burners. There's a trick to getting the back one to turn on high and—"

I followed Jillian through their Sausalito house Sunday afternoon, while Simon went through the same thing in the garage with Benjamin. House-sitting isn't what it used to be; you can't just bring in the mail and have a party.

As we toured the house, taking notice of everything we'd need to know while staying there, I was reminded of how perfect it really was. Situated in the hills just above the main street, the house was two stories in almost a triangular shape, so that practically each room had a view of the bay and, in the distance, San Francisco. Along with a multiterraced outdoor seating area, dotted with benches and fire pits, there was the in-ground hot tub they'd installed. Perfectly isolated, perfectly private, with a killer view.

The hot tub is where we found Simon and Benjamin, hunched down by the controls. Simon was having a great time, turning the interior lights from pink to blue to green to purple with a big grin.

"Caroline, look! It's like having a light show!" he exclaimed excitedly.

"And I think that's everything," Jillian said. "Car keys are in the bowl by the front door, alarm codes you've got written down, you know how to work the hillevator. Oh what am I forgetting?" She pulled her notebook out, frantically checking her notes.

"Don't worry about anything—we've got this. You two just enjoy your trip," I replied. "And you're not allowed to call and check in for at least a week. Go have sex with your husband."

"Yes, go have sex with your husband," Benjamin chimed in, closing her notebook and wrapping his arms around her from behind. "Thanks, guys, we really appreciate it."

"You sure you don't mind? You don't have to stay here every night; just maybe a few nights a week?" Jillian asked.

"Oh my God, shut up already, will you? It's a real big hardship, staying here— what a sacrifice." I laughed, gesturing to the house.

Benjamin said, "All right, let them get outta here. Simon, thanks again for everything. And make sure you check out those bike trails; I left the maps with everything else." As Jillian went for her notebook once more he told us, "I'd make a run for it if I were you."

"Oh, let go you big oaf, I need to hug her," she protested, engulfing me in her arms. "Thank you; you have no idea how much I need this," she whispered. When she let me go, there were tears in her eyes. "And remember, I'm just a phone call away."

I hugged them both and let Simon pack me into the Range Rover for our trip back over the bridge. We were both quiet as we entered the city, winding through the streets toward our apartment building.

He parked, then walked around to my side to open my door.

Taking my hand, he said, "You know, this might not be so boring after all. It could be fun, having a house."

Later on that night, Clive and I were playing Kill the Ponytail—a game we'd created a few years ago when I made the mistake of lying down next to where he was sleeping, and swishing my ponytail in front of him. He woke up to a giant piece of dancing hair in his face and went utterly apeshit. The object of the game, as closely as I could understand, was for Clive to chew on, bat about, and all but dangle from my ponytail.

Did I have to wash my hair thoroughly after this game? I did, but to see his eyes light up, and his little sideways crab walk across the floor when he knew it was time to play, was worth it. The game was taking place under the coffee table when Simon came over.

"Kill the Ponytail?" he asked as I poked my head out.

"Yup," I replied, wincing as Clive took my inattention to grab a mouthful and tug.

"Who's winning?"

"Who do you think? Ow!"

I turned under the table, intending to give chase, but laughed when Clive curled onto his back, purring loud enough to rattle the windows.

"Truce?" I asked him, rumpling the fur on his belly. The half-lidded eyes and the upside-down kitty grin was answer enough for me. Dusting myself off, I crawled out from under the coffee table to join Simon in the kitchen.

After our trip across the bay, I'd worked for a few hours while he napped, sleeping off his jet lag. I took my Clive break when he ran out to pick up some dinner. Now I got a whiff of Vietnamese, and quickened my steps toward the kitchen. A bowl of pho on a chilly evening was the best thing ever.

I got out bowls while Simon unwrapped containers. I grabbed

chopsticks and he poured wine. We settled in at the kitchen table and in between slurps and sips, he went through his mail. It piled up when he was gone, so it was always a chore when he got back. We chatted about the day, different takes on what it would be like living part-time in Sausalito, when I noticed he'd stopped slurping.

"What's that?" I asked as he stared at an opened letter.

"Huh? Oh, it's a letter from the alumni association."

"Stanford?"

"No, my high school, actually. It's an invitation to my ten-year reunion."

I stayed quiet, watching his face work through a few things. When he picked up his chopsticks and started on his noodles again, I asked, "So, you think you'll go?"

"I'm not sure. I didn't think I'd want to go, but now that it's here—maybe?"

He changed the subject, but I saw his eyes wander over to the letter more than once. And while I was cleaning up after dinner, I saw him reading it again.

"You should go," I said, hours later. We were in bed, the news was on, Clive in between us. Simon knew instantly what I was talking about.

"I don't know if I can. It's between Thanksgiving and Christmas; I'm sure I'll be traveling. I must have missed the notice somewhere," he said, eyes on the screen. He was tense.

"You'd have known about it if you were on Facebook. I bet you anything your classmates have been looking for you on there."

"I doubt most of them would remember me," he scoffed.

I bit down a response. Though I didn't know him back then, every high school had a Simon Parker. Couple that with his parents passing away so unexpectedly, and yeah, they all remembered him.

With a sigh, he turned toward me, hand reaching out across the pillows. I curled on my side as well, my fingers tangling with his. He tucked his other arm under his head. In the light from the television, he looked young. And a little sad.

"I never planned to go back. I mean, I really had no reason to." I squeezed his hand.

"I don't know, maybe I should? Might be kind of fun to see some of those guys again, right?"

I smiled and said nothing.

"I'll look at my calendar tomorrow. Maybe I can swing it."

"Want me to check mine?" I asked.

"You think you can? I mean, I know how busy you are."

"I think I can get away for a weekend. Besides, I've never been to Philadelphia. Can we go for cheesesteaks?"

He groaned. "Oh my God, do you have any idea how long it's been since I had a cheesesteak? That may have just made up my mind."

I slid across the bed and straddled him, moving his hands to my hips. I leaned down and brushed his hair back from his face and kissed him square on the lips.

"Tell me about your favorite place for cheesesteaks," I said as he wrapped his arms around me and pulled me down on top of him.

For the next twenty-seven minutes I lay on top of Simon, listening to him talk about a mom-and-pop sandwich shop. And the importance of both sweet *and* hot peppers. In doing so, he told me more about his family and the place he'd grown up than he had in the entire year we'd been together. I realized that I'd never even seen a picture of his parents, had no idea what they'd looked like.

I'd ask him about that soon. Not tonight, but soon. Tonight was all about cheesesteaks, and everything that came with them. And I'm not talking just about the sweet and hot peppers.

"Caroline, there's a call from someone over at the Design Center. They want to know if Jillian would be teaching her class again next month? Can you take it?"

"Caroline, Mrs. Crabtree is calling again, Jillian's client. She needs to know exactly what shade Jillian painted the trim in her sitting room ten years ago, and if we have any kind of guarantee that it shouldn't be yellowing? She also mentioned to me that she smokes two packs a day in that room and never opens a window; you want to handle this?"

"Caroline, there's a guy from the heating and cooling company in the lobby, says we're due for our fall maintenance check. Did Jillian mention this to you?"

"Caroline, I think I accidentally deleted the last few billing invoices on the Peterson account, but I know Jillian always keeps paper copies of those. Any idea where?"

"Caroline, can you—"

"Caroline, will I need—"

"Caroline, I superglued this doorknob to my—"

I gazed out the window of my new office, realizing that with the bigger office came not only bigger responsibilities but also bigger headaches. And the one I currently had was a whopper. I'd officially been in charge of the office for one week, and I was ready to throw myself to the sea lions. How the hell did Jillian manage all this? She had her own clients, she had her team to mentor, she was the answer woman and the puter-outer of all fires, and she managed to do it with her signature calm style.

I was frazzled, freaked, and fucked.

I could have called Jillian, of course. But she was on her honeymoon; I didn't want to interrupt her and Benjamin while they were . . . well, while they were. Besides, I didn't want to admit that there was so much to running this business that I wasn't aware of. I was determined to handle it on my own, figuring it out as I went, so when Jillian checked in after a few days, I lied through my teeth and told her everything was great.

After the office, house-sitting was a piece of cake.

That week we spent two nights in the Sausalito house, and

two nights in our own apartments. I worked round the clock, while Simon enjoyed some time off before his next trip. The two nights we spent across the bay he stayed the entire next day, hiking in the headlands, biking through the town, and by the weekend, he was asking when we were heading over.

I worked late Friday night while Simon had a night out with the guys, and Saturday morning we packed our bags and left. Our neighbors Euan and Antonio agreed to baby-sit for Clive; it didn't seem fair to him to transport him all the way over there for just a few days. If it seemed like we were really going to enjoy it, then I'd consider moving him in. For now though, I was enjoying the perks of being Jillian. Namely, racing her Mercedes convertible through the winding streets up into the hills, with Simon riding shotgun.

"Pretty sure Jillian wanted me to drive her car while she was gone," he insisted, grimacing as I took a turn too fast.

"Bullshit, she wanted me to enjoy myself. Get over it." I laughed, punching my foot to the floor as we took off into the breeze.

We ran errands, hit the market, then headed back home to fire up the grill before Mimi and Ryan came over. We'd decided to christen our first weekend with a quiet dinner, and since we couldn't agree on whether to invite Sophia, or Neil, or both, we settled on just the couple we could count on not bumping chairs.

Sitting on the terrace, Mimi and I watched the boys grill burgers as we munched on carrots. There was a late fog moving in, blanketing the bay with gray clouds and shrouding the city entirely. Shivering a bit, I moved closer to one of the heat lamps that was stationed around each patio.

"We have really pretty boys, don't we?" Mimi sighed, crunching down on a carrot. I looked at them and sighed as well.

"We really do."

"Speaking of pretty boys, has Sophia seen Barry Derry since the wedding?"

"Nope, the curb got that one. Good thing too—that man was so dull." Mimi mimed falling asleep in her chair, snoring.

"We boring you, dear?" Ryan asked, buttering his buns.

"Nope, just thinking about Barry Derry and his insurance ways," she piped back.

Simon looked over at me and mouthed the words "Barry Derry?"

"The guy Sophia brought to the wedding," I answered, pulling Mimi out of her chair and ushering her inside the house, the guys following us with their meat. Ahem.

"Oh, that guy? He tried to sell me travel insurance. Was telling me all these statistics about air travel and why I really needed to make sure I was covered." Simon laughed, setting down the burgers.

I poured more wine for everyone and we each grabbed a seat and a bun.

"Did she ever agree to talk to Neil?" Ryan asked

Mimi and I exchanged a look. Laughing about Barry Derry was one thing, talking about Neil and Sophia was another conversation entirely. One that never seemed to end well.

"No, I don't think so," I answered, passing the pickles.

"Jeez, that's cold," he responded, slapping a burger onto everyone's plate. "And if you don't mind me saying so, a little ridiculous."

"I do mind you saying so, a little. Who's got the ketchup?" I asked. "And besides, why should she talk to him, she didn't do anything wrong."

Simon passed me the ketchup with a side of stink eye.

"I agree with Caroline; Neil is the one that needs to work for this here, not her. Why should she bend? Who wants onions?" Mimi offered.

"I'll take the onions, and I think you both are being as ridiculous as your friend. How can he work for it when she won't even return his phone calls?" Simon said, giving "work for it" air quotes and spilling onions on the floor. "Shit. Babe, throw me that dish towel, will you?"

"Here's your dish towel, and before you ask, here's your mustard and your lettuce and your tomato," I said, setting the plates down a little harder than necessary. "And for your information, *your* boy, not *our* girl, is the one who cheated. Ergo, she doesn't have to return anything."

"Ergo? When did you become a lawyer? And thank you, this is everything I ever wanted in a burger," Simon said, making a great flourish out of dressing his patty. "She should at least hear him out; is that too much to ask?"

"Do you even know why she's so hurt? Why she can't get over that he cheated?" Mimi said, squeezing the ketchup bottle so hard it squirted all over her plate.

"Okay, can we stop saying cheated? He didn't cheat, he just kissed his ex-girlfriend," Ryan interjected, taking a bite of his burger. "Tha's na cheeinh."

"Of course it's cheating!" Mimi and I yelled in unison.

"Okay! That's enough. No one talks for one minute. Everyone take a bite," Simon commanded, looking as serious as anyone could, with a burger that was stacked almost nine inches tall.

We all bit. Then chewed. Simon took the longest. He had nine inches, after all.

"Now, can we discuss this like adults?" he asked.

"You've got mustard on your lip, Simon," I said, biting back a laugh. He blushed, then licked his lips.

"I can discuss this as an adult, if you two can admit that what he did was wrong," I offered, pointing my pickle spear at the boys.

"If I can speak for Simon here, neither of us ever said that what he did wasn't wrong. We just don't think he needs to be tarred, feathered, and driven out of town," Ryan said. "He kissed someone—would you rather he fucked someone?"

"But that's the thing: he didn't just kiss *someone*, he kissed an *ex- girlfriend. The* ex-girlfriend, from what you told me," Mimi answered.

"What do you mean, *the* ex-girlfriend. You didn't tell me it was *the* ex-girlfriend," I exclaimed, turning to Simon.

"I did too!"

"You did not."

"I did too!"

"So much for adults." Ryan snorted, taking another bite of his burger.

"You said it was *an* ex-girlfriend. You didn't say it was *the* ex-girlfriend," I snapped.

"What's the difference?" Simon asked, and Mimi's head exploded.

"*An* ex-girlfriend just means she's, like, one of many. No one special. *The* ex-girlfriend is suuuuuch a bigger deal," she explained

I could see Simon still didn't get it.

"You're talking to someone who doesn't have *any* ex-girlfriends, much less *the* ex-girlfriend," I told Mimi, signaling her that I had this one. "Simon, *an* ex-girlfriend is someone you're happy to see every now and again, you wish her well, but it doesn't matter in the long run. *The* ex-girlfriend matters: there's a connection there, there's shared history, she's even maybe the one that got away. *An* ex-girlfriend, we wouldn't be so pissed over. *The* ex-girlfriend, yeah."

"Wait a minute, just wait a minute. You're telling me if I kissed an ex-girlfriend, you wouldn't be pissed?" he asked, mustard on his lip again.

I closed my eyes. "Of course that's what a guy would hear—no! We're pissed if you kiss any ex, but *an* ex isn't as big a deal as *the* ex. *An* ex, *the* ex—big difference."

"Okay, please stop saying *an* ex. I realize it's grammatically correct, but it just sounds weird. Plus it sounds like you're saying *annex*. The point is, you're pissed because he kissed a girl he had a connection with—or at least you assume he had a connection with, right?" Simon asked. Still with the mustard. This time I wasn't telling him; he was in charge of his own mouth.

"Ryan, you told me this was the girl he almost asked to marry him, right?" Mimi asked.

"Yes."

"I rest my case," she shouted, dusting off her hands.

"Christ, this is going nowhere fast. Okay, so let me ask you this. Which would have been worse: if he kissed this particular ex, or had sex with some random woman he was never going to see again?" Ryan asked.

"Depends," I said.

"Random. No, ex. No, random. No, it depends," Mimi said, shaking her head.

"I give up," Simon said.

"Do you have any Tums in your purse?" Ryan asked Mimi.

"I'm getting more wine," I announced.

"You've got mustard on your lip, Simon," Mimi said.

They left. Simon and I did the dishes in silence, passing plates back and forth to dry. He went back outside to the patio; I stayed inside.

Mimi texted me:

Do you think Sophia should
talk to Neil?

Yes, she probably should.

You gonna tell her?

I think you should.

Together?

At the diner tomorrow?

Deal. Tell Simon thanks for
dinner, it really was nice.

I will, tell Ryan thanks for
coming.

They just don't get it do they?

Eh, they're boys.

They're pretty great boys.

That they are. I'm gonna
go kiss on mine. See you
in the a.m.

XO

I walked outside, bringing coffee for both of us.

"This seat taken?" I asked him.

He shook his head and lifted a corner of the blanket he was under. I sat down and handed him a mug. He sipped, then raised an eyebrow.

"I wanted a little Irish with my coffee tonight. Thought we both could use it," I explained.

"Agreed."

We sat together for a moment, silent.

"We can't keep arguing over this. This isn't our fight."

"I know it isn't. It's just hard to watch." I sighed, looking out over the bay. It was quiet tonight, the fog softening all the sounds.

"I get that, but you have to let them work it out."

"I know."

"And they can't work it out if they don't talk."

"I know."

We were both quiet, under the blanket.

"You said something tonight that I didn't like."

Surprised, I turned to him. "I did?"

"Just because I don't have *the ex-girlfriend* you guys were going on and on about, that doesn't mean I didn't have real connections with the people I dated. I don't have ex- girlfriends because I didn't have girlfriends in the traditional sense, but that doesn't mean I don't understand the difference."

I nodded. "You're right."

"You can't just negate my past because it wasn't the same as yours."

"You're totally right." I turned to look at him.

"Okay?" he said.

"Okay," I replied. He was in a very different place with me than he'd ever been before. "Are *we* okay?"

"Of course we're okay. Isn't this how people in relationships resolve conflicts? You said something I didn't like, so I let you know," he said, puffing his chest out a bit.

"Well, good goddamn, Dr. Phil, color me impressed," I said, clinking my coffee cup to his. "So what do we do next? Y'know, as people in a relationship after they've resolved a conflict."

"Pretty sure a blow job should follow this," he said seriously.

"Hmm, that does seem fair." I traced my fingers up his leg and snuck over to his hi-there. "Did you want that right here or—"

"Christ no, it's cold out here. Let's go inside, where it's warm, to conflict resolutize," he exclaimed, jumping up and tugging me inside.

"Pretty sure that's not a word."

"Blow job is." He locked the patio door and faced me with a knowing smile.

"I think it's two words, actually."

"Talking too much is what got you into trouble in the first place," he said, pointing me in the direction of the bedroom. "Now get in there."

I resolved him twice that night.

chapter nine

Sounds like everything is going great at work; everyone is saying what a great job you're doing. I even got an e-mail from Max Camden, who said the work is coming along even earlier than anticipated based on the guys you recommended to hire instead of his usual crew—way to go, kiddo! Hey, how's Monica doing? Don't work her too hard. I know you won't, but the boss in me requires me to say it. I bet she's a godsend! And I'd tell you not to work too hard, but I know better, right?

Things are amazing here; I almost don't want to tell you. But I totally will—I am *in love with France*. Seriously, I could live here. The food alone is a reason to chuck my passport and *stay*. Did you know you can harvest your own oysters and eat them on the beach in Brittany? Crazy. But now we're off to Italy, stopping first in Lake Como to stay in a villa that one of Benjamin's partners owns. No, it's not Clooney, but I will tell him hello if I see him ;)

Oh, I meant to tell you. Make sure you meet with the accountant this week; he said he's going to call you to set something up. I need you to e-mail me some files.

• • •

Text from Sophia to Caroline:

Okay. I talked to him. Big woo.

Big woo? Like he was wooing you?

Whoa. No woo. I meant like, big woo we talked, no big deal. You know, "big woo."

Did he try to woo you?

Caroline, dammit, no. That's not the point. He wanted to talk, you all convinced me to let him talk, so he talked. I listened.

Did you yell?

A little.

Did he tell you what happened?

Yes, he kissed her.

Anything else?

Does there need to be anything else?

No, just asking.

Well, stop asking.

How'd it end?

With yelling. He yelled too, though; it wasn't just me.

So it's really over?

What did you expect? That he'd come over, we'd talk, and I'd magically forget everything that happened?

Of course not. So it's really over.

It's impossible for me to hang up on you since we're texting, but know that I am hanging up on you.

Text from Caroline to Mimi:

They talked.

I know! It didn't go well . . .

I know!

So now what?

What do you mean? Did you think she'd just magically forget everything that happened?

You must have just been texting with Sophia; you're taking a tone.

I know! Sorry . . .

It doesn't matter. What matters is I don't think those two are over yet . . .

What? She's pretty sure they are.

I have a hunch. Let me think on it.

Mimi . . . don't meddle.

Have you met me?

Text from Simon to Caroline

Just sent you a picture, did you get it?

Mmm, should I close the door to my office?

No no, not like that, but I like the way you're thinking. Did you get it yet?

I did, I wish I was there. The beach looks amazing. How are things in Bora Bora?

Amazing. But it'd be better if you were here. Still can't believe you turned down a trip here . . .

You'd believe it if you saw my desk right now. I'm literally swimming in paperwork.

I'm literally swimming in the ocean. Or I was a few minutes ago

Honestly Simon, sometimes . . .

Sorry, babe. Just wish you were here.

Me too. I gotta go; my inbox just exploded.

Text from Simon to Neil:

So you talked to her.

Dude . . .

That bad?

Dude!

Sorry, man . . .

Text from Mimi to Caroline:

So I'm thinking we should have a game night—you know, play Pictionary and stuff like that?

I'd love to, but I'm slammed. When were you thinking?

Maybe the Saturday night before Thanksgiving? Can you spare a few hours over the weekend?

I can spare a few hours, yes, that's about it. You guys wanna come out to Sausalito? Be nice not to have to go back into the city.

We can do that. I was thinking we should invite Sophia.

Of course we should.

And Neil.

Oh boy.

Trust me.

There's an entire wall of windows in Jillian's house, Mimi. The last thing I need is someone throwing things.

Trust me.

Think Barry Derry sells party insurance?

Text from Mimi to Sophia:

Hey girl! Game night next Saturday, you in?

No.

What?

No. I've already peeped
your game, you're inviting
Neil, aren't you?

Yes.

No.

We'll see.

I'm not coming if he is.

We'll see.

Text from Ryan to Neil:

Game night? Next Saturday?

Cool! I smoked your ass
last time at Pictionary.

Sophia's invited.

Not cool, dude. I'm not
going if she's going.

Pussy—that's exactly what
she said.

She said she wouldn't
come if I came?

Isn't that what you just said?

I'm totally coming. Can I
bring someone?

Is that wise?

Who says wise? I'm
bringing someone.

Text from Mimi to Sophia:

So . . .

No.

Come on! Neil said he
wasn't coming—

Good! I'll come.

—if you were coming

What? What a baby; he
can't handle it if I'm there?

Well, he's handling it, he's
coming. And he's bringing
someone.

Well I'm bringing
someone too.

I thought you weren't
coming.

Shut up. What time?

It was late. I was once again at the office, alone. It was almost
midnight, and the shitty part was Simon had just gotten home
from Bora Bora this morning. In a previous life, when I wasn't
responsible for someone else's design firm, I'd have taken a long

lunch break to go home, see him, have a nooner, and then head back to work. But not anymore.

Now it was almost 11:00 p.m., and I was putting the finishing touches on my first payroll report, since the accountant wasn't able to pull all the hours he needed from his computer at home. Which is where he was. Which is where *most* people were.

I felt like I was finally getting on top of everything workwise; turns out you *can* get everything done when you work twelve-hour days. And weekends. With Simon away on a job, I could do it. I ate, slept, and peed Jillian Designs. But it was worth it; I was getting a taste of what it would be like to run my own business someday. Jillian had been an amazing mentor to me, she still was, and I wanted to do a great job for her. Could I have asked her for a little more help? Maybe, but I wanted her to enjoy herself. So I barely managed to keep my head above water.

My phone rang just as I clicked send on payroll. Yawning, I answered. "I promise I'm leaving."

"You said that an hour ago."

"But this time I really am. Can you hear that? Those are my shoes, walking down the hallway. And hear that? That's me getting out my keys to lock the door."

"I don't like the idea of you being out so late at night all alone."

"Babe, I am capable of handling myself. Besides, how do you think I get home most nights?"

"I still can't believe you wouldn't let me come pick you up. What if some weirdo is out tonight, and likes the way you look in your red heels?"

"Well then, that weirdo's gonna get an ass full of red heels if he tries anything— Wait, how did you know I'm wearing red heels?" I asked, whirling around.

Parked just a few feet from the front door was Simon's car.

"What are you doing here?"

"I can't believe you really thought I wasn't going to come pick you up," he said into the phone, hanging it up and getting out of the car.

If he was sun kissed when he was in Africa, he was sun baked while he was in Bora Bora. Which made his eyes even more blue, his face even more handsome, his jet-black messy hair even more enticing. He caught me into a hug so tight he even picked me up a little bit and my feet hung.

"You're so pretty," I whispered, kissing his cheeks and his forehead and his nose and finally his sweet lips. Which were now grinning. "How long have you been out here? Have you been here all night?" I asked as he opened the car door, and I saw the stacks of coffee cups.

"Not *all* night." He walked around to his side, getting in and turning the car on. "Just since about nine thirty."

"Oh my God, why didn't you tell me? I would've come down. I would've stopped working."

"I knew you needed to get your work done; no biggie." He yawned.

"Uh, yeah, it's a biggie," I insisted, then leaned across the seat to kiss his cheek again. "You glad to be home?"

"You have no idea—I'm going to sleep for days. After I get some sugar," he said, shooting me a waggly eyebrow.

"Maybe tonight, no sugar. Maybe tonight, just sleep."

"I'm tired, but I'm not that tired," he said, even as a yawn cracked open his face.

"We'll see," I conceded. "You should sleep so you're ready for Game Night tomorrow."

"Good point. I've gotta make sure we kill everyone at Pictionary. Is everyone coming?"

"Yep, should be interesting."

"If you girls can behave yourselves," he teased.

We cruised. He yawned.

"How's the ninth looking for you?" he asked suddenly.

"The ninth?"

"Of December. The reunion? You still want to go with me?"

"I do. Bring on the cheesesteaks!" I smiled, resting my hand on his leg and making little circles there.

"Sugar," he quipped.

"Sleep," I insisted, as he gave me a look that said he was a man intent on getting some sugar.

But this woman knew better, and I made sure to take a little longer than normal in the bathroom. I didn't need to exfoliate, but I did. I didn't need to condition my hair twice, but I did. When I finally came out, my Wallbanger was dead to the world and telling everyone about it with his snores. Next to him? Clive. Making the most ridiculous little kitty snores.

I slipped under the covers and burrowed into Simon's nook. Some nights, that *was* my sugar.

As soon as I was up, I left the city and headed over to the Sausalito house. I let Simon sleep in, allowing me some time to walk through the hotel alone. Sometimes it was easier to check on projects when there was no one else there. I could explore the space with my notebook and camera, taking pictures and generally getting a feel for how things were going.

The hotel was going to be beautiful. Still just a shell, but I could see what it was going to be. And as shells took shape, sometimes the design dictated a change to the original plans. Maybe a new palette suggested itself, or certain lines weren't as strong in real life as they were on paper. It wasn't second-guessing, it was adapting. And I missed my Master Adapter.

Jillian had the best eye for detail of any designer I'd ever worked with. And she was great at helping me solidify my vision, boosting my confidence; she was my gut check. My sounding board. So as I walked the plank flooring, I wished she was there. I did projects by myself all the time, but she was always in the wings, propping me up when I needed it. I had to prop myself up this time.

I'd never seriously considered having my own design firm. Of course every young designer thinks about it, some even dream about it—but that wasn't me. So much work, so much risk, taken on solely. Your name, your failure.

I'd literally lucked into a dream when Jillian hired me after my internship. I followed her around like a puppy my first few weeks, soaking it all up, taking it all in. I sat in her office, marveling over how she managed it all. She was always calm under pressure, always the cucumber when everything else was jalapeños. She was who I wanted to be when I grew up. I just never thought I'd get there.

Jillian didn't come from money; she'd worked for every penny she had. She'd left a successful position at a very high profile design firm in the city, and invested everything in her own tiny shop in the Castro. The stories I'd heard from some of her long-term clients were legendary. Receiving tile shipments at midnight, dog walking for her toniest clients, installing lighting fixtures twenty feet in the air when an electrician didn't show—you name it, she'd done it.

And from her own stories, she taught me how to barter and how to haggle, how to get the best discounts, how to school a contractor who thought he was going to get one over on a female project lead, and how to deal with clients who were complete and total assholes. And there were a lot of them.

She'd made a name for herself, scratching and clawing her way to a highly successful business while looking like she'd just rolled off a runway in Milan.

She did it all.

Was *I* doing it all? I knew I was a good designer, but I'd never be a Jillian. I could wear her shoes for a little while, though.

I took my pictures, made my notes, and hiked back up the

hill to the house. It was close enough to the main drag that I'd taken to walking into town when the mood struck. I usually walked most nights that I was there, sometimes to look at the hotel, yes, but sometimes to just explore the neighborhoods. Hidden pathways, rounded garden doors, high hedges and last summer's hollyhocks . . . It was a little magical.

When I rounded the street corner, I was thrilled by the sight of a black Range Rover parked outside. Simon was awake and on this side of the bay. With a secret smile, I hurried inside.

As I brushed out my hair that night, I realized that it was the first time in almost two weeks that it wasn't piled on top of my head in a bun held together with colored pencils. Simon was now working at the dining room table, checking all of his shots on his laptop. I passed by on my way to the kitchen, and was stopped by a hand on my ass.

"Hi?"

"Hi," he answered, his eyes still on the computer.

"You need something?"

"Always," he answered, maneuvering my ass so it was on his lap.

"Not always; you were sleeping earlier," I pouted.

"I'm not sleeping now."

"I've got turnovers."

"I already like where this is going," he murmured, his hands tightening around my waist.

"No no, I mean I have turnovers that I need to put in the oven."

"Wait, those are like tiny pies, right?"

"Yes, Simon, they're like tiny pies."

"Apple?"

"Cherry."

"Have mercy."

"You know what it does to me when you go Uncle Jesse on me."

His eyes widened, and something else hardened. "I do indeed."

Kissed me fierce, he did, and while I did my best to remind him of my turnovers, he did his best to make me forget. And I did, until the doorbell rang.

"Dammit," he muttered, releasing me.

"Saved by the bell," I sang out, rising off his lap.

"You know what it does to me when you go Kelly Kapowski on me."

"I do indeed. And if you're a good boy tonight, I'll give you my own special *Bayside* cheer later on." I winked and danced away from his grabby hands. "Now go do something with that," I instructed, pointing at his enthusiasm.

He strutted away, and I headed to the front door. I could see Ryan through the glass, but no Mimi.

"Hey, where's your girl?" I asked, but then heard a *wheeeeee* coming from up above.

"She's ridden it twice already," he replied, rolling his eyes but smiling at his girlfriend as she came down the hill in the hillevator, peeking over the side.

"That will never get old. I love this thing," she announced when she got to the bottom, opening the door and climbing out. She had a basket full of treats and an armful of board games, which Ryan hurried to assist with. "See, this thing is actually useful."

"Well, it's not just a carnival ride, no." I laughed, grabbing a bag as well. "Good lord, how many games did you bring?"

"I thought it would be best to plan for any and all hiccups tonight. And speaking of hiccups, I brought plenty of booze," she stated, nodding to the box from the liquor store.

"Sure, because what goes better with tension than alcohol?" I snorted, catching Ryan's eye.

"I tried to tell her," he said under his breath.

"I heard that," she sang out as she trotted into the house.

"I meant you to," he sang back. "'Sup?" He nodded to Simon, who had parked himself behind a wing chair.

I chuckled to myself at his technique for hiding his enthusiasm. I winked at him, feeling a thrill rumble through me when he looked at me with those heavy lidded eyes. Damn, that man got to me.

I led Mimi into the kitchen, letting her set up the bar while I finally got the turnovers into the oven.

We chatted while we put together snacks for the evening. Since I didn't have the time I used to, it nearly killed me to get the turnovers together in time. But taking a page from the Barefoot Contessa, I managed to put together a respectable spread. I arranged several cheeses from a local shop, including a runny Brie and a stinky Stilton, some French bread, and little bowls of spicy almonds and salty olives. Slices of salami, capicola, pepperoni, and mortadella covered another wooden board, along with bowls of marinated artichoke hearts and roasted red peppers. A few containers of garlicky hummus and pillowy pita completed the nosh. I finished up just as Mimi was putting the final touches on her drink stations.

"Whiskey sours, martinis, and look! Wallbangers!" she cried, setting out a bottle of Galliano just as Simon and Ryan came in to join us.

"Perfect. Caroline was just saying before you two got here that she was dying for some more of me," he teased, making me blush as the timer went off on my turnovers.

"Mix yourself up there, Simon," I said over my shoulder, pulling the flaky triangles from the oven. The look he gave me told me I would indeed be getting turned over later on that night. You wouldn't catch me complaining.

Just as Simon handed me a drink, we heard the doorbell.

"Showtime," Mimi mumbled, heading off to the door. It was Sophia, with the tallest man I'd ever seen. But not just tall, he was crazy good looking. He was like NBA meets surfer.

"Why, hello there!" I said, looking up and up. "I'm Caroline."

"Hey," he said down to me in a voice that was incredibly deep. "Zach."

He shuffled off to shake hands with the guys as I took Sophia's coat.

"When I say that's a tall drink of water, I'm not exaggerating," I whispered to her, checking him out as he towered over Ryan and Simon, neither of whom were short.

"Thanks. He plays basketball in France; he's home for the holidays. I met him at the gym."

"Damn, I need to switch to your gym. The cute boy quotient is considerably higher than mine," I replied, hanging up her coat.

She scanned the room, breathing a little easier when she saw that Neil wasn't there. "Can I help with anything?"

The doorbell rang again.

"Like right now, can I help with anything? How about I make sure the bars okay," she said, heels clicking across the floor as she grabbed Tall Zach and pulled him toward the alcohol.

Simon walked over to me, reaching around me to open the door for the only friend who hadn't yet arrived.

"Hey, man, what's up?" Neil said, handing Simon a bottle of scotch. "Caroline, thanks for inviting me," he added, sneaking a kiss on my cheek before I could react.

"Hi, Neil," I managed, trying to remember that this was Simon's friend and I was making an effort. I had to *really* make an effort when I got an eyeful of who he brought with him.

I can't say for sure that she'd ever appeared in *Playboy*. But if she hadn't, she should have.

"Hi! I'm Missy," she said, and I smiled at Neil through clenched teeth. I could tell it was putting Simon in physical pain not to laugh.

"Hi there, Missy," I managed. "Let me take your coat, Missy."

"Wow, look at all those windows!" She giggled as I led them inside.

I knew how much a window wall that size cost to install, and I wondered how much it would cost to repair . . .

chapter ten

"Airplane. Airplane people. Airplane holding a sponge."

"Airplane with hands, hands? Okay, hands. Airplane hands. Sponge hands."

"Sponge hands! Airplane sponge. Bird sponge. Bird! Okay, bird. Hand bird."

"SpongeBob HandBird. Stop pointing at the airplane, we know it's not an airplane!"

"Time's up."

"*Dammit!*"

Sophia sat down in a huff, throwing her Sharpie across the room. Neil stuck his hand straight up in the air and caught it as she huffed, "I can't believe you guys couldn't get that! It was so obvious that it was—"

"Ah-ah-ah, don't say another word. We get a chance to steal," Simon said from his place on the couch.

It was girls against guys, and the guys were currently kicking our ass. They were up forty points. Stupid boys.

"Go ahead, you'll never get it. Don't worry, they'll never get it," Sophia assured us, sipping her cocktail and winking at Zach over the rim.

"Now just give us a minute. We have thirty seconds to examine the picture and see if we can guess what you were trying to draw," Ryan said, standing up and going over to the board where Sophia had been drawing.

"We know how the game is played!" Mimi yelled from her perch on the back of the couch. She was Drunky Mimi tonight; her cocktail station had served her well. And overserved her—she was Loud Drunky Mimi. "You don't have to say that each time you try to steal!"

As Simon and Ryan puzzled over the drawing while Mimi counted down from thirty, Zach flirted with Sophia. And by flirting, I mean licked the rim of his glass. All the way around. He looked like a giraffe.

Shuddering, I looked at Sophia, who wasn't even watching. She was watching Neil, who was watching Missy, who was adjusting her bra. I knew this because it was hanging half out of her shirt.

Ryan and Simon continued to argue over the picture while Zach giraffed, and I just held my head. Disaster.

"Ten! Nine! Eight! Seven!" Mimi shouted, staring at her watch.

"It's not New Year's—just give us a few more seconds, we can get this!" Ryan shouted back, looking back and forth from the picture to Simon.

"Shit, I don't know, is it, is it—shit!" Simon yelled, bouncing from one foot to the other.

"Six! Five! Four! Three!" Mimi continued. Missy crossed her legs. Neil stared at her legs. Zach burped, but continued licking. Sophia steamed.

"Two!"

"A bird in the hand is worth two in the bush," Neil stated, his gaze on Sophia.

"One! Ha, you didn't— Wait, what?" Mimi asked, looking at Neil, then Sophia. Simon and Ryan looked hopeful.

Silence.

"That's right." Sophia scowled, wincing when Simon and Ryan erupted into cheers.

"No way, no way! No fair, I had almost said one! I had almost said one!" Mimi cried, jumping across the room and landing on Ryan's back, pummeling him with her fists. Zach burped again. Missy took her hair out of her ponytail, and everyone with a penis stopped to watch.

"That's it," Sophia snapped, and stormed into the kitchen.

"I'm calling time-out!" I yelled as I left the room to follow her.

"Time-out from what?" Zach asked, and I just shook my head.

Sophia was angrily taking things out of the fridge, then putting them back again. "I can't believe he got that!"

"I can't believe we didn't. How embarrassing!" I answered, holding the fridge door open for her as a rotisserie chicken made its way out.

"No kidding! I mean, come on, how are we losing to these guys?" she asked, rifling through the condiment door and coming up with a bottle of Sriracha.

"We're losing because we're not concentrating. We need to get our heads in the game." I watched as she put away a jar of pickles and grabbed a jug of milk.

"Pfft, maybe you're not concentrating because you're drooling over my b'ball player." She smirked, removing a plastic container of leftover peas.

"I'm sure that's it," I remarked, trying to keep the incredulous out of my voice. Without question, Tall Zach was great looking, but what a drip.

"What am I looking for?" she asked, holding a container of sour cream in one hand and a cucumber in the other.

"You got me," I answered, spying Neil coming around the corner. "But thanks for cleaning out the fridge."

As Sophia stuck her head back in, Neil came into the kitchen.

"Funny how I knew exactly what you were trying to draw, huh, Soph?" he started, and she froze. I knew she froze because the sour cream dropped to the floor. I sidestepped away as she shut the door, pointing her cucumber at him.

"Don't give me *you knew exactly what I was trying to draw.* You must have seen the card."

"How could I have seen the card? You were holding it the entire time."

"Well, maybe you turned away from Titty McBoobs over there to look."

"Oh please, you think that—"

I walked away just as Simon came around the corner, and I quickly turned him back from where he came.

"I wouldn't go in there right now. Sophia's got a cucumber and she knows how to use it."

He snorted.

"Wait, that came out wrong. They're in there talking," I said, tugging him along.

We both winced as their voices rose.

"Well, they're talking loudly—but they're talking." I sighed.

In the end, Game Night totally sucked. Mimi almost passed out, still grumbling about being cheated out of SpongeBob HandBird. Ryan spent the rest of the night memorizing the Pictionary rulebook for next time, while Simon and I cleaned sour cream off the kitchen floor and picked cucumber seeds out from between the tiles.

"She squeezed the seeds right out, with her hand! It wasn't even peeled!" he kept saying, amazed and more than a little scared.

And Frick and Frack? Made out with Tall and Tits. Actually made out with their dates in front of each other. I've never seen anything like it. I wanted to look away, I felt like I *should* look away, but I couldn't. Simon and I stood there, covered in seeds, watching the make-out contest. Sophia was pushed up against the wall, so then Tits got pushed up against a wall. Neil got an impromptu lap dance; so did Tall.

"It's like we're at some kind of swingers' party," Simon whispered when a shoe flew by, kicked off by a Playboy bunny.

"Or WrestleMania," I whispered back when another shoe flew the other way. Don't think Sophia didn't notice Shoeless Tits.

When the groaning finally drowned out Mimi's muttering, it was time to stick a fork in the entire evening. And then never speak of that fork again.

Glaring at each other, Neil and Sophia walked out together, hot dates in tow. Ryan carried Mimi out to the hillevator, telling us he'd come back the next day to pick up their things. "I've got to get her home before she pukes," he said, shaking his head. "No more drink stations."

As they rode up the hill, I could hear snippets floating back from Neil and Sophia, arguing all the way to the cars.

We headed back inside, looking at the drawing board. Which was now decorated with phallic imagery, courtesy of Tall Zach.

Simon began, "I love our friends, but—"

"How the hell are they our friends?" I finished, and he nodded.

Laughing ruefully, he flipped back to the picture that ended the game. "A bird in the hand. How did we not get this?"

"Because she drew an airplane with sponges—that's why." I sighed. "Wanna go to bed?"

"Hell yes," he answered. As we headed to the bedroom, he helped me unzip my dress. "She still loves him, doesn't she?"

"Of course she does," I answered. I let my dress fall to the floor, and I climbed into bed in my bra and panties. I watched through tired eyes as Simon undressed.

"Did you set the alarm?" I asked.

"It's Sunday. Why do we need to set the alarm?" he asked, turning back his covers.

"I have to work for a few hours in the morning. Monica's meeting me at the coffee shop down the street."

"Babe." He shook his head before turning out the light. After he set the alarm. "You're working too hard."

"Lots to do. If I work tomorrow, I'll have some time this week during the evening. It'll be fine. You sleep in, and by the time you're up, I'll be almost home. We can go for a drive."

"It's not that. I just think you're working too much; you need to slow down a bit," he grumbled, pulling me across the bed and into his side.

"Things will slow down after the holidays, you'll see. Besides, I'm in charge right now—kind of don't have a choice," I reminded him.

"I know, I just— I know," he said, kissing the top of my head.

I kissed his chest. "It'll ease up, I swear in the name of Sponge-Bob HandBird."

A moment later, the bed was shaking from laughter. And a few minutes later, the bed was shaking for a different reason.

Eh, sleep is overrated. Being turned over by a Wallbanger? Priceless.

The week of Thanksgiving started out okay. The morning after the Pictionary party, I left a sleeping Simon behind while I headed over to work for a few hours, came home, and then ate naked turnovers with Simon in bed. Or, ate turnovers in bed with Simon, naked? Whatever, that was the high point of the week.

Without a family to speak of, Simon had always kept himself busy over Thanksgiving as well as Christmas. This year, I'd been hoping he'd take my family up on their offer of spending Thanksgiving together, but he wasn't quite ready for that.

He'd met my folks on several occasions, and holy shit on a shingle, I have never seen Simon more nervous than he was the first time. Meeting the parents is a big deal in any relationship, but he'd never been involved with anyone long enough to make this step before. He totally won them over, though. He flirted like hell with my mom, won my dad over by sharing stories of Formula 1 races he'd attended over the years, and now he looked forward to spending time with them when they came to San Francisco. But a turkey dinner in a house filled to bursting with family?

"I just can't. Maybe next year," he explained, while I handed him socks I'd folded for him. He dropped them into the suitcase, then headed into his closet to grab some sweaters. "They won't be mad, will they? I mean, I always work this time of year; it's just what I do."

"No no, they get it. And I get it. But I've finally got some time off, and just wish we could spend it together," I said quietly, watching as the sweaters went into the bag. I'd be working like crazy right up until Thursday, but I'd planned on spending the rest of the week at home with my folks.

"I know, babe. You've been so busy lately even when I am here, I hardly see you," he answered, dropping a kiss on my forehead and disappearing back into the closet.

"What's that supposed to mean?" I asked, my nose wrinkling a bit.

"It's not supposed to mean anything," he said, rolling a few pairs of jeans.

"You hardly see me because I'm busy, Simon. It's not like you don't know everything I'm trying to juggle right now." I frowned, sliding off the bed and standing in front of him.

"Don't get so defensive, it wasn't a criticism. I get it; you're busy. Chill."

My eyes bugged out of my head. Did he just tell me to—*chill*?

"Christ, I'm sorry. Forget I said anything." He sighed.

I started to snap back, then took a deep breath. *Let this one go.* I reached out and pulled him toward me by the belt loops, letting my head drop onto his chest. A few seconds later, I felt him sigh and then his arms were around me. I breathed him in, then turned my face up toward his.

"We'll have lots of time to spend together in Philadelphia."

His face shuttered. He kissed my forehead again, then turned to zip the suitcase closed. "Tell your folks I said happy Thanksgiving," he said with a tight smile.

Guess that subject was closed.

He left the following day. He was heading back east, doing a photo shoot on Thanksgiving in Plymouth, the pilgrims and all that. It was to be featured the following year in travel magazines and regional newspapers to boost the local economy. But he was going, and I was staying—and that was the beginning of my shit week.

I came home Monday night after spending the entire weekend in Sausalito, to find that Clive had decided he'd had enough of me being gone. Maybe it was time to consider bringing him over to Sausalito, as creative as he was being with showing me his displeasure. He'd left me presents. Multiple presents. In multiple shoes. I missed him too; I just didn't show it by shitting in his shoes. The image of what size his shoes might be if he *did* wear shoes wouldn't leave my brain, so I spent a conference call with Camden's people not paying attention and doodling cat shoes all over some documents.

You try explaining to your intern why there were tiny paws in pumps all over a contract that she now had to reprint.

The lowest point came on Wednesday afternoon after I sent everyone home early, and then I realized that I *wasn't* going to be able to see my family for Thanksgiving. I'd thought I was on top of things, I thought my in-box was finally cleared out enough to sneak away for two days, when I found an e-mail in spam for a job I'd agreed to months ago. To come in and decorate for a client who was having thirty people over to her Nob Hill home for Thanksgiving dinner, and needed the dining room dressed. And the living room. And an entire autumn-in-New-England scene designed for her conservatory, where drinks *might* be served but *might* not, but just in case, could I please make it look like pilgrims might have lived there?

I lost my mind.

I didn't even close the door, since there was no one left there but me.

I was still wiping the sob snot from my face when I heard Skype ringing on my computer. Dammit.

Crawling around the desk—yes I was on the floor, that's the best place for a breakdown— I popped up and saw that it was Jillian.

Should I answer? Should I not? She'd know I was upset. Oh hell, let her.

I pulled myself into my chair, answering her call with one last nose blow.

"Do you have a cold?" she asked, the video coming through instantly. I saw myself in the tiny window, red eyes and red face, and I lied.

"I do, how're you?" I asked, trying to keep my voice light.

"Great! We're just about to take the train into Venice. I never thought I'd be having Thanksgiving dinner in Venice, can you imagine? It won't be a true Thanksgiving dinner, but we were thinking maybe we'd have something with chicken. That'll be close enough, right?" She laughed.

"I'd think so. What can I do for you, Jillian? You just caught me."

"I wasn't sure you'd still be there. When are you leaving for your folks'?"

"Um, in a few minutes, just finishing up a few last-minute details," I answered, struggling to keep my voice from breaking. Mentally, I was going through the stockroom, thinking about how many yards of brown silk I'd need to fashion into a tablecloth.

"Well, good. I just thought I'd check in and see how things were going, wish you a happy Thanksgiving."

I bit my tongue, wanting to say something but keeping it in check. "Happy Thanksgiving to you too, Jillian. How's Benjamin?" I managed to ask.

"He's great, he sends his love. Where's Simon this year?"

"Back east, taking pictures in Plymouth. Fucking pilgrims. I mean—you know what I—"

"You okay, kiddo?" she interrupted.

I didn't need her worrying about anything, so I forced a smile. "Everything's great here, I'm just trying to finish a few things so I can get down to my folks'."

"Okay, if you're sure that's all—"

"It's all good here, Jillian. Talk to you later, okay?" I hurried, knowing I couldn't hold the tears back much longer. We said our good-byes and hung up, just as a fresh wave started.

I couldn't take another call like that, so I chickened out and texted my mom to let her know the change in plans, promising to call her a little later. I couldn't speak to her until I'd calmed down; I didn't want to worry her. She knew how many hours I'd been putting in; she was so proud of me and how well everything was going. Ha.

I texted Simon to let him know that I was no longer going home for Thanksgiving, that I was working on a last-minute project, and that I'd call him later on when I took a break.

A break! Pffft.

He tried calling me back almost immediately, but I let it go to voice mail. I needed to work, not wallow.

I spent the next nine hours working on table settings and centerpieces, and then spent six hours Thanksgiving morning dressing a conservatory to make it look like very wealthy pilgrims had wandered by and decided *this* would be the place they wanted to have spiced squash soup accented by thyme and chervil.

Thanksgiving night, I was on the couch eating ramen in my pajamas with Clive, watching reruns on Food Network of *Ina's Best Thanksgiving* shows. It was like disaster porn; I couldn't look away. Now that I'd saved the day for another family, I could wallow. And wallow I did.

Which is why my wallow was so surprised when Clive began to pace at the front door, seconds before Simon came in.

I looked at him, covered in November rain, his eyes warm.

"I didn't want you to spend Thanksgiving alone," he said, shaking off the rain. "And maybe I don't either."

I burst into tears for the second time in twenty-four hours.

He just picked me up off the couch and settled me into his lap, his North Face getting my PJs soaked. He held me, soothing me, running his hands over my back and making little circles on my shoulders.

"You . . . are . . . the best . . . boyfriend . . . ever!" I wailed, wiping my nose on my arm. Clive ran in and out of Simon's legs, threading himself as close as he could get without appearing too needy. Hell, I was idling at needy, ready to downshift into pitiful.

By the time my sobs tapered off, I was shivering, the chill from the rainy night moving into my bones.

"Come on, sweet girl, let's get you changed into something warm," he said. Reluctant to be set down, I clung to him. So he stood with me wrapped around him in front, and walked us back to the bedroom.

"I can't put into words how happy I am to see you, Simon. I really can't," I whispered, arms tight around his neck.

"I missed you too," he answered, trying to set me down on the bed, but I was fighting him. "Babe, let's get you into some dry clothes."

"Kiss me, please," I asked, pulling him down to me.

He kissed me. And I kissed him back, needing to feel him. I wrapped my arms back around his neck, around his back, under his North Face, needing skin. He rocked against me, needing it too. "Caroline," he groaned, pulling back to look into my eyes. That made me tear up again, just seeing his face so unexpectedly close to mine.

When you were in a long-distance relationship, of course you made the most of the time you were together. But sometimes, it was the unexpected that really made the difference. The unexpected emotions you were hit with when you saw that face, looked into those eyes, felt those lips. The unexpected reminder of why you fell in love with this person could hit you so powerfully. And this was that time.

I memorized his face, felt every line and every pattern, drew his temple, his nose, his dimple, the bow of his lip, drew it all with my fingertips and memorized it once more.

"I love you, Simon. Love you, love you, love you so much," I chanted as he laid me down, peeled the clothes from my body and his own, and entered me.

He groaned my name, answering my cries with his own, loving me sweetly. And when my orgasm crashed through me, it was wonderful and secondary to what this was.

He was here with me. Not photographing pilgrims.

chapter eleven

The time between Thanksgiving and when we left for Philadelphia flew by. I was always at work before everyone else, and almost without fail I closed the office every day. I put out fires, I trained Monica, I even did payroll a few more times. It was crazy, hectic, impossibly frantic. There were days when I barely saw daylight, ate every meal straight from the microwave, and the only time I sat down was to pee. And even then, I was reading e-mails. Please, like everyone doesn't bring their phone to the bathroom to read?

And through the crazy, the hectic, the impossibly frantic life that I was leading, I was getting my shit done. I was not only handling it, I was actually now ahead of the curve. I'd turned some kind of time management corner and was holding my own. I walked not with a drag but with a bounce; I rushed from meeting to meeting and job site to job site with a renewed sense of purpose. I was tired, but I was happy in a weird way. I was getting the swing of things. I was still stressed, but it was a good stressed.

I was ahead of schedule on the hotel project, and I was even able to start working on a few Christmas projects. If you were very wealthy, you didn't do your own Christmas decorating—heavens, no! You hired it out. Initially I thought that with Jillian being gone

I'd need to contact some of the other design firms we were good neighbors with to farm some of it out, but I couldn't do it. I needed to make sure that everything at Jillian Designs functioned the same way as when Jillian was actually in residence. So I slept less. And got to work on decking the halls with boughs of Red Bull.

Simon was home. His trip to Plymouth should have kept him busy until right before the reunion, but now he had some free time. Something he usually didn't have much of. But now he did. After coming home one night to a present in his own shoe from Clive, he agreed that instead of spending a few nights a week over in Sausalito, it would be easier to just move out there and bring the little shoe pooer. So Clive was now a country cat. And he had a stay-at-home daddy.

The two of them had a ball, exploring the new house and spending hours looking out the window wall. Clive had never had so much room, and he relished all the closets and beds he could hide in and under. Simon took over the nightly game of Hide the Pounce, something that I unfortunately didn't have time for anymore. One chilly night I came home late and found Simon holding Clive up to the window, making paw prints where it was foggy and talking about how far away the city of San Francisco was.

He grinned when he saw me, but didn't stop talking about how cold the water was and how Clive should not try to swim back to the city. Clive nodded sagely and pressed another print to the window.

Now that Simon had so much free time, he was biking most days, sending me texts and pictures from all over Marin County. He had a favorite restaurant, a favorite place to get coffee in the morning, a favorite deli; he had a new favorite everything.

For the record, his favorite *position* remained whichever one I was in when he was inside me. And while I was exhausted most nights, I still managed to sneak in naked times with my Wallbanger. Such a hardship.

And with all this free time came unexpected visits. Office pop-ins. Several phone calls a day. He was around all the time, and didn't seem to understand why *I* wasn't around all the time. He logically got that I was working more than ever, and that I was happy. Didn't stop him from trying to pull me back into bed each morning.

And shit, that was hard. Because it is incredibly difficult to get out of bed every morning when you have a rumpled Wallbanger holding on to your pajamas. Because, and I say this with pride, *his favorite position remained whichever one I was in when he was inside me.*

Seriously, though, he was around *all* the time. He'd also reminded me several times that I was not. Hmm.

Jillian and Benjamin were leaving Italy and heading to Prague, planning on spending a few days in the city and then exploring the Czech countryside. I marveled over the pictures she e-mailed me, letting her tell me all about the amazing time she was having with her husband. She was relaxed in a way I hadn't seen her in years, and she was sure to tell me how much she appreciated her "office dynamo" handling everything so that she could take this time with her new husband. It was weird hearing her refer to Benjamin as her husband; they'd been engaged for so long he'd been her fiancé the entire time I'd known her.

I'd asked her once what made them finally decide to go ahead and set a date. We'd been sitting in the conference room, sampling cakes the baker had brought by one morning, trying to decide which one would be the wedding cake. I caught her looking down at her ring, smiling a secretive smile, and I asked her.

"I don't know. One day I just looked at him and knew I was ready to be his wife. I'd built my business, I'd accomplished all of the goals I'd set in my twenties and a bunch I'd set in my thirties, and it just felt like the right time." She grinned, pulling the chocolate buttercream with raspberry filling back toward her for another taste. I had a feeling this one was going to be the winner. It was. "Plus, have you seen his ass? Oh, look who I'm asking, the president of the Benjamin Fan Club," she joked.

"I'll have you know I won that election fair and square. It's not my fault Mimi and Sophia didn't know we were voting that day. Fair and square," I explained.

Speaking of my friends, all was quiet on the Sophia and Neil front. They hadn't seen each other since Game Night, and Mimi was planning to try again before Christmas—something I was trying to talk her out of. But when she invited them both to her Christmas party, neither one tried to get out of it. In fact, they both seemed to be looking forward to it. Who knew who they'd bring this time? They both continued to date, and often, but it rarely went beyond to a second date.

Color me surprised.

In order to jet off to Philadelphia for an entire weekend in the middle of one of my busiest seasons, I worked practically round the clock, evenings, and Saturdays to clear my schedule enough so that I could leave everything behind and just be with Simon. It was never a question of not going; there was no way on earth I was going to let him do this alone.

He was so nervous.

The night before we left he had a nightmare, and today on the plane he barely spoke. When he did speak, he was curt and quick. When the plane touched down, he turned to me and said, "I'm going to apologize right now for being a dick this weekend, in case I am. I'm not planning on it, but if it does happen, I'm sorry."

I patted his hand, and kissed his nose. "Apology preaccepted. Now show me your hometown— I can't wait to see your Liberty Bell."

He half smiled, and took my hand as we left the plane.

• • •

Philadelphia was a city I'd never been to, and I wished I had even more time to explore. But this weekend wasn't about indulging my reenactment of the Rocky Run up the steps of the art museum, but more about me being wherever and whatever Simon needed. Besides, apparently they moved the Rocky statue from the top of the stairs off to the side anyway. Pffft.

We picked up the rental car, threw our bags into the back, and headed to the hotel. With the trip cross country, it was already dark by the time we got to the part of town Simon grew up, but he lit up when he began to call out places he recognized. And places he didn't.

"When did that bike shop close down? Oh man, this was the place I got my first bike without training wheels. Why is a mini-mall there; when did that go up?"

"When's the last time you were here, Simon?" I asked.

"Um, a few weeks after graduation, I think," he said distractedly, his eyes going back and forth on both sides of the street.

"You really haven't been here since you were eighteen?" I asked, astonished.

"Why would I have been back?" he asked, making a turn and taking us right into the middle of the town square.

When Simon said he grew up in Philadelphia, that wasn't technically true. He grew up in one of the many feeder communities, the smaller townships that made up the outlying areas. I knew he came from money, but I didn't know he came from Moneyville, USA.

His hometown was plush. And darling in the way all northeastern towns looked to anyone who grew up in California. There was something to be said for growing up in a town that was almost three hundred years older than the one I grew up in. Most of the houses we passed could only be described as estates.

The town square was quaint, with tidy little shops framing

City Hall in the center. Two story mostly, with a few turreted three stories on each corner. People were shopping as the lightest dusting of snow fell, sparkling on the wrought-iron railings and—oh my God—honest to goodness real iron horse head hitching posts! Like, where people used to tie their horses to! Like, in olden times!

"Simon, we have to walk around a little, look how cute your town is! Look at all the shops, and, oh, look at the Christmas tree in the middle!" I cried, pointing. In front of City Hall was a large tree, bedecked with red bows, gold ornaments, and white lights.

"Babe, they put up a Christmas tree in front of City Hall in San Francisco every year."

"This is different; this is so stinking *cute*! Everything is so old! What's that?" I asked, pointing to an old Gothic house with a plaque outside. Each window had a wreath; the windows upstairs even had candles too. It was so pretty, it must be of some historical significance.

"It used to be . . . Yep, it's still a Subway."

"Station?" I asked, confused.

"No, like the sandwich shop," he replied, laughing at my fallen expression. "I can't believe it's still open; no one eats there. Not when there's Little Luigi's. You still want a cheesesteak?"

"Am I breathing?"

"One cheesesteak coming up," he said, turning the car down the last corner of the town square. "You gotta understand, everything here is old. Every building used to be something else; every building gets reused for something else," he explained, pulling into one of the parking spots that was diagonal along the square. "Except for that stupid strip mall where my bike shop used to be."

He turned off the car and walked around to my side. Stepping out, I breathed in the snowy air, feeling it prickle in my lungs. The cold felt good after the long plane ride, and it was nice to stretch my legs a bit as we walked down the block.

As we walked, he pointed out the different shops: the bakery where they made the best sugar cookies, the place where he got his new shoes every year for school, and as we walked and he talked, he seemed less and less nervous.

"Thank God, it's still here. Little Luigi's," he said, where there was a line out the door into the cold night. It moved fast though, and soon we were inside. It was a hole in the wall, with only three tables and a counter. They were grilling the steaks on a big black griddle, peppers and onions sizzling. People were barking out orders, wrapping sandwiches, and the smell was heavenly.

When it was our turn, Simon ordered for both of us. Two steaks, cheese, onions, mushrooms, with both sweet and hot peppers on the side. And the funniest thing happened. When he ordered? This accent came out of nowhere. I'd never heard it before. Not New York or New Jersey; this was very specific. As I listened to everyone around me, they all had it. Some thicker than others, and Simon's was fairly light, but it had definitely popped up. Huh.

Grabbing a handful of napkins, he spied a family leaving one of the tables and was able to nab it. Leaving me with the table, he went back up for the sandwiches. I'd seen Simon order from a man with ten baskets of spring rolls on his head in Saigon. I'd seen him order sausages from a giant woman in an apron in Salzburg. And nowhere had I ever seen him more at home than he was in this sandwich shop in suburban Philadelphia.

With a wide grin, he returned to the table. He showed me how to spread out the paper to catch the drips, added salt and pepper, then how to hold it so it didn't spill out over the sides. Then he bit down, and pure bliss came over his face. And he made a sound I'd only ever heard him make once. And he was very happy when he made it.

"Simon Parker?" a voice said from behind, and he turned with a mouthful of cheesesteak. He quickly swallowed, and stood. An older woman with a sleek silver chignon and a strand of pearls that could choke a horse was looking at him in amazement.

"Mrs. White?" he asked, running a hand through his hair.

"Oh my goodness, it *is* you! I never thought we'd see you around here again!" She pulled him into a hug. "Where in the world have you been? Last I heard, you were off to Stanford."

"Yes, ma'am, and I'm still out on the West Coast—San Francisco, actually. How are you, how's the family?"

"Oh fine, fine! Todd's with the firm now and practicing corporate law. He's married, with their first little one on the way, and Kitty just got married last summer, and— You must be here for the reunion; I just can't believe it's you!" she said again, hugging him tight. He rocked forward on his feet, off balance, while I looked on, grinning.

She spied me over his shoulder, and looked me up and down with shrewd interest. "And who might this be, Simon?"

He ran his hand through his hair nervously again. "This is Caroline Reynolds. Caroline, this was our neighbor from next door, Mrs. White." He patted me on the shoulder so hard that I almost took a nosedive into what remained of my cheesesteak. Which was basically just a grease stain.

I reached a hand out to her. "Mrs. White, it's lovely to meet you. You must be the one to go to for stories about how much trouble Simon used to get into, am I right?"

"I remember everything, Caroline—my mind is like a steel trap," she said, tapping her temple. "But tonight I forgot to remind Arthur to grab the chicken out of the freezer, so it's hoagies in the TV room," she said, waving at the counter man who was holding up two torpedo-looking bundles.

Looking at Simon carefully, she patted him on the cheek. "Simon, I can't tell you how good it is to see you. You'll stop by while you're in town? I won't take no for an answer."

"Well, Mrs. White, I'm not sure if we'll have time since the reunion is tomorrow night, and before that I was going to show Caroline around a bit more. We're leaving on Sunday, so—"

"Lunch."

"Lunch?" he asked.

"Lunch tomorrow. You have to eat, right?"

He nodded. I smiled. I liked her.

"Then it's settled. I'll see you at twelve." She nodded, settling the matter. "Oh, I can't wait to tell Arthur you're coming over tomorrow; he'll be so pleased!"

"Thank you, ma'am," he agreed.

"I've got to run, see you then!" she called over her shoulder, heading out into the night.

"She's great," I remarked, watching as Simon balled up the remaining papers and napkins and threw them into the wastebasket.

"Mmm-hmm."

"That was good," I said, patting my stomach.

"Mmm-hmm."

"So what now?" I asked, raising my eyebrows at the sudden change. The nerves were back.

"What? Oh, um, let's head to the hotel, get checked in? Yep, let's do that," he said, ushering me out of the shop.

We walked silently to the car in the lightly falling snow. This trip was a big deal for him, and I'd just realized what lunch meant: he was going to be next door to the house he grew up in. For the first time in ten years.

He reached for my hand, and into his it went.

I took a few minutes to clear out my in-box when we got back to the hotel. I was trying really hard to leave the office behind, so I limited it to a few moments here and there, answering only the questions I couldn't put off until Monday. Then I took a shower, wanting to get rid of the airplane and the cheesesteak smell, both of which lingered. Still damp, I padded out to the bedroom in my towel with another on my head, finding Simon lying on the bed. Hands clasped behind his head, he was staring at the ceiling.

"Hey," I said softly.

"Hey, how was your shower?"

"Fantastic, they've got one of those rain showers? You should take one before bed."

"I might."

Silence fell once more, and I crossed to the bed, sitting down beside him.

"Thanks for bringing me here. It's nice, seeing the place you came from."

"Sure," he said, looking at me for the first time.

I laid my hand on his chest gently. "Hey."

"Hey," he whispered back.

I leaned down slowly, watching his eyes. I gently grazed my lips over his, light and quick. When he didn't pull away, I kissed him again. He let me, my lips taking his for a third time. I pressed a little harder, and he let me in. I stroked his tongue with my own, feeling him respond as we tangled and twisted. His breathing deepened, his pulse quickened beneath me, and I propped myself above. Not removing my mouth from his, I let my fingers undo his buttons, exposing the skin beneath. Kissing along his jawline, I let my lips tease just below his ear, feeling the sandpaper scruff. I knew what that scruff felt like on the inside of my thighs, and how great was that?

I felt him tense as I flicked my tongue against his earlobe, eliciting a hiss. His hands came up to my waist as I crept back along his neck, kissing lower along his collarbone. Pulling at his shirt, untucking it from his waistband, I threw it wide, pressing myself along his torso. His skin was warm; it felt divine against my own. I needed to feel more of it.

Standing, I kept my hands on him at all times while I gently removed his shirt, then belt, then socks and pants, until I had him naked and wanting. Standing in the moonlight, I dropped my towel.

"Caroline," he breathed, and I crawled back on top of him. Straddling him low on his legs, I took him in hand. His hands came up to my breasts, needy and kneading. I stroked him, grasping the base and working upward, swirling my hand over the head and letting his hips tell me what he needed.

He panted, his chest rising and falling as I worked him. Up and down and swirly twirly, he was hard in my hands and the single most erotic man I'd ever seen in my life. I gently grazed one finger along the underside, and he thrust hard.

"Not going to last long if you keep that up." He groaned, his fingers teasing at my nipples.

"That's not what this is about," I answered, rising above him. I positioned him, and slid him inside. Slick from just the way he was looking at me, I sank down inch by perfect inch, slowly. Exquisitely so, as he strained to stay still.

Once he was seated fully inside I gave one slow roll of my hips, gasping as I felt him grow harder and thicker. Impossible.

"What's . . . impossible?" he grunted, every muscle taunt and lean. I didn't know I'd spoken aloud. No matter, he should know.

"That I will ever get tired of this, of what it feels like to have you inside me," I said, shuddering as he thrust up. I leaned backward a bit, resting my hands on his thighs for leverage as I took him in again. Rising onto his elbows, he watched in fascination at the sight of him sliding in and out of my body. One of his hands swept my hair back from my face, then dragged down my neck, between my breasts, down my tummy and dipped down below.

That hand, making those perfect circles, right at the center of my world, and my hips took over. I rode him hard, rising up and down, as he watched me writhe above him.

"Simon. That's. Perfect!" I called out, feeling my orgasm approaching. He sat up underneath me, wrapping my legs around his waist, pistoning into me in an unrelenting rhythm, crushing me to him. I shook as I came, his own release chasing him down in a fury.

I held him to me, not letting go, not letting him get away, my body molded to his in a mess of sticky, sweaty skin, sliding and thrusting together, frantic and furious.

He was silent when he came, his eyes burning into mine as I held him to my breast, as he shattered. His head threw back, his strength washed over me, then he fell into me. I held him, rocking, still feeling him inside me as he softened, cradling him against my skin.

"It's impossible for me to love you more," I whispered, kissing his forehead.

He clutched me even tighter.

He was white-faced when we turned onto his street the next day, his lips in a tight line. And speaking of tight, with the grip he had on the steering wheel, he was close to tearing it off. When I wasn't looking at Simon, I was gaping at the houses we were passing. This was old-ass money, moldy blue-blood money. Not a McMansion in sight, only actual estates. Tennis courts, pool houses, and miles of fencing. Still a neighborhood, though; the houses weren't so far apart that they were isolated. Just a neighborhood lined with stately oaks and gas lamps.

And three security cars. So far.

But it was beautiful. We pulled up to an elegant fieldstone and brick home, Tudor style with black shutters. The little bit of snow that had fallen was neatly shoveled, the path and drive neatly edged. Christmas lights twinkled from inside, hinting at a mammoth tree, and a wreath as big as my bed was on the front door. The house to the left must have been Simon's, as it was the one he was avoiding looking at entirely. Pine trees along the property line softened the view, but it looked like a brick center style colonial, as grand as the rest of the neighborhood. There were bikes in the driveway. Kids' bikes.

As we walked up the pathway to the house, Simon let out a chortle. "I can't believe that's still here."

"What?"

"They redid the pavers when I was in elementary school, and her son and I wrote our names in the cement. Boy, did we hear about that one." He pointed to the first step, and on the corner I could just make out his name. Simon Parker.

"You wouldn't have made a very good vandal; you signed your full name, for pity's sake," I said as he rang the doorbell. I reached out and gave his buns a squeeze, and as he looked at me in surprise, the door opened.

"There you are, right on time!" Mrs. White sang out, opening the door and hurrying a blushing Simon inside. He insisted I go first and I got my own bun squeeze. "It's so cold out, look at your cheeks, bright red! Good thing I had Arthur make a fire. Arthur, come down here!"

Exchanging hugs and kisses on the cheek, we were ushered into a formal but very comfortable sitting room, where there was in fact a fire crackling. I made small talk with Mrs. White while Simon surreptitiously took everything in: the picture window, the antique desk, the ship in a bottle on the mantel. I saw him take a deep breath, turning as Mr. White came in.

"Simon, so great to see you!" he said, walking right up and shaking Simon's hand, then pulling him into a one-armed hug.

"Mr. White, good to see you too, sir."

"I can't tell you how Penny went on and on about seeing you when she came home last night. How've you been?"

"Good, I've been good. I heard Todd is married?"

"Oh yes, nice gal. But more importantly, how are you? What

have you been up to all these years? Photography we heard, tell me all about that." Mr. White clapped an arm around Simon's shoulders and walked him into the library, which was all wood and full of books, enough to require one of those sliding ladders.

As they disappeared around the corner, I looked over at Mrs. White. She was smiling, but her eyes looked a bit damp.

"Mrs. White, your home is beautiful," I started, and she turned her glassy gaze to mine.

"Call me Penny."

"Not until Simon does." I grinned.

"Mrs. White it is, then; that boy will never call me anything but. Can I get you something to drink, dear?" she asked, gesturing for me to follow her over to where there was lemonade, coffee, and—

"Is that a Bloody Mary bar?" I asked.

"Oh heavens, yes." She nodded, sweeping under her eyes a bit with a manicured hand. "Olive or celery?"

"Both?"

"I always knew Simon would end up with a smart girl." She winked, and poured. Lots of Mary in that Bloody . . .

We sat on the couch and chatted, keeping things light. We discussed the design of her home; she was fascinated by interiors and had helped with every room in the house. We talked a little bit about the town, and how many years her family had lived here. Many. And since the men seemed to be taking a while in the library, we eventually moved on to Simon.

"I can't tell you how good it is to see him. Everyone here had resigned themselves to never seeing him again, after he graduated."

"I didn't realize he hadn't been back since . . . Well, since."

"No, he left that June and that was the last anyone saw him. He kept in touch with a few of his friends for a little while, but he seemed to need the break. We all understood, losing his family so suddenly."

"I'm glad he came back; this seems like a lovely place to grow up."

"It was, and it is. Gail and Thomas, his parents, were wonderful people. So tragic . . ." She trailed off, then turned toward the desk. "I think I have some pictures of them, out on their farm. We spent time out there with them almost every summer. Did you know the Parkers had a farm?"

I shook my head. I knew nothing. He shared nothing. Not about this. She rifled through some drawers, then brought out an album. "I think this is it—yes! Yes, here it is. This is the summer Todd and Simon got caught skinny-dipping with the Wilson girls. Those two!"

She laughed, mulling over the pictures. "Take a look at this one," she said, handing a picture to me.

I hesitated. Simon had never shown me anything about his family. Should he be the one to show me? Curiosity won out, and I took the picture.

First, we must be clear: The word *farm* means different things to different people. This was no vegetable patch. In this scenario it meant rolling hills, a three-story house, and a picture-perfect red barn peeking through the trees. This was a Pottery Barn farm. But it's what was at the center of the picture that filled my eyes with tears and made me want to hug Simon for the rest of my days.

His father was tan, tall, and fantastic looking. His mother? Gorgeous. Healthy and vibrant, they stood with their son, just shy of his teenage years. He was at that age when everyone is all elbows and knees, but you could see that this guy was going to be devastating. As I scrutinized their faces, I could see that Simon got his incredible blue eyes from his father, his blinding smile from his mother.

Though I'd never meet them, I'd never have a conversation with the people who shaped Simon into the wonderfully perfect imperfect man that he was today, I knew I was looking at an extraordinary little family.

"Oh," was all I could say.

"So tragic," Mrs. White repeated, shaking her head and tsking in a comforting way.

I handed her back the picture, breathing deeply and making sure the tears that had sprung up were under control.

She took the picture, the album, and tucked it away. Taking a breath, she threw her shoulders back and the rest of her drink as well. "Now, what in the world are those boys up to? Arthur? Where have you taken Simon?" she called out, jumping to her feet. I asked if she would mind sending me a copy of that picture. She smiled and said she'd send me the original.

We headed into the library where we found another fireplace, with another crackling fire. Mr. White and Simon were sitting in leather chairs, with glasses next to both of them. Simon's was empty, but Mr. White's still had a trace of dark-colored liquor.

Simon's face wasn't pale anymore, but his eyes were the tiniest bit red. As were Mr. White's. They both stood when they saw us, and Simon crossed to me. I mouthed, Okay? He nodded, and took my hand.

"I believe lunch is ready," Mrs. White announced, and led the way to the dining room.

She disappeared for a moment while everyone settled around an enormous table, with yet another cozy fireplace behind us. As she took her place across from her husband, I asked her if there was anything I could do to help.

"Thank you, Caroline, but I've asked our housekeeper to assist us today," she said.

It didn't seem at all out of place that for lunch that day, I was served roasted sea bass with fennel and leeks on white china, by a housekeeper named Fran.

Old-ass money.

Very sweet people.

In the end, it was a really nice time. The Whites fawned over Simon and showed me pictures of him that were taken with their family growing up. They told stories, Simon told stories, and we all laughed a lot.

Simon asked about the family that lived in the house now.

"Very nice people, moved into town from Boston after they were married. They're both physicians, had their children later in life. Two girls, eight and six. There are several new families in the neighborhood; it's nice to have kids around again," Mrs. White said.

"That's good. It was a good house to be a kid in." Simon cleared his throat and went to the window, his shoulders tight. The window faced his home.

The fire crackled and popped.

"We should get going. I wanted to drive Caroline around a bit before we get ready for the reunion tonight," he said, his voice gruff. I started to go to him as he turned. "Thank you so much for having us here today, Mrs. White, Mr. White. I can't tell you how much— Thank you."

Time to go.

Mrs. White went to him and kissed him on the cheek. "You come back anytime you like, you promise?"

He nodded.

We left in a flurry of good-byes and number exchanges. I promised to send them pictures from San Francisco when we got back home, and as Arthur and Simon were saying their good-byes, Penny pulled me aside.

"You take care of him. He's still got a ball of hurt in there that's never come out, and when it does, it's going to be hell."

I nodded. "I'm on it."

She studied me a moment. "I believe you are, Caroline." She caught me into a surprise hug.

As we got settled in the car, they waved from the front steps before going back inside.

"They seem like very nice people," I said.

"They're the best," he replied.

As we pulled down the driveway, the trees cleared and I could see the house next door. It was magnificent. Brick for days, circular drive, festive for the holidays. Trimmed hedges, wreathes in every window, even the attic windows under the eaves. An expansive lawn with what looked to be the original carriage house set back from the main house.

"Simon," I breathed as he slowed down just a bit. "It's a beautiful home."

"It was, yes."

He turned the car away.

Brain wanted to push it, Heart said leave it. I listened to Heart.

I wasn't sure if Simon would still want to go to the reunion. He seemed so blue when we left the Whites, after having such a good visit with them. I think seeing the house had shaken him more than he thought it would. But once we got back into town, he seemed to rally. His spirits up, he drove me by his high school, the field where he played Little League, and the place down by the creek where everyone went to make out.

I offered. Can't blame a girl . . .

But once we got back to the hotel, we did share a shower. To conserve water, obviously. And to make sure my Simon had a little extra pep in his step, I dropped to my knees and sucked him off right there in the shower. Because I'm thoughtful like that.

As Simon and I pep-stepped into the lobby of the Wainwright Hotel, he was cool, calm, and collected. With a touch of afterglow. Dressed in black pants, a white button-down, and a leather jacket, he was sophisticated but cool. A man about town, a globetrotter, a secret cat whisperer who would sell his soul for an apple pie. And he was mine.

We followed the signs for the Newbury High School Ten-Year Reunion, stopping outside the ballroom to check my coat. As he helped me slip the coat down my arms, he whistled.

"Babe," he said in a low voice, "I realize I said this earlier, but you look fucking fantastic."

I grinned, spinning around so he could see my dress. I went bombshell, as you do when you're going to your boyfriend's high school reunion. Red skirt, black leather boots, and wouldn't he be surprised later on when he found out that's *all* I had on. I figured, go big or go home. And if he needed some cheering up later on, I wasn't opposed to sneaking his hand under my skirt and letting him get a little touch.

Now we were less than ten feet from the check-in desk, and as we neared the group that was gathered there, he stalled just the tiniest bit. I squeezed his hand, and his eyes met mine. Those sapphires were bright tonight.

"Come on, Wallbanger, show me off," I teased, and he grinned.

We moved toward the desk, and when he told the lady his name, I heard a gasp behind us in line.

"No fucking way. Simon Parker's here? He came?"

Word quickly spread, and by the time I had his name tag affixed to the front of his jacket, everyone was buzzing. Walking inside, I suddenly could appreciate the feeling movie stars must have when they get out of a limo at a premiere.

Everyone was staring at us.

chapter twelve

We walked into the ballroom amid whispers and darting glances. The place was packed, young professionals decked out in their finest junior partner/corporate raider/banking magnate's kid check-me-out clothes. And the guys were impressive too.

High schools were the same across the country. This one happened to be set down in one of the wealthiest towns in America, but there are still universal truths. Every single one of the Breakfast Club archetypes was represented here, and a few hybrids as well. And they all had their eyes on Simon.

Who was oddly relaxed. Once we hit the room, his shoulders went back, his stride lengthened, and he cruised. Along the walls were blown-up pictures from yearbooks: cheerleaders, football players, someone in a wig from a play, and someone in a wig streaking the soccer field. And there was Simon, up on the wall with a crown on his head and a hottie on his arm. Homecoming king.

"I just got it," I said, looking up at him a little starry-eyed.

"You just got what?"

"You were the shit in high school!"

His eyes crinkled, and he blushed the tiniest bit.

"Well, I'll be goddamned. I wondered if you'd show," I heard behind us, and as we turned, a strange look appeared on Simon's face. Johnny Wall Street stood there, backed by the Billionaire Boys Club. All of them great looking. All of them bigger than life.

Simon looked at them all, narrowing down on the guy in the middle. "Henderson."

"Parker."

I watched the testosterone spark. If it had been a Western, tumbleweeds would have blown through. But since it was Wall Street . . .

Cue cocaine.

The tension only lasted as long as a chorus of Usher's "Yeah" before—

"What the fuck, dude! I can't believe you're really here! Fucking A, man— Parker's back in town!"

Wall Street backslapped a now-grinning Simon and pulled him into a giant, swarming man hug amid calls of, "Now, that's what I'm *talking* about" and "So fucking stoked that you're here, man" and "Dude, Tammy Watkins got new tits and they're fucking huge, you gotta see 'em!"

I stood back and watched as he was swallowed whole by this group of guys. I'd never met them, never heard him mention any of them before, but they knew Simon in a way that I never could.

These guys were there when Simon was growing up, when his entire world was midterms and *Jackass* and getting some girl to take her sweater off. My money was on Tammy Watkins.

And into this privileged enclave of white-bread preppies came the death of Simon's family. And Simon retreated, taking the first opportunity he had to remove himself entirely, moving as far across the country as one can for college, short of Hawaii. He went into a profession that took him all over the world, and chose to live in his adopted city of San Francisco. The only tie that he had to anyone in this world was Benjamin, for whom I was more grateful than ever.

But he'd come home, and *this* family was ready to make sure he knew he'd been missed.

Simon grinned big, shaking hands and high-fiving with his crew, and then he spotted me out of the corner of his eye. "Caroline, c'mere—you gotta meet these guys."

The penis sea parted, and I walked to the center, where he stood. "This is Caroline," he started, and I heard at least one wolf whistle. Glad I wore the boots. "And this is Trevor Henderson." Wall Street stuck his hand out and I shook it, looking up into his handsome face. Warm brown eyes twinkled down at me, not letting go when I was also introduced to Matthew, Mark, Luke, and John.

I'm not kidding. The apostles were all around us. Was it blasphemous that they were all hot? No matter, Trevor was still holding my hand.

"Seriously, dude, she's smoking," he said.

Simon removed my hand from his, laughing. "Cut it out, dick." This guy was harmless. And had good taste.

"Come on, they're serving dinner soon. You can sit at our table. You remember Megan Littlefield?" Trevor asked as the group moved together into the dining room.

"Um, maybe. Littlefield sounds familiar," Simon puzzled as we walked.

"It's Henderson now; she's my wife."

"You're married? Wow," Simon exclaimed, shaking his head.

"Yep, this past summer," he said proudly, waggling his ring finger in Simon's face.

"Wow," he repeated, and looked at me.

I just laughed and crooked my arm through his. "Come on, Homecoming King."

We grabbed a drink at the bar, said hello to a few more people, and sat down with his friends. And I say that broadly, because *everyone* here seemed to have been friends with him at one time or another. As I sipped my cocktail, I watched some of the girls begin to circle. Simon had obviously been a big swinging dick around here, and I wondered how many of them had taken a turn on that swing . . .

I met Trevor's wife before they started serving dinner, and as Simon left me to go say hello to an old teacher, I chatted with her. Megan had gone to school with them, two years younger.

"Didn't matter, though; *everyone* knew Simon. He was the guy every girl wanted." She sighed, a dreamy look on her face. Then she caught herself, and looked guiltily at me. "Sorry, is that weird?"

"Nope, I totally get it." I smiled, maybe smirking a little bit. He was shaking hands with an older gentleman, the teacher, I assumed. "So you just got married, huh? Congratulations."

"Thanks! It was great. We had it here, even though we live in New York now. It was just easier with the families being here."

"New York? State or city?"

"City. So both, right?" She laughed.

"And what do you do there?" I asked.

"I'm not working anymore. I worked until we got engaged, for the Food Network? I was a food stylist. Anyway, once we started planning the wedding, it was just too hard, commuting here to organize everything, so I quit. We got married at—"

I was seeing stars.

"Sorry, I can't even pretend to have heard anything you said after Food Network. You *worked* there! And you *quit* there! Why, woman—why in God's name?" I cried, my jaw hanging open so wide it was a good thing we were sitting down. Otherwise I'd trip.

She laughed and raised her eyebrows. "Let me guess. *Barefoot Contessa?*"

"*Yes!*" I screamed. Everyone stopped to look at us, and I turned red. Simon looked over from the bar, and I gave him the all clear.

I regrouped. "I mean, yes, I am a fan," I said coolly.

"Me too. She's super nice."

"*You've met her?*"

This time Simon excused himself from who he was talking to and started toward me, Trevor and the apostles in tow.

I know it's not logical; I know it's not even physically possible—

but I swear on all that is holy, they walked in slow motion. Like in some kind of action movie. Simon took point, Trevor just off to his left, and the rest slightly behind, like geese in a V. Everyone stopped to watch. It was like the sexiest train wreck ever; no one could look away.

I'd say it was quiet enough to hear a pin drop, but music from the early 2000s was on heavy rotation, and 50 Cent's "In Da Club" gave the boys their own soundtrack. All I saw were the sapphires, and they were laser locked and speaking volumes. I was familiar with this Simon.

Strong Simon. Authoritative Simon. Big Swinging Dick Simon. And on this, I could confirm.

Wallbanger Simon.

He reached our table, sat down next to me with an amused look on his face, and slid his arm around my shoulder.

Oh. My. God. Simon Parker put his arm around me! Like, in front of everyone!

Wait, this wasn't high school. This wasn't even *my* high school. But that didn't stop girls from throwing eye daggers at me from all corners of the room. I smirked a little, preening with my shoulder candy.

"You want to tell me why you're over here screaming?" he whispered into my ear, and I melted. But before I melted totally, I got control.

"Your girl Megan here has met Ina Garten, in person!" I announced, looking fondly at her. "You're my new best friend!"

"I bet I could get you a signed cookbook," she offered.

"Trevor, your wife is the coolest person ever," I gushed. "I'm buying you a drink—what're you drinking?"

"Just club soda," she said, casting a shy smile at Trevor, who beamed.

I looked between them, then arched my eyebrow at Megan, who nodded. "Congratulations! Wow, that's great! You must not be far along, you're so tiny!" I gushed.

"Wait, what'd I miss?" Simon asked.

"She's only about eight weeks—we just found out." Trevor grinned, taking her hand across the table.

"Wait, what'd I *miss*?"

"That's so great," I said. "And so soon after the wedding. What a year for you— What, Simon?" He was tapping me on the shoulder.

"I don't get it. What's eight weeks?" he asked, looking bewildered.

"She's pregnant," I said, rolling my eyes at Megan, who responded in kind.

Simon looked at Trevor in shock. "Dude?"

Trevor nodded. "Dude."

Simon digested, then grinned wide. "Dude!"

Take a lesson, girls: *That's* how you communicate with someone you haven't seen in ten years.

Dinner was fantastic, his friends were fantastic, the entire evening was fantastic. Once dinner had been served, everyone mingled again and people were truly happy to see Simon. From what I could glean from tidbits here and there, most of his classmates knew he was a photographer, and some even knew how successful he was in his field. But hearing him tell his story, telling people what he'd been up to over the last ten years, was *really* fantastic.

And you should have seen his face when the apostles started whipping out their wallets to show him pictures of their kids! All of them, married; all of them, kids; all of them, settled into the good life. The good life that was preordained for apostles from Moneyville, USA. I had to bite down on my lip to keep from laughing when Luke copped to having triplets. Simon looked like he was going to pass out. I just made circles on his back with my hand and sent him back into the fray when another wave of old friends made their way by the table.

No one said a word about his family, and I'd been paying attention, ready to swoop in with my no-panties alternative. They were just all glad he'd finally popped back up on the radar, and to know he was doing well, that he was happy.

After dinner we walked around the room and I saw more yearbook pictures on the wall, including Senior Superlatives: Class Clown, Cutest Couple, that sort of thing. After what I'd seen tonight, I knew he was on here somewhere; it was just a question of where. Best Hair? Best Smile? Best Looking? I could see all three, but it turned out to be the one on the end: Most Likely to Succeed.

"Well, look at you. Everyone knew you were going places way back then," I joked, pulling him in front of the picture and comparing what ten years did. In the picture he was tall and handsome, eyes bright and hopeful, an easy grin on his face. A little leaner than he was now, of course; just the tiniest hint of a laugh line here or there.

He looked at the picture and smiled ruefully. "I can't believe they put those pictures up. How embarrassing."

"No, it's nice. I like seeing you back then."

"It's funny, seeing this now. You know why I got this one?"

"As opposed to Most Fuckable? Because you have my vote for that one."

"Because I was going into business with my dad," he answered, his eyes darkening a bit.

"I'm sorry, Simon," I breathed as he pulled me closer by the hand that'd been on my back all night.

He was silent for a moment, looking at the picture. He took a deep breath. I wondered whether I should tell him about what I wasn't wearing under my dress; there was a dark corner not too far away—

"No, it's okay," he said. "It's actually been nice to think about these things again. Makes it seem not so far away."

"Far away, my ass. Far away is Istanbul," a female voice said behind us. We turned and saw a petite girl with closely cropped jet-black hair, a nose ring, several eyebrow piercings, and the most piercing green eyes I'd ever seen. The tiny black dress, fishnet stockings, and Dr. Martens took your eyes to her body right away, and when you put it all together, the girl was a fucking knockout. With killer arm ink.

"Istanbul, where you *left* my ass," she finished.

"Viv Franklin," Simon breathed, his eyes lighting up.

Uh-oh.

"Left your ass? Like hell! My job was over, you knew I was leaving. You were just too involved with that tour guide to notice."

"You never could hold your liquor."

"Hold this."

"Ha! In your dreams, Parker." She grinned and launched herself at him, wrapping her arms around him in the biggest bear hug I'd ever seen. He swung her around and actually patted her on the ass. I wasn't wearing underwear, but I could still kick some butt. Although to be fair, she looked tough.

Setting her down but keeping his arm snugly around her waist, he turned back to me. "Caroline, this is Viv Franklin. Viv, this is my girlfriend—"

"Girlfriend? *You?*"

"—Caroline Reynolds," he finished, releasing her to tug me over.

"No shit—Parker's got a girlfriend. What a night," she cackled, smacking him on the shoulder and reaching for my hand. I shook it, not sure what else to do.

"Nice to meet you," I offered, but those two were off and running.

"What are you doing now? Working for your old man?" he asked.

"Nah, I went out on my own. Data mining."

Oh, she was a miner?

"Wow, good for you. You still writing?"

Oh, she was a writer?

"Yeah, I just sold a new app to one of the big guys. Niiiiice paycheck, know what I'm saying?"

Oh, she wrote an app for, wait. What the hell *did* she do?

"I bet," Simon said. "You know, I ran into one of your brothers when I was in Cairo last year. He was there working on some new system, seemed like a pretty big deal."

"Oh, you know my family. They're always on to the latest and greatest."

"Yeah, your brother was *not* on to the latest and greatest when he snuck some porn into my backpack when I wasn't looking. You wouldn't believe the trouble I got into when I—"

"What the *hell* is going on? What do you *do*? Where did you two go together? And who the *hell* was putting porn in your backpack?" I yelled, for the third time tonight. I needed to get out more; my party manners were out of practice.

"Sorry, babe. Viv and I went to high school together—"

"Obviously," I said, in a quieter tone. Viv just looked at Simon like he had just lassoed the moon and stuffed it in her bra. Which was already pretty full; for a tiny person, she had a great rack.

"—but I hadn't seen her for years, until I literally ran into her in a bar in Instanbul."

"And spent the next week trying to weasel into my tour group. I was on a grand tour, backpacking my way across Europe until I ran into this guy," Viv chimed in, patting him firmly on that sweet ass. Okay, that was going to stop.

"Yes, and the night I allegedly 'left her' she was making out with her tour guide like the world was about to end." He grinned, rumpling her hair like a kid sister.

Kid sister—I can handle that.

"And now *you're* here—I can't believe it! I bet you surprised the shit out of everyone here. No one thought you'd come back, after your parents died and all."

I winced, waiting for Simon to tense up and shut down.

"I figured now was as good a time as any, right? It's been good to be back, you know?" Then he went right on to ask her more about the app she just sold.

Unbelievable.

Ten minutes later, the three of us were at the bar. With shots. They continued to talk, fast and furious, and I began to piece it together. Viv and Simon were friends back in high school, her parents were friends with his parents, blah blah blah. Her father owned a computer software company, and all five, yes, count them, five of her older brothers had gone into the same field. Trying to break out of that mold, she'd gone a different route, studying a general liberal arts curriculum and spending semesters and summers abroad. But the numbers game eventually bit her as well, and she wound up in the family business.

"I hated math in high school. Hated it! But I'm good at it; that stuff just makes sense to me," she explained to me between shots. "Eventually I went out on my own, small-time initially, but then I got lucky a few times with the right programs at just the right time, you know?"

I didn't, but I nodded along.

When she and Simon were in Istanbul together, no hanky-panky happened. She was real clear on that. They were always just friends, friends who were thrown back together in an unreal setting and bonded quickly.

"Simon's just that guy, you know? The guy that I might only see once every five years, but if I needed something, he'd be there in a second," she told me, and I bought her another shot. "He's a great fucking guy."

Simon stepped away to say good-bye to someone who was leaving.

"You two seem serious. You're not gonna break his heart are you?" Viv asked.

"What?" I sputtered, taken off guard.

"Are you?" she asked, her green eyes narrowing on me.

"Is this where you tell me if I break his heart, you'll break my face?"

"Shit, no— I'll kill you." She grinned. I really shouldn't like this girl, but I did.

"Well, I have no intention of dying anytime soon. Good enough?"

"Good enough for me. Seriously, though, he was messed up for a long time. He tries to be all playboy suave, that whole girl-in-every-town bullshit—thank God that's over. He seems happy with you, so I'm happy."

"I'm . . . glad."

"He and I come from a similar background, same upbringing. If his parents hadn't been killed, he likely never would've left this life. Which is a great life, don't get me wrong. But Simon always seemed like a guy who needed more. Shitty way for it to happen, but after his parents were gone he went out and explored a bit, did something else with his life," she mused thoughtfully, swirling her drink in her glass.

"He's an adventurer, no mistaking that," I agreed. "You must be too."

"Me? Maybe once, but now I'm pretty settled. I've got my business; it's doing well—what do I need adventure for?"

I looked at this girl, who looked so different from everyone else in this place. She was almost vibrating with energy; she looked like she could handle anything. And her eyes sparkled at the idea of an adventure. Yet she worked with computers all day?

"Yeah, you look like you're really settled," I replied, arching an eyebrow.

She swung her gaze back to me, challenging. "You just met me—how in the world do you think you're entitled to make an observation like that?"

"*You* had your hands on my boyfriend's ass—that pretty much entitles me to call it as I see it."

"Marry this girl, Simon," she said without taking her eyes off me. He'd just appeared behind her, something she knew without having to look. "Marry this girl and make globe-trotting babies with her. Like tomorrow."

She clinked my glass, drained her own, kissed Simon soundly on the mouth, and sauntered off into the crowd of trust funds, her fishnets clashing with the twinsets in the most delightful way.

"Oh, I love her," I said, laughing even harder when I saw Simon's face. "Relax, Wallbanger. No one's getting married tomorrow."

He studied me for a moment, then grinned. "You about ready to go?"

"Really? Already? You don't want to stay?"

"I've seen the people I wanted to see, and it's been great. But there's something I've been thinking about all night," he said, resting his hand in the small of my back and bringing me into his dance space.

"What's that?"

"You're not wearing anything under that dress, are you?" he murmured, dipping his nose along my jawbone, making me shiver.

"Busted," I admitted. His hand moved just south of the small of my back, but not so low as to be indecent.

"Wicked girl," he breathed.

"Let's go say good-bye to the apostles," I replied, making his brow furrow in confusion. "I feel like fucking the Homecoming King."

We said our good-byes to everyone, offering congratulations again to Trevor and Megan. Simon seemed to be truly happy for them, and a little sad to say good-bye. Amid promises to keep in touch and last-minute retellings of past glory, he laughed until he damn near cried. The apostles gathered, they wished him well, and made him swear he wouldn't stay away so long. He promised to return.

We finally saw Tammy Watkins. And they were indeed huge.

Simon and Viv exchanged phone numbers, then she hugged him tightly.

We made the quick drive back to our hotel, his hand tangled with mine on the console in between, his thumb making tiny circles on the inside of my palm. When his eyes met mine, they burned. We didn't speak much, and when we walked down the hallway to our room, he kept that hand solidly in the small of my back.

Once inside the room however, that hand roamed.

I was pressed up against the inside of the door, his mouth fierce and demanding. My hands went to his shoulders immediately, struggling to remove his coat. "Do you know how intoxicating tonight was for me?" I said, panting. His hands closed briefly around my throat as he turned my face to kiss my neck. Mmm, possessive. I wanted to be possessed by this man, tonight and every night. "To watch all those women, all those girls who probably had their first orgasm back in high school thinking about you."

He pulled back to look at me, full of crazy lust.

"Half the women there tonight wanted to fuck you, Simon—but they don't get to." I undid his buttons, yanking when my fingers wouldn't work fast enough. "*I* do."

He had me out of the dress in seconds, bra off a second after. "Leave the boots," he instructed, undoing his pants. "And get on the bed."

I laid back, the cool comforter sliding against my heated skin. He appeared over me, shirt gone, pants unbuckled, hair tousled from my frantic hands. He looked down at me, his eyes raking over my body as I shivered just from his look alone.

"You're fucking stunning," he murmured, pulling himself out

of his pants and stroking the long length. "You have no idea, do you?"

"Christ, Simon," I breathed, watching him run his hands up and down his cock, pumping firmly.

"Spread your legs for me," he instructed, and my knees fell open as though he'd cast a spell. "Touch yourself, Caroline."

My heart exploded out of my chest, desire pulsing through me at the thought that he wanted to watch me. My hands drifted down to my breasts, circling with my fingers and just barely grazing my nipples. They stiffened instantly, and I closed my eyes. I could see the way Simon looked when he was nuzzling me, torturing me with his tongue and nibbling with those damnable teeth. I pinched my nipples, imagining his mouth, sucking and teasing with pleasure than bordered on pain.

"Lower," he commanded, and my back bowed off the bed once more. I let my right hand travel farther south, dipping down to discover I was soaked for him, big surprise. At the first pass with my fingers, he took a staggered breath. At the second pass I brushed against my clit, taking my own staggered breath as my knees closed the tiniest bit, the sensations overwhelming.

"Ah-ah-ah, keep those legs open," he said, and I felt his hands on my knees, just barely on the inside of my thighs. "How else can I see you make yourself come?"

I cried out, my hand now exploring my sex with abandon. Behind closed eyes, I felt Simon's fingers swirling through and plunging inside, making those perfect circles exactly where I needed him, pressing and slipping and sliding.

I was going to come, and I was going to come hard. I told him so.

I opened my eyes to see Simon staring down at me, his eyes heavy lidded and drunk with lust, his fist moving over his own excitement. I came in a rush, one hand on my breasts, my fingers buried deep inside, and his name falling from my lips. I'd barely recovered when he moved his hands underneath me.

"Turn over—get on your hands and knees for me." His voice was throaty and full, making me shudder once more. I did as directed and turned back to look at him. One strong hand shot out to grasp my shoulder, the other smoothed over my bottom. Angled just so, he thrust into me in one hard surge, burying his considerable length all at once. I groaned as he pushed me farther down onto the bed before his hands settled on my hips.

He plowed into me, hard and thick, impaling me with every pump of his hips. Unrelenting. Unforgiving. Unbelievable.

He took me hard, sexy, and wild. I cried out as I came all around him, my swollen flesh tender and responsive to his every move, his every plunge. Sparks burst behind my eyes, my entire body caught up as he thrust into me.

"You can't imagine, how it feels," he said, his voice low in my ear as he leaned over me, "to have you come on my cock."

I exploded once more as he drove himself into me a final time, his hands digging into my skin as he rode out his orgasm deep within me.

We fell onto the bed into a heap of sweaty skin and heavy breathing. After I regained use of my limbs, I struggled to roll us both over, pushing the mass of my hair out of my face as I rested my chin on his chest. "If I get a cheerleading uniform, can we play Homecoming King again sometime?"

"As long as you wear the boots, babe," he replied, kissing me thoroughly.

We didn't play Homecoming King again that night, but we did play Reverse Cowgirl meets the Student Council President.

chapter thirteen

Once we flew back to the West Coast, holiday planning was in
full swing. I was as busy as ever, trying to get as much done as I
could before work crews began taking breaks for Christmas. We
worked on Christmas decorating at a few key homes and hotels
around town, and the Sausalito project kept trucking along. We
were ahead of schedule, and Mr. Camden seemed very pleased
with not only the construction but the interest that was being generated around town.

Mimi and Ryan were planning their holiday party for a week
before Christmas and it promised to be a fabulous evening. Hosting
in their new apartment, they'd invited friends and work colleagues
on both sides. And Sophia and Neil would *both* be attendance. Of
course they were *both* bringing dates. I was hoping the lack of Pictionary would keep them a little more in line. Wishful Thinking:
Party of One.

And Simon? Well, I don't know how to describe what Simon
was. He was . . . around. I can't explain it any better than that.
He just seemed to always be—around. He'd canceled a trip he'd
planned to Vancouver; he'd canceled a trip he'd had planned to
Honduras. He was supposed to be gone almost the entire month

of December, but now the only thing on his books was our trip to Rio. He hadn't had downtime like this in, well, I don't know when. Not since I'd known him. He biked most mornings, then spent most afternoons poring over old disks of his pictures, cataloging and dating them.

He was . . . *around*.

The thing was, I wasn't. I thought I should feel bad for working so much, but the thing was, I wasn't. I mean, this was my busy season, and if he was traveling like he usually did, he wouldn't be around so much to notice it. Should I feel bad?

He said he understood. He brought me lunch most days, tried once again coaxing me back into bed in the morning with promises of dirty things..

And my God, I loved him, but I'd almost be glad when . . .

Okay, I'm going to say the thing you're not supposed to say.

I'd be glad when I had the bed to myself again.

I hate to say it, but sometimes I slept better when he was on the road. But you're not supposed to say that, right? You're supposed to curl up each and every night for eight solid hours of spooning and cuddling . . . But the truth? I needed my own bed occasionally. I liked some alone time. Is that bad?

But he knew I had work to get done. There was no way I'd be able to get away for our Christmas trip unless I got all my work done now. And there was no way I was missing that: This girl was going to Ipanema.

The morning of Mimi's Christmas party, I had planned on a little quality alone time with my KitchenAid. Mimi had asked me to bake some cookies for her party and I'd jumped at the chance, even though I was stupid busy.

Every woman needed a little self-love once in a while. Am I right? And my self-love machine was stainless steel, powerful, and came with an optional sausage attachment. Ahem.

I was almost finished for the day when Jillian called. When I answered, I almost didn't hear her at first with all the sneezing and nose blowing.

"What the hell, Jillian. Is the bubonic plague making a comeback?"

"Ugh, don't ever get sick in Europe; you'll spend hours just trying to explain your symptoms. But never mind that—what have you got for me?"

"What do you mean?" I asked, flipping through my planner. I needed to have Monica run over to a client's house in Pacific Heights and drop off a wreath, and there were two more deliveries after that, and—

"Caroline. Hey, Caroline, did you hear what I said?"

"Sorry, just a busy day. What's up?"

"I asked what you had for me—your list? Don't you have any questions? Any fires to put out? I'm all ears; whatcha got?"

"Oh, I'm sorry. Um, let's see. Actually, things are pretty well under control. I'm taking off soon; Mimi and Ryan are hosting a holiday party tonight, and that should be fun," I said, looking at my watch under the desk. I really needed to get Monica going on her errands so she could leave on time. "Things are running pretty smoothly."

"Oh. Oh, well that's good. I just thought I'd check in and see if you needed anything, but it sounds like—"

"Sorry, Jillian," I interrupted as Monica walked by the door. "Hey, Monica, can you run this by the Nelson's on your way to drop off the place settings? Thanks!" I waved a good-bye. "Okay, where were we?"

"You're having an intern drop setup Christmas decorations to one of our most important clients?"

"No, I'm having Monica drop off a wreath. She helped me to design their entire living and dining room this year, and they love her. Mrs. Nelson practically adopted her last time we were over there. Why, is there a problem?" I asked, confused. She'd put me in charge, right?

"No, no problem; just surprised you've got an intern doing that. But I suppose everyone has their way of doing things, right?"

I squeezed my fists under the table. We were both silent. I breathed in, hating this tension. "Anyway, how's the world tour? Where are you spending Christmas?"

"Benjamin has some friends in Munich who wanted us to spend the holidays with them, so we're heading there tomorrow."

"That sounds nice."

"Yes, it should be. So sorry to hear about Rio—maybe you guys can go next year."

"Yes, me too—wait. What?"

"Rio. Benjamin said it fell through, that you guys were spending Christmas in San Francisco? That's kind of a big deal, isn't it? Way to go, Simon! That's a first for him."

"Whuh?"

Monica appeared at the door again, and I whispered to her that I'd just be a minute.

Jillian caught it. "Sounds like you've got your hands full, so I'll let you go. Have fun at your party tonight!"

She hung up. I hung up. You could have knocked me over with an Ipanema.

I headed back to my apartment as soon as I was done with work, the conversation playing over and over in my head. I *really* needed the quiet time now. I'd texted Simon and told him to meet me at my apartment right before the party. I didn't mention anything about Rio; I wanted to see his face when I brought it up. I didn't understand what in the world was going on.

I let myself into my apartment with a big sigh of relief, the sound escaping me before I realized it. The air was a little stuffy; it'd been a while since I was here. I cracked a few windows, running my hand along the deep windowsills as I did. Clive loved a deep windowsill. I looked around at the thoughtfully chosen knicks and knacks, remembering how I delighted in selecting all the pieces, the first apartment I'd ever had on my own. Through the kitchen doorway I caught sight of gleaming metal, all curves and heaven. My KitchenAid mixer.

I cracked my back, rolled my neck, and thought about all the cookies I was about to bake. I took off my heels; they'd been pinching my feet all day. And while I was at it, I took off my snug pencil skirt too.

I baked better when I was comfortable.

I had literally worked through every lunch hour and stayed late almost every day, just so I could knock off a few hours early and bake the cookies I'd promised Mimi. I'd tried mixing up a few batches of dough at Jillian's the night before, but it wasn't the same. Off-brand mixer. Subpar paddle. Eh.

Tuning my stereo to an all-Christmas station, I wrapped my apron on, pulled my hair into a bun on top of my head, and got to work. I stroked my KitchenAid, feeling the cool metal soothe my frayed nerves.

While Bing serenaded me, I scooped balls of chocolate chip and plopped them onto a parchment paper–lined cookie sheet. While Frank told me I'd better watch out and I'd better not cry, I mixed up a batch of snickerdoodles, rolled in extra cinnamon sugar. While Judy sang to me of having a merry little Christmas, I doused pecan sandies in powdered sugar, gently setting them to cool on wire racks that covered the dining room table. And when Elvis was blue, I was frosting red and green sugar cookies, cut into snowmen, angels, and evergreen tree shapes.

As I rolled and dipped, sugared and iced, my mind kept playing over the conversation with Jillian. Why in the world would Simon have canceled the trip without asking me? Maybe she'd gotten it wrong. Maybe she hadn't heard Benjamin correctly. But why would Benjamin have gotten the idea that we were spending Christmas here?

I was irritated. More than irritated. If this was true, I was downright pissed. While there was no place like home for the holidays (thank you, Perry Como), and I wanted nothing in the world than to bring my boyfriend home for said holidays, *this* holiday I wanted Rio!

As I baked, I got more and more irritated. Adult Caroline said things like, "Just talk to Simon; find out what's really going on." Pissed Off Caroline was saying things like, "I already bought a new bikini, dammit, and I want to wear it!"

Guess which one was winning? By the time Simon came waltzing in, I squeezed a poor gingerbread man right where his gingerbread nuts would have been.

"Do you think this is what heaven looks like?" he asked happily. Simon, not the nutless gingerbread man.

"Cookie heaven?"

"No, *my* heaven: cookies *and* you in panties," he replied, picking up a snickerdoodle and inhaling deeply.

I blushed. I'd forgotten about the panties. I turned around to grab the last round of gingerbread men from out of the oven. "So I talked to Jillian today. She said the funniest thing about—"

"You're killing me, bent over like that, and with cookies! Dreaming, I'm dreaming," he joked, coming up behind me and unexpectedly grabbing my hips.

Startled, I dropped the pan, gingerbread men spilling all over the floor and shattering. It looked like a disaster scene; legs broken, arms severed, even a few decapitations.

"*Dammit!*" I set the pan down a little louder than was necessary, then turned to face Simon with my hands on my hips, eyebrows arched.

"Oh, I'm so sorry, Caroline. I didn't mean—wow. They're kind of scary like that, aren't they?" he said, looking around at my feet.

I took a breath, held it, counted to thirteen, then let it out.

"Did you cancel our trip to Brazil?"

"Brazil?" he asked, looking guilty.

"Yes, Brazil. When I talked to Jillian today, she told me about a conversation you had with Benjamin—that you'd canceled our trip. Did you?"

He was quiet for a minute, his eyes unreadable.

"Yes."

He had. He really *had*.

"You want to tell me why?"

"I was going to surprise you," he started, walking over to me, dodging ginger parts.

"Most guys surprise their girlfriends *with* trips, Simon—not the opposite," I snapped, throwing the cookie sheets into the sink and squeezing soap all over them. I scrubbed at them furiously, splashing suds everywhere. "Why in the world would you *do* that?"

"I wanted to—"

"Do you have any idea how *hard* I've been working? How much I was looking *forward* to that trip?"

"I know; I just thought that—"

"You can't just up and cancel something like that without *talking* to me! I literally can't *believe* that you—"

"Would you just listen to me for a second? Jesus!" he exploded, slamming his hand down on the counter, crushing more ginger-bread men. "I wanted to spend Christmas with your folks, Caroline. I invited them here."

The sponge fell from my hand. "You . . . *what*?"

"I wanted us to have a real Christmas this year, so I called your mom and dad and invited them to stay with us. I thought I'd surprise you. They'll be here the day before we were supposed to leave. I know how disappointed you were when you couldn't go home for Thanksgiving, so I thought they could come here," he said. "I had no idea you'd get so upset, believe me, or I would have talked to you about it first."

My thoughts whirled; emotions crashed and banged around inside. Touched? Overwhelmed? Surprised? My eyes filled with tears as I crossed to him through the gingerbread carnage.

"You really want to spend Christmas with my family?" I asked, taking his face in my hands.

"I do," he murmured, his eyes full of something I couldn't pinpoint. "Weird?"

"No, babe. So sweet," I whispered, holding him tightly.

His arms slipped around my waist and he kissed the top of my head. "Are you still mad?"

"I was, but I'm not now," I replied, leaning in closer to his ear. "But next time, just talk to me, okay?"

"Promise," he whispered into my ear, then kissed me fierce. "I'm going to get us the biggest Christmas tree you've ever seen." He grinned, his face full of excitement. Crisis over. He took off his jacket and surveyed the cookie damage. "Now, what can I do to help?"

"You can start by helping me clean up this mess. Then we need to get these packed up if we're going to make it to the party before Sophia and Neil Round Three begins," I said, handing him a broom.

He started to clean up, whistling along to "Frosty the Snowman." I turned back to the soapy sink, wiping my tears away. One of them belonged to Rio.

The stage for Sophia vs. Neil Round Three (known in conventional circles as Mimi and Ryan's Christmas Party) was set the second Neil showed up with a hot nerd. A hot nerd, you ask? Let me back up a bit . . .

Sophia had met a new guy at a symphony benefit. Bernard Fitzsimmons, associate professor of applied physics at Berkeley and vice president of the Bay Area Musical Appreciation Society, had the pleasure of meeting Sophia at a Music in Schools program fund-raiser she was performing at. Being incredibly talented as well as gorgeous, she was often called upon to perform at charitable functions, especially ones that were musically inclined.

They shared a cab and a kiss after the event, and Sophia invited him to the party. He was wicked smart and wicked cute, both attributes complementing each other nicely.

Neil got wind of this development, orchestrated carefully and quite purposefully by Mimi to be clear—"Oh, she's going for the hot nerds now, huh?"—and he went on the hunt for his own Hot Nerd. He ended up meeting Polly Pinkerton, the head of a research lab at UCSF Medical Center, specializing in the effects of pesticides and insecticides on child development. She was appearing on the morning show on the local NBC affiliate, and Neil spent the entire time in the green room flirting with her over a pot of hazelnut French roast. Hopped up on caffeine, he saw her as the perfect Hot Nerd to bring to the party. But he also genuinely enjoyed her company, and had seen her a couple of times before the party.

They both brought nerds to an ex fight, and neither was ready for the outcome.

Bernard? Cute, yes. Smart, yes. Boring, *yes*. I'd been stuck in the kitchen with him and Sophia for almost thirty minutes discussing beige walls and their place in home interiors, because Bernard loved HGTV, don't you know. Sophia had been giving me the "sorry" eye all night, but I understood.

He was what Carrie Bradshaw had called a "great on paper" guy. Unfortunately he was as dull as paper too. I was in the middle of discussing sand vs. stone *and* trying to stop myself from biting off my own arm so I had something to beat him with, when I heard Neil's voice from the entryway.

Sophia froze. I froze. Bernard waxed poetic on the beauty of a periodic table painted in the softest hues of putty and bone.

"Putty and Bone," I told Sophia, "what a great name for a—"

"Oh, shush with your great name for a band—here comes Neil," Sophia hissed, wrapping her arm around Bernard, who was coaxed from his beige oration by very soft breasts pressed into his side. His eyes widened and he shifted his feet nervously. I almost felt a little sorry for him; the poor guy had no idea what he was caught up in.

"Putty and Bone *is* a great name for a band," I mumbled to myself, taking my leave and a shrimp puff from the potluck table.

The party was in full swing; beautiful couples swaying to rockabilly Christmas songs on the stereo, hot toddies and spiked cider being poured generously by Ryan, while Mimi set out tray after tray of goodies.

As I shrimp puffed, I scanned the crowd for Simon. He was talking to one of Ryan's friends from work. I caught his eye and pointed toward the hallway, where Neil was making his way to the kitchen. The girl he had in tow was darling; sharp eyes and a curious look on her face as she took in the crowd. They were on a collision course for Sophia and Beige Bernard. I stuffed another puff in my mouth and spy-walked back toward the kitchen, meeting up with Simon, who had also alerted Mimi and Ryan, around the corner.

"You know, this is getting ridiculous," I said as we four took up a watch-and-wait stance, flanking either entrance to the kitchen.

"We're just watching out for our friends," Simon said, flattening himself against the wall. When did this become *Mission Impossible*?

Right about when Sophia and Neil laid eyes on each other for the first time since Game Night, and remembered that while Beige Bernard and Pretty Polly were fine and dandy, they weren't ever going to blow their hair back. They were never going to be the "one." But that didn't stop them from trying.

"Sophia."

"Neil."

So dramatic, these two.

"Bernard?"

"Polly?"

Wait, what?

The four of us peeked around the corner like totem poles, watching as Pretty and Beige collided in the center of the room in a tangle of arms and laughter.

"Wow, Polly! I haven't seen you since the symposium on genetic rehabilitation at the Hilton in Anaheim," Bernard said, looking thrilled to see her.

"Has it been that long? I looked for you at the Quantum Summit in San Diego; I thought for sure you'd be there," Polly replied, looking up shyly through her eyelashes.

"I was in Switzerland—the Hadron," he said, puffing out his chest a bit. I didn't get it, but she sure looked impressed.

"Large Hadron Collider, it's at CERN in Switzerland," Ryan whispered across the entryway. Mimi looked impressed too. With Ryan.

"Uh, Bernard, why don't you introduce me to your friend," Sophia interjected, tugging at his arm. He didn't notice. She pushed her boobs out. He noticed.

"Oh, I'm so sorry, Polly. These are, I mean, this is Sophia," he said, flushing. "Sophia, this is Polly. She heads up a lab over at UCSF—"

"I play cello with the San Francisco Symphony," Sophia spat out, looking surprised at her own word vomit.

I bit down on my fist to keep from laughing.

"Very nice to meet you, Sophia, This is Neil. We just met; he—"

"Hi. NBC. Channel 11," Neil said, pumping Bernard's hand up and down furiously. "Sports?" he finished, when Bernard looked at him in puzzlement. "I'm the sportscaster? You know, Neil makes the call every day at six and eleven?" he finished in his best broadcasting voice.

"Oh, sure, hi. Nice to meet you . . . Neil?"

Simon choked back his own laughter.

Polly and Bernard continued to talk in the center of the room while Neil and Sophia backed into their own corners, confused. I went back to the shrimp puffs with Simon, content that this night would work itself out.

An hour later I was huddled in the bathroom with Sophia and Mimi, debating the benefits of an on-purpose nip slip. Bernard and Polly had continued to reminisce about conferences they'd attended, who had published what article in which journal, and now they were talking about some charming guy named quark who was a bottom? Ryan had attempted to explain the latter, but when he launched into fundamental forces and particle decay, I couldn't listen anymore. Mainly because Mimi was panting so loudly; she loved it when Ryan gave good science.

So now here we were, debating the slip of said nip, and whether it would be enough to get Sophia's night back on track. A little tipsy from too many toddies and still thrown by the fact that I wasn't going to Rio, I was losing interest quickly.

"Oh, for God's sake, just go flash some cleave at Professor Boring over there, will you?" I snapped, pushing back out to the party. Pretty Polly and Beige Bernard were on the couch, noses practically touching, and I was pretty sure more body parts were on their way.

Their chemistry was the kind that was cultivated in a petri dish and simmered over a Bunsen burner until hot and horny. Someone's hadron was colliding tonight, that was for sure.

I spied Neil heading over to where Sophia had just appeared from the bathroom, and I rolled my eyes.

"How ya doin', babe?" Simon asked, taking my arm.

"Great! How 'bout you?"

"You sure you're okay?"

"Why wouldn't I be?" I drained my toddy and looked around for another.

"Because half your boob is out of your shirt," he replied, turning me into the wall and away from some rather delighted guests.

"Shit," I exclaimed, tucking myself back in. "I was demonstrating how to—oh, never mind."

"Maybe we should think about heading home," he suggested.

I was about to tell him what *I* thought about this when we heard a crash from the kitchen. We all got there at the same time to find Neil wearing a bowl of potato salad and Sophia holding a plate of shrimp puffs over his head. With a nip purposefully slipped. Neil's eyes were locked on the nip, rage burning through the potato salad.

"Cover yourself!" he growled.

"Cover *this*!" she shouted.

"My shrimp puffs!" Mimi moaned.

"How far is your car?" Polly asked as she and Bernard sailed out the front door.

I shook my head, gathered up my cookies and my Wallbanger, and headed for Sausalito.

Simon and I had been together over a year now, and of course there were nights that we didn't have sex when he was home. Headache? Sometimes I got them. That time of the month? Definitely not happening. But this was the first time I said no because I was irritated.

And he was now irritated that I was irritated.

It's fair to say I blamed it on Rio.

chapter fourteen

The following montage has been reproduced from the television special **Caroline's Christmas Spectacular.** *If you are able to listen to* "It's Beginning to Look a Lot Like Christmas," *preferably the Johnny Mathis version, please do so now.*

We open on a driveway. A beat-up black Range Rover is parked there, covered almost entirely with an enormous blue spruce Christmas tree. A devastatingly gorgeous man with jet-black hair and a grin that sparkles with mischief is untying the tree, catching it just before it falls onto the concrete. He laughs, tossing a look over his shoulder at a pretty—no, a stunning—blonde who watches from the sidewalk. Her full, perky breasts push out against a sweater decorated with reindeer. The luckiest reindeer ever to grace wool. Ahem. As she watches the handsome man wrestle with the tree, she calls out to him, and he laughs again. He also notices the reindeer . . . How could he not?

Cut to the same couple, now joined with another happy young pair. A man with wavy blond hair, horn-rimmed glasses, and a scholarly look about him sits next to a tiny Asian woman with impeccably groomed shiny black hair and an impossibly short skirt. The four are tucked into a red leather booth in Chinatown, and as they crack into a round of fortune cookies, the brunette woman slides a festively wrapped present across the table to her friend, the stunning blonde. The four friends smile at each other as they read their fortunes. The man with blond hair looks up and spies a bundle of mistletoe, prompting him to steal a kiss from the tiny brunette.

Cut to a buxom redhead, dressed in a long black dress. She is on a stage surrounded by an entire symphony as she plays a solo on a cello. While the music swells, bringing merry tunes to all the concertgoers, she inclines her head in appreciation of the applause. As her music is absorbed by the rest of the musicians once again, she seems to have a far-off look in her eyes . . . hinting at sadness, perhaps? What could a girl this lovely have to be sad about at Christmas?

Cut to a television studio, where an athletic man with curly dark hair and a winning smile tells his audience about the latest sports news. In between the football highlights and the blooper reel, one can imagine all the viewers tuning in. Is one of them the buxom redhead? Does he hope so?

Cut to the pretty blonde sitting in front of a giant window wall. Through the window we can see the deep gray-blue of a large body of water, and in the distance we can see the outline of a great city. The skyline suggests San Francisco. In the reflection of the window we can see an enormous Christmas tree, decorated with twinkly lights and sparkly baubles. The gorgeous man enters, a majestic cat at his heels. As he sits down next to the pretty blonde, we see that she was reading a magazine. She hurriedly closes it, but before she can, we see over her shoulder that it was open to an article about Brazil.

Cut to a bedroom where we can see . . . Fade to black. Family program.

Cut back to our original couple, now seated at a table piled high with Christmas delights. Dishes of buttery mashed potatoes, bowls of green beans and sweet potatoes, crowned by a perfectly roasted turkey. As the pretty blonde brings an apple pie to the sideboard, the gorgeous man gives her a secret smile that makes her blush. Does he know something we don't know?

Joining them at the table is an older couple. The woman is a spitting image of the pretty blonde; her mother? Ah yes, and this must be her father, shaking hands with the gorgeous man. As they sit down together, we zoom in on the pretty blonde. She seems very happy to have her family around her on this Christmas Eve, but as the gorgeous man squeezes her hand under the table, we can see an almost wistful look in her eye. What could she be dreaming of on this magical night?

Cut to the sideboard, where we are the only ones to see a cat perched, nibbling at the edge of the piecrust.

Cut to all four gathered around a Christmas tree. Discarded wrapping paper in shades of green and red, silver and gold, is scattered all around. Occasionally one of the piles rumbles, and we can see whiskers poking through. As her parents head to the kitchen, the pretty blonde retrieves a package from behind the couch. The gorgeous man looks surprised; he didn't know there were any gifts left to give. The pretty blonde offers it to him, perching on the arm of the couch next to him. He smiles as he takes it, unwrapping this last gift.

We zoom in, and can see it's a picture frame. We can't see the photo, but it makes the gorgeous man tense up. We see emotions flit across his face. Unease. Raw sorrow. The pretty blonde holds her breath. And then, the gorgeous man begins to smile. And it's breathtaking.

As he pulls the pretty blonde onto his lap for a close hug, we pull back and see her parents start to come back into the living room. Spying the two on the couch, they retreat into the kitchen.

chapter fifteen

Text from Sophia to Mimi:

I can't believe you're still
mad . . .

> I can't believe you can't
> believe I'm still mad.

I'm sorry, okay? Again! How
many times can I say I'm sorry?

> Once more should do it.

OK. I. Am. Sorry. I. Ruined.
Your. Christmas. Party.

> Forgiven. Now you want
> to tell me what that was all
> about?

I don't know.

Oh, I know, and I know you know; I just want to hear you say it.

I'm taking back my apology . . .

Can't. How's the professor?

Now you're asking for it.

Snicker.

Text from Simon to Neil:

You wanna go bike riding tomorrow?

Can't we just hold hands and skip?

Dude.

Can't. Working. Speaking of, you've been home awhile now. When are you heading back out on the road?

Taking a bit of a break

Come on, really, when are you heading back out?

No really, I'm taking some time off.

Huh.

Huh what?

Just huh. Anyway, can't
tomorrow; but how 'bout
this weekend?

Done. You wanna text the
idiot or should I?

I'll do it. Blow me.

See ya.

Text from Mimi to Caroline:

Can you do the diner Saturday
morning?

Yes, if you can do early. I
need to work afterward.

How about 7:30?

Perfect.

Holy shit, Caroline, I was
kidding.

Oh, when were you
thinking?

9?

I've got meetings in the
afternoon. Did I tell you I
just picked up a new job
in Sausalito? Someone
walked by the Claremont

the other day, liked what
she saw, came by the
office, and BAM I'm doing
a remodel over here.

Wow, my girl is going for
Designer of the Year!

No kidding. Okay,
breakfast. How about we
say 8:15, in the middle?

Wow, okay, I'll see if I can
get Soph up that early. She
still owes me from the party.

She really does; the
throwing of food is never
okay.

They're both so stupid! Ryan
said that Neil's tried to call
her again, but she just won't
budge.

Maybe it's time to sit this
one out. I mean, what
are the odds that 3 best
friends and 3 best friends
would all magically meet,
fuck, and live happily ever
after?

Pfft, true. What a romance
novel that would make. But
2 out of 3 isn't bad. And I

still think they're gonna get
back together . . .

                     You old softie.

You guys want to see a
movie next weekend? Or is
Simon out of town?

                     Oh no. He's here. He's
                     very much here.

???

                     Forget it. We'll see. Gotta
                     get back to work.

Portion of an e-mail from Jillian to Caroline:

   . . . So it looks like we'll be heading over to Spain sooner than
we thought. I have an old friend from college who's renovating
an estate just outside of Nerja. Isn't that where you and Simon
stayed? And how is he? Benjamin said he's not traveling as much?
     I spoke to the accountant; he's sending me everything FedEx
for year-end taxes. Looks like you've kept up on everything really
well. I did notice, however, that you need to be itemizing your
meals when you're out with clients—we need the actual receipt
with the items ordered, not just the cc receipt. I can have him
show you some examples if that's easier? Let me know, and I'll
have it sent over.
     Sounds like your Christmas was interesting, Vienna was
enchanting! What a wonderful city to spend the holidays in.

   I scrolled through that e-mail once more, then thought back
to the conversation we had right before Christmas. She'd said they

were going to Munich for the holidays, I was sure of it. She'd mentioned Benjamin's friends and everything. But now she said they were in Vienna?

Something stinks in Vienna.

I put my phone away as I walked toward the hotel site. I was meeting with Camden's assistant to make the final decision about some light fixtures in the bar downstairs. Taking advantage of the natural light, and being aware of the sometimes very foggy mornings, I had designed a space that could transition from a place to share a quiet drink in the afternoon or even a business meeting, to something infinitely more sexy at nighttime.

I tried to focus on the meeting at hand, but I couldn't shake the feeling that something was going on. When Jillian first left, she was in almost constant contact—as much as a newlywed could be. But as the weeks went by, turning into months, the e-mails and phone calls had lessened significantly. Initially, I was so busy I didn't realize how those phone calls were beginning to dwindle. Once the holidays were in full swing and we went back east for the reunion, I was in control enough to not *need* the calls, but that wasn't really the point.

And when was she coming home? There seemed to be no end in sight. I needed to have a come-to-Jesus meeting with Jillian, but I wasn't quite sure how to go about it. And I was *positive* that she had told me she was going to Munich . . .

"Caroline? You been waiting long?" A voice broke me out of my head. Camden's assistant, looking at me expectantly.

"Sorry, no, not at all. Ready to get started?" I asked, and plastered on a smile.

That night when I got home, Simon was there and had made spaghetti and meatballs. Of course he was. Home, I mean.

"It's shocking, how much I need balls right now," I quipped, sitting at the table in my jacket and scarf, my knife and fork pointed up.

"I had a feeling. I found this great Italian market this morning on my bike ride, and they're one of the only places I've ever found stateside that will grind the pork, veal, and beef together," he said, pouring me a glass of red and putting the pasta into the boiling water. "Makes for a more tender ball," he said, deadpan.

"So that's your secret," I said, sipping the wine. The night was chilly, but inside it was cozy and warm. A fire was ablaze in the living room, its light bouncing off the window wall. Clive was curled into a ball inside the cat condo that Simon had bought for him. Orange carpet, multileveled with a scratching post and a bouncy ball on top of the entire thing, it was hideous. I'd told him Clive would never go for something so garish, so obviously *cat,* but he fucking loved it.

My boys had a simpatico thing going on. *They certainly spent enough time together . . .*

There it was again. That corner of something I kept running into my head; the very edge of something cooking in there. It disappeared when Simon set down the salad, then kissed me stupid.

"How'd the meeting go about the bar?" he asked.

He'd been listening the night before when I told him what I had going on today.

"Good, though I was a little distracted. I got an e-mail from Jillian."

"How're they doing? I haven't heard from Benjamin for a while, but we're talking next week about some investments."

"Is he still managing everything for you?"

"He's got someone on them more day to day while he's gone, but he's keeping his eye on it too. She say when they're coming home?"

"No, and that's the thing. Every time I try to bring it up, she changes the subject," I said, chewing on a piece of escarole I stole from the salad bowl. Lemon and mustard vinaigrette. Nice.

"Benjamin too. I figured with their honeymoon and all, they're having too much fun to think about coming home."

"Must be nice to have zero responsibilities," I muttered, bumping into that corner again.

"I wouldn't say that," he chided, tossing the pasta with tongs. "You want to shred that cheese?"

"I *would* say that." I grabbed the cheese and began to shred. "I don't know; maybe I'll say something to the girls tomorrow, see what they think."

"The girls?"

"Yeah, breakfast at the diner? I haven't seen them for a while," I said, still shredding. He mumbled something under his breath about me being gone again, but I ignored it. "And another thing—when we talked before Christmas, she told me they were going to Munich for Christmas. But I got an e-mail from her today that said they were in Vienna."

"I think I heard Vienna. At least that's what Benjamin said."

"I know she said Munich; she said it was because Benjamin had friends there." I continued to shred.

"Benjamin has friends everywhere," he said, testing the pasta and calling it good.

"The point isn't whether or not he has friends there. The point is I know what I heard," I said, shredding furiously.

"Is it at all possible, and I'm just asking here," he said, tossing the pasta with a little bit of the sauce and then pouring it all into a bowl, "that you didn't hear her correctly?"

"No." I shredded.

"Not at all possible?" he asked, setting the bowl down on the table and then going back for the meatballs. "No chance in the slightest."

"Of course there's a chance," I said through gritted teeth. "I just know what I heard."

"Well then, ask her. That'll solve it, won't it? Better than shredding your fingernails into that bowl," he replied calmly, covering my hand with his and stopping me right before I did that very thing.

I looked down. I'd shredded the entire wedge.

"I can't ask her, she's depending on me," I said, releasing the shredder and heading for the sink to wash my hands.

"She is, but she's also your friend. If there's a problem, she'd want to know about it, don't you think?" he asked, pulling out my chair for me.

"She's my friend, but she's my boss first. And yes, I should probably talk to her," I replied, sitting down and smiling briefly when he placed a kiss on my shoulder before sitting down across from me. "Dammit, I hate when you're right."

"That's a lot of hating, then. I had no idea," he teased, passing me the bowl with several pounds of grated Parmesan.

I took the bowl, and then showed him a particular finger.

For the record, they were amazing balls.

"Whole wheat pancakes, blueberry sauce, and a side of turkey sausage, please."

"Egg white omelette with ham and green onions and a cup of berries, please."

"Scrambled eggs, hash browns with no butter, rye toast. And could I also please get a grapefruit half?"

We sat at our regular table at the diner, Sophia and Mimi nursing extra big cups of coffee.

"Thanks for coming so early. I know you both like to sleep in on Saturdays," I said, sipping on my own extra big cup. I had an art installation being set up today, and I knew it was going to be a day for extra caffeine.

"How's it going over at the hotel? Think you'll be able to slow down a bit when that's all complete?" Mimi asked.

"Not likely. We've slowed down on some of our residential design to take on this project, but once that's done, we've got clients who have literally put their remodels on hold a few months in order to work with us," I said proudly. "But some of that depends on Jillian."

"Still no word on when she's coming back?"

"Nope, but let's not talk about that. Let's talk about your wedding—how's the planning coming?" I asked, changing the subject smoothly. I hadn't made any progress on what I was going to say to Jillian about everything, unsure how to broach the subject, so I was eager to think about something else.

I could tell you Mimi had begun planning her wedding the day Ryan put a two-karat solitaire on her finger, but that would be a lie. She'd been planning it since she knew what a wedding *was*. She had notebooks and binders full of tear sheets that she'd been collecting over the years. Table settings, flowers, dresses, linens—you name it, she had it in a binder. Ryan didn't ask any questions or make a single suggestion; he just sat back and let the Mimi Train run.

"It was so great seeing Jillian's wedding, and how she planned. It gave me so many ideas, and really helped me to focus in on what I want and what I don't want. If you'll look here on page seventeen—"

She had a binder out on the table.

"—you can see how I'll be capturing the light of the chapel to accentuate not only the soft pastel pinks and peaches of the flowers, but also to set off the natural golden tone of my skin."

"Well, sure, but that depends on the time of day," Sophia said, casting a mischievous look my way.

Mimi flipped her binder. "Based on the sun's position in the sky that week, I've timed the ceremony to reflect as much light into the church as possible." She pointed to a sun chart.

"Oh my God, I was kidding," Sophia said, turning the binder around to see. "This is impressive, woman."

"Thank you. You'll also be glad to know that I took into account your skin tone and Caroline's when I chose your dresses."

"Our dresses? You chose our dresses?" Sophia asked.

"Hold up, you haven't even officially asked us yet! Don't you think you better choose us before you choose the dresses?" I snorted, passing the butter as the plates were set down.

"Please, like I need to ask. Obviously you're both bridesmaids," she scoffed, cutting her sausage into quarter-inch slices and centering them on either side of the plate.

"Well, obviously," I mimicked, laughing at her when she looked up in surprise. "Of course we'll be your bridesmaids."

"Makes sense, since Simon and Neil will be groomsmen. And I see that look on your face, Sophia," she said, not looking up but anticipating her reaction. "He's in the wedding and that's final. And there will be no throwing of food."

I muffled a laugh into my napkin.

"Make sure Simon knows the date. I don't want him missing the wedding week because he's off taking pictures of zebras in Australia," Mimi continued, pointing her knife at me.

"Zebras are in Africa. Kangaroos are in Australia," Sophia interjected.

"Australia, Africa, I don't care if he's in Akron—just make sure he'll be home," she said, crossing something off in her bridal planner.

"Oh, he'll be home. Don't worry about that," I muttered. Before she could say anything else, I brandished my own knife. "And don't think I didn't notice you using phrases like *wedding week*. It's a wedding *day*, Miss Thing."

"I have so much planned for this wedding that I need an entire week, and Ryan says I can. And don't think I didn't notice you snarking under your breath about Simon being home. What's going on?" she asked.

"There's nothing going on. He's just taking some time off, that's all."

They both looked at me.

"What? You're always saying he's never home—well, he's home now."

They both still looked at me. I looked back.

"It's great. Really. Great."

One more moment of silence, then we all returned to our plates.

"So Ryan found out that there's a group interested in sponsoring a chapter of his charity in San Diego," Mimi offered, and the news portion of our breakfast began.

"There's a new krav maga studio opening up down the street, and I'm thinking of taking it. As long as I can protect my hands," Sophia remarked.

"Clive has finally figured out that the cat that's running back and forth outside the window wall and anticipating his every move is his own reflection," I said.

We chewed.

"I think I finally talked Ryan into taking ballroom dancing lessons for the wedding. We get to learn how to tango!"

"I heard from Professor Bernard Fitzsimmons; he and Polly just moved in together."

"I think Jillian is lying to me about something."

Forks clattered.

"Wait, what?" Mimi asked as Sophia looked at me in confusion.

"I can't explain it. I just think something's going on and she's not telling me." As soon as I said it out loud, I was even more convinced. "I don't know what's going on, but something's up."

They listened as I told them about everything that had been going on: the phone calls, the non–phone calls, the e-mails, everything. I sat back and waited for them to see it, to agree with me.

"You're basing this all on the fact that she might have said Munich when she meant Vienna?" Sophia asked, shaking a sugar packet.

"No. I mean, partly, but—I don't know, I just feel like something's off," I insisted, not understanding why no one else was seeing it too.

"She's on her honeymoon. If I was riding that Benjamin train every night, you can be damn sure I'd be forgetful. Mmm, you think he likes it dirty? Do you think he likes it when—"

"Good Lord, Mimi!"

"Jesus Christ, woman!"

We stared at Mimi. To be fair, we'd all fantasized about it. But we never discussed it.

She had the decency to blush into her sausage circles.

"Anyway, no, it's not just mixing up the names of the cities. She was supposed to be gone awhile, but this is almost getting ridiculous. And she hardly ever checks in anymore—"

Mimi laughed. "How could she check in, when she's too busy checking out Benjamin in one of those tiny little European bathing suits? I bet they do it in—"

"Enough!" I said, slamming my hand down and making the silverware bounce. "I don't have time for this; I'm trying to tell you that—forget it. You know what? I need to get to work," I snapped, throwing a twenty down on the table and getting up.

"Are you really leaving?" Sophia asked as I put my coat on.

"Yes, I'm really leaving. I have to go receive an art installation for the hotel in Sausalito!"

I slammed out of the restaurant, my heart pounding. I was *so* mad, and I had gotten there *so* fast. Dammit.

I went back inside to where they were still sitting, wide-eyed. "Thank you very much for asking me to be a bridesmaid; that was really very sweet." Then I left again.

I got into Jillian's Mercedes and drove back across the bridge to wait for my art installation. Which never showed up.

Hey, art installation? Suck my dick.

That night, I was frustrated beyond belief that I'd wasted an entire morning and the better part of the afternoon when my free time was at a premium. Waiting around for the artwork after repeated calls to the delivery service, which just kept telling me it was "in transit," just further irritated my already foul mood. I felt frazzled, so I decided to tune out and get turned on. I wasn't going to think about work anymore.

I found Simon in the kitchen, looking through Chinese take-out menus. He asked me if I wanted to just stay in tonight and pig out on pot stickers. It was exactly what I needed and I told him so.

I needed to relax. Everyone else got free time, I was going to get some too.

After pot sticking, we retreated to the hot tub. Simon turned on some Count Basie and we hurried down the chilly path. Sitting under a blanket of stars, I leaned back into the bubbly water with a glass of wine and tried to relax. I tried to let go of the unease I'd been feeling about Jillian, my stress about work, and the mini fight I'd had with Mimi and Sophia that morning.

I'd texted both of them with apologies that were met with an "Oh please, it's fine" and "You're an asshole but I love you anyway."

"You seem quiet tonight," Simon remarked, his strong arms curved behind him on the edge of the hot tub. A wet Wallbanger was something that can never be described. But I will try.

It was . . . Oh, hell, it was really good.

"I'm relaxing, can't you tell?" I replied, making a great show of settling back and letting out a contented sigh.

"That's good. You need to relax more, if you ask me." He tilted his face toward the sky, throwing his jaw, and his stubble, into stark relief against the cold night.

As I admired him, I noticed his jaw was not only strong, it was tense. "You okay?"

"Never better," he replied as he breathed out heavily.

Had I been ignoring Simon? Surely not; how could anyone ignore someone this good looking? But just to be sure . . .

Feeling a spark below, I pushed across the water to his side, sitting on his lap. His hands wrapped around my waist, fingers tangling into the edges of my bikini bottom. "You remember the first time we hot tubbed, Wallbanger?"

"I do. You were quite randy," he remembered, the hint of a smirk appearing.

"I really was. You were hot to trot as well, as I recall." I rolled my eyes. And my hips. Which did not go unnoticed. "Until you put the brakes on my advances."

"You will never know how hard that was."

"Oh I *know* how hard that was." I laughed as he thrust up against me. I turned around, sitting with my back to his chest, and looked out across the bay, the lights from the city sparkling on the water. From this vantage point, I could see the town below, its own light reflecting in the waves. It was so peaceful over here, I'd miss it when we moved back to the city full-time.

A moment of tension crept in, but I shook it away. I breathed deep, inhaling the scent of laurel and pine, the saltiness of the sea air that was always in the background. He pushed my hair off my shoulders, leaving a trail of warm wet kisses behind. Passion was one thing, but that quiet comfort of unhurried touching?

It was really good.

"This is nice." I sighed, leaning back against him.

"I agree," he murmured into my skin, his hands beginning to roam across my belly.

"I meant being out here in Sausalito." I laughed, shivering as his mouth dipped into the hollow between my shoulder and ear.

"I know what you meant, and I agree," he answered, nibbling me like an ear of corn. "I didn't think I would, but I really like it over here. It's homey."

I squealed, his touch causing me to break out into gooseflesh. "Who you callin' homey?" I giggled.

"Shush, I'm seducing you," he instructed, raising my arm and kissing the length of it like a villain in an old-timey cartoon. "You'll soon be putty in my hands; I'll be able to have my wicked way with you."

"Then by all means, continue." I fell back against him, doing my putty imitation.

"Wow, you're easy."

"You're just now figuring this out?" I laughed, bouncing on his lap, splashing water all around.

His response was dunking me under the water. I came up spitting and sputtering. While I was grumbling and wiping my face off, I felt him tugging at my bikini top.

I feigned a look of surprise. "Now look what you did."

"I'm looking." And then he was touching. And then he was doing other things to me. Wanton naked licking loving sucking biting thrusting things.

It was *really* good.

chapter sixteen

The free time continued into Sunday; I desperately needed a day off. I could have been at the Claremont. I should be approving curtains and rod placement; I should be eyeballing the marble tiles in the bathrooms and whether they should be hung vertically for a touch of whimsy; I should be approving a slab of reclaimed wood for an entryway table that was being custom designed; I should be . . . I should be . . . I should be playing hooky. So I did.

I slept in, I ate eggs sitting down instead of toast on the way out the door, and I was presently on an afternoon stroll with Simon, with absolutely no direction and nowhere to be. Hooky. Doing it.

We'd started off walking down the main drag, stopped to get coffee, and then turned down a hidden pathway through an old garden gate back up into the hills. We chatted as we walked, our hands linked. He was telling me about a call he'd had with Trevor from back east. They'd kept in touch after the reunion, and his wife had indeed sent me an autographed cookbook that had been signed by none other than Ina Garten herself.

She'd *touched* it. Touched the book that now lived on my nightstand. I wonder if her husband, Jeffrey, had touched it. Perhaps the day she'd been signing countless cookbooks, he'd stopped by her office. Maybe as they'd chatted about rosemary bushes and lobster rolls (as you do), he'd patted her hand, weary from signing her own name. Maybe her hand (and now Jeffrey's) was resting on the cookbook that became *my* cookbook! It could have happened.

We stopped at a corner, not quite sure where we were. I could see peekaboo Pacific here and there, but not enough to orient myself.

"Where's the house?" I asked, looking back up to the hillside. No landmarks I recognized.

"We're a few blocks away. I think I zigged when I should have zagged. No problem, it shouldn't be too far," he said, looking left, then right, then left again. "I think it's this way," he said. As we walked, my phone rang. I reached into my pocket and turned it off.

"I don't think I've seen you do that in weeks," he remarked, and I smiled ruefully.

"I'll feel guilty Monday, but today I can't think about anything work related. My head will literally burst."

He nodded, squeezing my hand as we walked. "Let's talk about what we should make for dinner tonight—I feel like cooking. How about we stop at that farmers' market you're so in love with and see if we can find something fun—"

Still continuing to walk, I didn't realize he had stopped dead in his tracks. I pulled on his arm. "Hey. Come on, pokey. Hey, Simon." I snapped my fingers to get his attention. He was staring at a house at the end of the street, partially hidden by trees and a jungle of weeds.

"Babe, look at that."

"Look at what—that shack? Yeah, it looks pretty abandoned. Let's head back. Farmers' market? Dinner?" I answered, pulling on his hand again. He stood fast, peering through the debris.

"No, *look* at that house. Isn't it interesting?"

"Interesting isn't the word I would use—" But he pulled me toward the house. Which had a For Sale sign in the yard.

Uh . . . what?

"You're kidding, right?" I asked, dragging my feet as he led me up the walk. As we got closer, I saw that it was probably once a very nice house. Victorian, but not froufrou. Peeling paint gave it a melancholy look, but it had clean lines and looked to be decent sized. I glanced around at the other houses on the street; rows of beautifully maintained homes. How had this house deteriorated so?

"It's pretty, isn't it?" a voice called, and we turned to see an older woman peering over her newspaper from her front porch.

"Um, well," I hedged, smiling at her.

"Well, it *used* to be pretty. Want to see the inside?" she asked.

"Oh no, we couldn't—" I started, only to be interrupted by Simon. "Yes, we'd love to."

"Babe, what are you doing?" I whispered through my teeth as the woman produced a set of keys from her pocket and threw them over to us. He caught them in midair, saying, "Thanks."

"No trouble at all. The Realtor has only shown it a few times, but I still have a set of keys. Mrs. Shrewsbury—she's the old owner—went to live with her daughter in Sacramento. She let the house get the best of her the last few years, but it's got good bones," she said, going back to her paper.

Good bones. I mentally snorted. Someone's been watching HGTV . . .

"Have you lost your mind?" I asked quietly as we made our way up the walk. Dodging clumps of grass and twigs, we headed up onto the porch.

"I don't know. I just want to see the inside; don't you?" he asked, and his eyes lit up with something I couldn't pinpoint.

"Sure?" As he fiddled with the lock I glanced around, noting the orange trees, the honeysuckle vines, the shrub roses. This Mrs. Shrewsbury was definitely a gardener. Looking past the debris, I could see the white clapboard, the faded shutters flanking an enormous picture window. A traditional two-story home, its porch curved away from the street and wrapped around toward the back.

"There we go," Simon announced, the door swinging inward. We walked in, the afternoon light showing us an outdated interior. I gazed at the mauve wallpaper with a calico cat border. But as we moved farther into the house, the entire back wall opened up into a view of the bay.

"Oh," I gasped, seeing the little lights of Sausalito just beginning to twinkle down below, and farther out, San Francisco. The porch wrapped all the way around the back, with two comfortable-looking lounge chairs positioned to take in the view. The grass needed mowing, the weeds needed weeding, but it was a killer porch.

I turned back toward Simon, who was leaning against the mantel of a stone fireplace flanked by bookshelves with leaded-glass doors. They were covered in shelf paper, but the craftsmanship was unmistakable.

Thumping my feet along the pink wall-to-wall carpeting, I made a guess. "There's hardwood under this Pepto rug, I bet you anything," I said, my heart racing a little.

Whoa, slow down Heart. What the hell were we even doing in here?

I passed Simon on the way toward the kitchen, finding avocado green appliances but ample space. My mind began to work. Not you too, Brain—settle down!

"Interesting?" he asked, reaching out his hand to me.

"Interesting," I allowed, letting him pull me toward the stairs. On the way we passed a formal dining room, complete with bay windows facing the . . . bay. The carpet on the stairs continued the pink, but was only a runner, exposing the hardwood underneath. As we made our way upstairs, golden sunlight broke through the stillness, another huge window hiding under an eave but making for great light. I held my breath as we reached the second floor, peeking inside rooms and counting one, two, three bedrooms, a hallway bath with subway tile, original probably, and heading into what was the . . . master bedroom.

High in the trees, overlooking the porch and the undeniable view, it was a large room with windows on two sides. The hardwood floor was stained a honey that could easily be lifted or darkened. My mind began to whirl, placing a highboy dresser on one wall, a desk in the nook in the corner. Would the bed be four poster or sleigh . . . Oh no, I was staging the room.

Simon came out of the bathroom with a smirk. "Holy shit, you are going to lose your mind when you see what's in here."

I pushed past him.

Claw.

Foot.

Tub.

"Sweet merciful God," I managed, leaning against the wall as he chuckled.

He caught me up in a close hug, leaning his forehead onto mine.

"Nightie Girl, we should totally buy this fucking house," he said, laughing when I shrieked.

My legs literally turned to jelly. Everything south of my navel liquefied, and if it were not for the core strength I possessed from hours spent in the yoga studio, I would have melted into the hardwood floor and dripped down onto the Pepto carpet below.

"Simon," I started, an eyebrow moving north.

"Caroline," he came right back, his eyebrow mocking mine.

"Simon," I repeated. "Slow down. And when did you start smoking the marijuana?"

He laughed again, then disappeared into one of the closets. I followed him, tamping down the hysteria that threatened inside.

"Listen to me. Seriously, are you high? You must be, because otherwise— Holy shit." I stopped, my voice echoing. It echoed, you see, because the closet was as big as our entire block. I immediately envisioned miles and miles of custom cabinets: drawers, open shelving, shoe racks. I let out a whimper.

Simon stood in front of the window (the closet had a *window.* I can't *even.*) and gestured at the view. "I wonder if my closet has a window too."

I gulped. "There's *another* closet?" I spun back into the bedroom. Yep, there it was. Two closets. I more than whimpered this time. I looked at Simon, who was leaving my closet (*the* closet) and coming toward me. I backed into the wall as each step came closer.

"No. No, Simon."

"We could totally do this."

"We could totally *not* do this! Not kidding."

"This house is incredible."

"This house is a money pit. Haven't you ever seen that movie?"

"Have you ever seen a view like the one from that porch?" he asked, placing his hands on either side of the wall, caging me in. "Quit trying to talk yourself out of this," he said with the tiniest bit of . . . annoyance?

"You haven't even seen the basement," I said.

"So we'll go to the basement."

"I'm scared of basements, Simon."

"Everyone's scared of basements, Caroline."

"You too? One time when I was a kid, I—"

But I couldn't finish my story about the time I gave myself a black eye racing up the basement steps with every Barbie I owned because of the werewolf that was chasing me, because I suddenly had a very insistent and very skilled tongue working past my lips and into my mouth.

I had barely caught my breath before the assault on my senses began again. His hands pressed into the small of my back, pulling me into him. His kiss ended, and he now rested his forehead against my own. There was want and need in his eyes, but in a different way than normal. I brought my hand up to his face and traced a path down his jaw.

"I'm not totally saying no," I whispered, and sudden joy broke across his face. I pushed him off me and looked again at the bedroom. He snuck his hands around my waist, which I allowed. Frankly, I needed the anchor. This was crazy.

"Since when did you want to live in Sausalito?"

"It's grown on me. Besides, they're turning our building into condos—we'd have to move sooner or later."

"That's a rumor."

"That's a fact. The lady in 2A told me."

"The lady in 2A just wants to get in your pants. Are we actually talking about this? And can we afford this?"

"I can, and you can help out. I know you're already thinking about all the things you want to change."

"We'd start with the carpet; that would come up immediately," I answered promptly, then slapped a hand over my mouth.

"I knew it." He laughed, and tugged me over to the window seat. For Christ's sake, a *window* seat. I never stood a chance. When he pulled me onto his lap, I let him.

"Okay, look," I said. "Let's just talk about this for a minute. A year ago, you had just left behind your harem. Now you want to move out to the suburbs with me?"

"I would hardly call this the suburbs."

"You know what I mean. This is just . . . Look, you have to admit that things have been different since . . ." I trailed off.

"Since?" he prodded.

"This just isn't what I was expecting. You're asking me to— Wait. What *are* you asking me?" I asked suddenly, my entire body going on point.

"I'm asking if you want to live together, silly girl. To buy this totally impractical, beautiful house that's way too big for two people, and live in it with me. Together."

And I'd thought we were just going out for a stroll today.

I looked around the bedroom, looked out the window at the killer view. I looked at him, looked him right in the eye, and tried to uncover what he was thinking. "You sure you want all this?" I asked, not just talking about the house.

"Hell, yes. I love you; that's not going to change. I want this, I want you, and I think . . . Oh hell, here comes the *Dawson's Creek*." He grimaced and I chuckled in spite of the moment.

His gaze grew wistful, and he looked so young. "I don't want to put things off, even though we haven't been together a really long time. I don't want to wait—you never know what can . . . Look. I adore you, and I want a home. Again. With you."

That did it. Cue the waterworks.

"You're killing me, Simon." I sniffled, tears and nose beginning to run.

"I know. I'm very cute when I'm vulnerable," he said, making me snort in a very unladylike way.

"So without knowing how much this house costs, without knowing anything about buying a house in Sausalito, without an inspection or a real estate agent *and* knowing there's a shit ton of work to be done, you want this? *All* of it—you really want this?"

He nodded, looking determined but a little afraid of my answer.

I got off his lap and walked around the bedroom once more. There were at least a hundred reasons why this was maybe not the best idea. I peered out the big window once more, looking down onto the old rosebushes in the brush. I bet this was beautiful in the spring.

I leaned on the windowsill, seeing the last of the afternoon sun leave the city across the bay. The windowsills were deep, exactly the right size for a very particular cat to doze in. I turned to Simon, now standing in the doorway with the most hopeful look ever.

Did *I* want this?

Is this what it was like, being grown up? Making big decisions, and then moving into a new phase of your life? Wasn't this too fast, too impulsive, too . . .

I *did* want this. And I wanted it with Simon. I nodded yes, and he grinned, laughed, then kissed me stupid.

Three hours later, he'd made an offer. It was accepted.

Grown-ups, right?

"Are we rushing into this?"

"No, we've been at this quite a while. It's called foreplay, Caroline," Simon murmured, south of my navel.

"I'm familiar with the concept," I replied, tightening my legs around his midsection and lifting up onto my elbows to peer down at him. "Not talking about the foreplay, although it's good."

"Good? Just good?" He crawled up my body, kissing it all the while. I shivered. "I was giving you some of my best stuff down there."

"Did I say good? I meant fantastic. Phenomenal." I kissed him square on the lips. "Out of this world."

"That's better. Now, what's this about rushing things?" He used my left breast as a pillow as his fingertips traced lightly over the right.

"With the house. Are we rushing into this?" I asked, running my hands through his hair and making it stand straight up. I twisted it this way and that, making Mohawks and no hawks, bowl cuts and bangs. I worried his hair around every finger, feeling the silky strands as he kissed my cleavage.

"You're still thinking about this?" he asked, sighing. "If I thought it was too soon, I wouldn't have made an offer." The barest hint of tongue now wet the tip of my breast. "If I thought it was too soon, I wouldn't have told the Realtor that I wanted that house no matter what was wrong with it."

His hips bumped mine, slipping between my legs, which automatically cradled him. I could feel him, hard and wanting and insistent. "If I thought it was too soon, I wouldn't be giving you an obscene design budget to turn that house into our home," he whispered, his voice husky and thick. And speaking of thick . . .

He nudged inside, just barely. "Heated floors, Caroline." My back arched. "Marble countertops." My legs fell open wide.

"Carrara?"

"I don't know what that means, babe," he said, panting, now hovering over my body. He rested his full weight on one hand, letting the other dip down below to begin drawing those perfect circles, exactly where he knew would send me flying.

"It's a kind of marble that—mmm . . . ." I moaned, my head falling back onto the pillow as he slid inside me entirely.

"Anything. You can have anything you want. Don't you know that?" He groaned, scooping under my back and pulling me closer into him, tilting my hips so that each thrust hit me right smack dab on the Carrara. "I just need you." His eyes burned into mine, stormy and full of want. "You—I need you," he repeated, thrusting deeply, stringing me out right on the edge.

It was those eyes that pushed me over that edge. And when he followed, it was epic. We lay together, tangled and out of breath. Holding him closely, I whispered in his ear how much I loved him, and how great this house, this home, would be.

I only hoped I could make it what he needed.

chapter seventeen

The next morning, I got an e-mail from Jillian. They were coming home in three weeks.

And in those weeks, my entire world turned upside down. I'd been running things for months now, and I'd pretty much gotten the swing of things. But not these last two weeks. No, sir. It was like the design gods all gathered, rubbed their hands together, and said, "Let's see how we can fuck up Caroline Reynolds."

And in case you're wondering, there are in fact design gods. And in case you're wondering, yes, they're fabulous.

The new job I'd agreed to take on in Sausalito was initially supposed to be a kitchen remodel. Which turned into a living room remodel. Which turned into "Couldn't we maybe add French doors out to the patio?" and "I think we could use a new patio, don't you?" and "I saw something called a pergola on HGTV the other night; could we put one of those over the patio?" This was all very good for the pocketbook, but it was way more work than I had planned on. We revised the timeline, revised the hell out of the budget, and I began work on the almost total renovation that this project now required.

We had a sprinkler malfunction at the office, resulting in the entire third floor being flooded. The sprinkler just went bananas one afternoon and sprayed for fifteen minutes until we could get it shut off. Offices had to be aired out, a team brought in to dry out the carpets, and some of the year-end tax forms now were blurred beyond comprehension. Luckily I had backup copies, but the panic I felt when I saw those forms? Might have caused my first gray hair ever.

The damned art installation was finally installed in the lobby of the Claremont. Max Camden took one look at it, pronounced it all wrong, and demanded we find something else. Which we did. All parties agreed that the new art was better for the space, but now everything else needed to be reconfigured to accommodate it. Which made me question the lighting placement. And the lighting in general. It was like pulling one loose thread on a sweater, and suddenly, poof, no sweater! And you're standing naked in a new hotel with terrible lighting.

I don't have time for naked.

Because the next blow to fall was that our building was indeed going condo. After Jillian forwarded an e-mail from her landlord, I learned they'd be going on the market in thirty days. Thirty *days*—is that even legal? During which the building owner would be coming in to make repairs and updates to all the units.

Simon took it all in stride, saying that it was a sign reaffirming that we were supposed to move to Sausalito. Sign or no sign, I was now faced with a new home that we were going to renovate top to bottom, and we'd lost the apartments we were going to live in while it happened. And with Jillian due home, I was losing my house-sitting gig.

So now on top of everything else, we had to pack up both our apartments in the city and move everything into a storage container until we were ready to move into the new house. Seriously. I hired help, of course, but I still needed to sort through things, purge things, and pack a few things on my own. There are certain things in a woman's apartment that she wants to pack herself. You know what I'm saying.

Nobody was getting their hands on my KitchenAid.

So, to recap. My already hectic work life was ramping up instead of slowing down. My boss was returning in a few days, and there were box fans all over the third floor of her office space in a historic Russian Hill mansion. And I was stealing a few hours I really didn't have to pack up my glorious apartment, to move into a nonglorious home going through a gut rehab.

I was going to be living on-site during a gut rehab.

Laugh all you want, design gods. I could handle it.

Right?

Brain laughed. Backbone curled up like it had scoliosis. Heart was still drawing her own image all over the imaginary mirror in her new master bath.

And Simon? Simon was . . . a pickle. A pickle who was packing up his apartment next door as we speak, and making a helluva lot of noise while doing it. I was in my bedroom, purging my sock drawer, when I heard a very distinct thumping coming through the wall. A banging, if you will. I smiled, remembering the first few times I heard that banging.

Clive jumped up on the bed, looking curiously at the wall.

Pretty sure that sometimes he still listened to see if Purina was going to come meowing through that wall again. Fat chance.

I crossed to the shared wall, placing my hand on the spot I imagined was right above his bed, and sure enough, I felt another thumpity thump. What the hell was he doing over there?

I grabbed my phone and sent him a text:

What the hell are you doing
over there?

> Taking apart my
> headboard.

Ah! No wonder. I was having
flashbacks.

His response was to bang on his wall again. I banged back.
Bang ba ba bang bang.
Bang bang.

I giggled, then listened. Would he . . . ? Sure enough, a moment later, Glen Miller came through the walls. Smooth.

I went back to packing, and he went back to taking apart his headboard. Clive attacked a roll of bubble wrap and made it his bitch. A few hours later, we met back in my apartment and looked around at the tiny dent I'd made in getting things ready to be moved.

"When is the storage container coming again?"

"Two days." I looked in my calendar to verify the date. "So you need to make sure anything you don't want in the container is already moved out before the crew gets here. They're taking care of everything else." It was still weird to think about the new house. I almost *couldn't,* with everything going on. One step at a time.

"We still staying here tonight?" he asked, peering over my shoulder at the calendar.

"I'd like to, if that's still cool with you. One more night, where it all began? Besides, I went to the trouble of bringing my pussy," I joked.

As if on cue, Clive ran through the kitchen and back out again like the hounds of hell were on his tail, towing a large piece of bubble wrap that streamed out behind him like a crinkly-sounding cape.

"You know I can't resist that," he murmured in my ear, arms sneaking around my waist. "By the way, you can erase that trip."

"What trip?" I asked, my voice all gooey. His arms did that to me.

"The one to Belize. I canceled it," he said, pointing to a date I had circled on my calendar.

"You canceled Belize?" I asked. That was three trips in a row.

"Yep, I wanted to be here to help with the house." He nuzzled my neck. "I'm pretty handy with a hammer, if you'll recall." He bumped his hips into mine.

I bumped them right back. A little harder than was necessary? Maybe. A little.

"I'm gonna go make sure I got everything in my room," I said, shrugging him off and heading back to my bedroom. I knew he didn't like it much when I questioned his schedule. And if he noticed that my voice was no longer gooey, he didn't say anything.

Pickle.

E very single one of my worlds collided on the same day. Friday dawned cold and clear. It was a good thing there was no fog, because the fog in my head by noon was enough for the entire Bay Area. Jillian and Benjamin were due in on a six o'clock plane. We wanted them to be able to enjoy their first night back without us hanging around, so when I left for work Friday morning I made sure everything was spick-and-span, with everything exactly how they'd left it.

Simon was closing on the new house at two thirty. He'd be signing the paperwork and picking up the keys, and I told him I'd meet him at our new address as soon as I could get away from work. Utilities were being turned on, we had a truckload of essential boxes being delivered, and Simon was in charge of buying and setting up our blow-up bed. Yep, a blow-up bed. Since we'd be living on the premises while our new home was renovated, we didn't want any real furniture there. Didn't want to have to keep moving it as we worked through the rooms, so we were living basic for a while.

Shit was about to get real. Really real.

Poor Clive didn't know what was going on. After moving from Jillian's house, back to the apartment, back to Jillian's, back to the apartment, he barely knew where his litter box was. Luckily, the Stanford sweatshirt was long gone.

Uncle Euan and Uncle Antonio had chosen to move out of our building when it went condo, so my cat sitters were gone. I didn't want Clive at the new house until I'd had time to kitty proof it, so off he went to kitty day care.

I felt like the shittiest mommy on the planet. And Simon's feelings on the matter were not helping.

My veterinarian had recommended this great pet hotel. I say hotel, because this was not your average boarding place. He had his own room, with his own flat-screen TV playing hummingbird porn 24/7.

"It's just temporary. I promise, sweetie." When we went to tour the place I'd brought Clive along, and he and Simon looked around with the same expression.

Are you kidding me?

"We can't leave him here, this place is ridiculous!" Simon whispered as we walked down the row of kitty rooms.

"This place is great. Don't *you* be ridiculous," I whispered right back as we followed the owner down the hallway.

"And this will be Clyde's suite!" she sang out, opening the door onto the cutest little room I'd ever seen.

"It's Clive. Not Clyde; Clive." Simon sighed, rolling his eyes at me. My eyes told him to shut up. I took Clive from him, setting him down to get the lay of the land. He looked around, scratched at one of the posts, and looked back at me. "Where's my window ledge?" he wordlessly asked.

These two. Honestly.

Simon and I argued about it on the way home. Clive sat regally on the console between us in the Range Rover, hind legs tucked into the cup holders. The pet hotel was a little cheesy but it was great. And it was a means to an end. It would only be for a few days while we got a feel for the new space. I'd been with Clive much longer than Simon, and I knew if there was one loose floorboard, one cupboard with a wonky door, he'd go exploring and it'd be impossible to find him later. Simon protested that I was being ridiculous and a control freak.

I simply wanted to kitty proof the joint. That's it. And in order to do so, my cat had to spend a few nights in an overpriced pet hotel with room service. The way Clive and Simon were acting, you'd think I'd suggested he spend a few nights on Alcatraz.

But here we were, moving day, and Simon had finally agreed it was in Clive's best interests, as well as his own, to take him to the pet hotel before closing on the house. I'd kissed them both that morning, telling Clive to enjoy his adventure. He arranged his paw in a way that one of his little kitty fingers was sticking straight up. Not an accident, I'm quite sure.

I planned on working through lunch that day, trying to get everything pulled together so that when Jillian came back to work on Monday, it would be like she'd never left. No, *better* than when she left. I really wanted her to know how seriously I'd taken running her business while she was gone, even bringing in a few new clients while taking care of our existing ones. And mentoring a new intern with the same patience and guidance that she'd given me when I walked through those doors for the first time.

And that while, yes, we'd lost the carpet on the third floor, I'd replaced it with something even better.

I'd put together storyboards showing the progress on the Claremont; very striking. I'd streamlined one of the payroll reports so she could see not only total hours worked for her hourly employees but how many hours had been allocated to each project. And I

almost had all the invoices for all active accounts and projects cat-
egorized and color coded in different colored folders, which were
spread out all over my office.

I was checking my math on a particularly long itemized receipt when Simon unexpectedly sailed in with a pizza box at twelve
thirty. He plunked it down square in the middle of my desk with
a flourish.

"Whoa, whoa, what's this?" I exclaimed, looking up from my
adding machine and realizing that I'd lost count for the third
time.

"It's called lunch, babe," he said with a proud smile, pulling so-
das out of a bag and looking for a place to put them down. "Damn,
woman, I've never seen your desk this messy."

"Simon, wait, don't—"

He'd picked up three of my folders and stacked them together
to make room, mixing up everything I was working on. "There we
go—much better."

I took off my glasses and glared at him. "Do you have any idea
how much time that took me to organize this morning?"

He looked guiltily at the stack. "Oops?" he offered.

"What are you doing here, anyway?" I took the stack from him
and started to separate them all over again.

"It's House Day, Nightie Girl." He looked at me like I was crazy.
"I thought we could celebrate with a little lunch, and I know what
you're going to say before you say it: You're too busy. No problem—
that's why I brought lunch to you!"

"Hey, Caroline, did you still want me to work on the cost projections for—oh, hey, Simon!" Monica said, breezing in from the
hallway and stopping short when she caught sight of my boyfriend.
She had a monster crush. It normally made me chuckle to watch
her stammer and stutter around him, but today I didn't even feel a
flash of amusement.

"Monica, how'd you like some pizza?" he offered, picking up

the box from my desk. The papers underneath were now stained with grease.

I pulled a colored pencil from my head and started to chew.

"Oh no, I already ate a pizza, I mean I didn't eat an entire pizza, I mean I went out for an entire pizza, I mean a slice! I had a small slice of pizza, and a salad, mostly salad and—"

I stopped her. It was embarrassing. "Yes, Monica, please work on the cost projections for the Anderson account and let me know if you have questions. Thank you."

"Okay, sure, no problem, I'll just be naked in the other room— I mean working! I just—crap. Bye!"

I dropped my head to my desk. Monica was the most talented, most mature young woman I knew. I would have killed for the poise she possessed at such a young age—except when Wallbanger was involved. Then she turned to goo. I could relate. And she didn't even know he had the power to move an entire bed with the strength of his hips alone.

Speaking of hips, they moved into my field of vision, along with the pizza box.

"So, lunch?"

I started to laugh. I couldn't help it. I was at that point when you either laugh or cry, and the scales just happened to tip toward laughter. I looked up at him, celebrating House Day in his own sweet and unaware way, and cackled like a loon. "Sure, Simon. Let's have some pizza."

I took the box from his hands, and right there on the top, surrounded by an army of dancing pepperoni and wearing a chef's hat, was a picture of the devil himself.

Cory Weinstein. Pizza chain owner. Discount giver. Self-described man about town.

And the jackrabbit fucker who'd hijacked my O.

My eye began to twitch. The floor, to pitch. My skin he'd seen just once now crawled and creeped and bunched and itched.

The laughter that was ringing out from my lips turned to a shriek that stopped traffic all over town, upset several fruit carts, and may very well have been the slight earthquake tremor that was reported that night on the news. And my knees were kissing my chin as my body turned roly-poly in an effort to protect itself at all costs.

"Oh, will you settle down? There are positively no anchovies on this pizza," Simon said, rolling his eyes and handing me a napkin.

I'd had flashbacks all afternoon.

Cory, cheers-ing me with his Natural Light beer when I met him for drinks on our one and only date.

Cory, grinning as he slid behind the wheel of his stupid souped-up yellow Small Dick Mobile with the license plate IEET-PIE. Point of order, he in fact does not.

Cory, poised over me grunting and blurry while his hips ran a race he would never win.

To be fair, I'd had every opportunity to stop this particular tragedy. And still chose to proceed with the single worst sexual experience of my life, resulting in the Great Orgasm Hiatus, as it came to be known to all mankind.

I now blinked my eyes hurriedly, trying to get the images to stop coming. I turned onto my new street a little too quickly and the contents of my bag spilled all over the floor of the delivery van.

Delivery van, you ask?

Yes, delivery van. In our haste to make real estate history with the fastest decision ever, we both forgot about my commute into the city. Sure, I could take the ferry, but I hadn't had a chance to figure out the ferry schedule. And I no longer had access to Jillian's very sporty Mercedes. So I'd purloined the Jillian Designs delivery van, and was using that to drive over the bridge to my new address. As I pulled up in front of the old Victorian that I now called home, my lipsticks rolled around on the floor. I sighed heavily as I turned the ignition off, looking through the windshield at the house.

From the street, it still looked melancholy and a bit run down. I knew that was temporary. Perhaps I was feeling a bit run down? This day had taken it out of me, and I wanted nothing more than to explore my new home, take a hot shower, and crawl into bed.

A bed on the floor.

Shit, I didn't care anymore. I just wanted a bed. As I shut the door to the van, it squeaked in a way reminiscent of Cory Weinstein's bed as he jackrabbited his teeny peeny in a mind-numbingly (and hoohah-numbingly) way, and I flinched once more.

I slammed the door shut and walked up the steps. I could see Simon through the front picture window, moving boxes.

I felt my load begin to lighten. And something else begin to tighten. This was my new home, and I was sharing it with Simon.

Suddenly the crappy day disappeared. I couldn't wait to get inside and make the sweet sweet love. And the nasty dirty love. And everything in between.

I opened the front door, looking past the mauve wallpaper and the Pepto pink carpet and the dingy baseboards and the fingerprinted doorjambs and all of our boxes, and saw my boyfriend. Tall and handsome, strong and lean. He turned when I came in, and shot me a devilish grin.

"Hey, babe."

"Hey, yourself," I answered back. I dropped my bags and started to walk across all that pink toward him.

"I waited to order some dinner till you got here. How does Thai sound to you?"

"Sounds great, you big, hot homeowner, you," I purred, and he looked up from his take-out menus. He grinned as he watched me walk toward him, so I threw an extra bounce into my step.

"What's got into you?"

"Nothing. Not yet, at least." I winked. "Now, where's that blow-up bed? Let's christen this pile of bricks."

I pulled him into me and kissed him deeply, winding my hands into his hair. He responded immediately, kissing me back urgently. I kissed along his jaw, along his cheekbones, drawing my tongue along his skin right where his neck met his shoulder. He always tasted amazing there.

He groaned into my ear. "Shit. I forgot to get the blow-up bed."

"Whuh?" I said, my mouth full of neck and shoulder.

"Yeah, sorry. I was so busy with everything this afternoon, it totally slipped my mind."

I pulled back and pulled my tongue back into my mouth. "So where are we going to sleep—aghh!" I danced away; something furry had brushed up against my legs. "What the hell was that?"

My mind instantly conjured a task force of mice determined to take the house back from the invading humans.

But it wasn't mice. It was Clive. Wide eyed and bushy tailed. Now weaving himself in and out of my legs, saying hello to Mommy. I looked at him, then back up to Simon. Who had the decency to look the tiniest bit guilty.

"I couldn't leave him there; they called him Clyde!"

It took me 120 seconds to fly around the house, closing each and every door to each and every room that had not been kitty proofed. And then another sixty seconds to unclench my fingernails from the inside of my palms.

I returned to the living room. Simon was showing Clive the coat closet.

"I can't believe you, Simon," I huffed, pushing past him to grab my bag from where I'd dropped it by the front door.

"Oh, come on, it's not that big a deal."

I whirled on him. "It *is* a big deal when this is something we'd already agreed on. I don't have time tonight to run around this huge fucking house and make sure there's nothing he can get into."

"I think you might be overreacting here a little. He's probably going to stick pretty close to us tonight. He'll snuggle up just like he always does and—"

"Snuggle up with us where, Simon? In the blow-up bed we don't have? Where the hell are we supposed to sleep tonight?"

Clive wisely retreated to the dining room, where he pretended to explore the window seat. He was totally listening to us.

"I forgot! It's not the end of the world; I'll run out and get one. No big deal," he snapped, grabbing his jacket and starting for the door. I stepped into his way to stop him when I heard a rattling of glass. I turned around and saw Clive, halfway out the big window over the window seat.

"Clive!" I shouted, and he froze, half in and half out. I snatched him up and held him close, Simon right behind me. The original casement windows were rusty, covered in years of old putty, and had no screens. Simon jiggled the window, finally got it shut, and turned back to face me.

Tears were running down my face. Clive was like my child. And like any mother who just saw her child go halfway through a window, I was half scared, half furious, and totally relieved. Clive was an indoor cat through and through; he'd never been outside a day in his life. He'd only seen streets from the comfort and safety of a window ledge. With a *real* window between him and the streets—not this rickety death trap.

"I'm so sorry," Simon said, and I nodded. I hugged Clive so tightly he squeaked.

"Where's his carrier?" I asked.

"I'll get it," he answered, and left the room.

I looked down at my cat, who turned in my arms to look up at me. "Don't ever do that again, you hear me?" I warned, stroking his silky fur. He put a paw over my mouth. I kissed it, smiling down at him. When Simon came back with the carrier, my smile faded.

"I'm going to run him over to the pet place, okay?" I said quietly, nudging him into his carrier.

He nodded. "I'll go buy one of those blow-up beds."

I started for the door. "Do you have my key? In case I get back before you do?"

"Oh, sure—here it is," he said, pulling a new key chain from his back pocket and handing me a key. I took it.

This didn't have quite the ceremony that I thought it might.

I left with my cat.

I checked Clive in to his hotel, bought at least a dozen I'm-sorry catnip mice, and left after he was passed out on a pillow watching *Lion King*. As I drove back home, thoughts flew in and out of my head almost faster than I could process. Emotions too many to count. I was pissed, no doubt about it. About the bed? Yes. About Clive almost going out the window? Yes.

But there was more going on than just that; shit that I couldn't even begin to ponder. Too tired to ponder this pickle, I winced once more as the car door squeaked, then plodded up the walk. I was exhausted, I was starving, and more than that, I felt terrible that this very exciting day had been turned into a crapshow.

I pushed open the door and found the biggest blow-up bed that had ever been created smack dab in the middle of the living room. Made up with sheets and blankets and mounds and mounds of pillows. And next to that? A table made out of a box covered with a furniture pad. And next to that? Two bags full of take-out Thai and a six-pack of beer cooling in a mop bucket full of ice.

And next to that? Simon. Sitting on the end of the bed. Which was very low to the ground. And quite squishy. So when he tried to stand? Not so much.

I bit down on the inside of my cheek as my very good looking and oh-so-athletic boyfriend struggled to stand up straight, and when he did? He was beet red.

"I got the bed," he said quietly.

"I see that."

"It's pretty low."

"It would seem."

He came and stood in front of me, his body tense. "I'm sorry about earlier."

"I know." I smoothed his hair back from his face and looked into his eyes. "I'm sorry too."

"Can I have that key back?"

"Already?" I asked.

"Gimme it," he muttered, one corner of his mouth lifting.

I looked at him curiously, but handed it back to him. He looked at it carefully, then back at me.

"I've never lived with anyone. You know that, right?"

I nodded.

He was quiet for a moment, his eyes thoughtful. Then he opened my hand and placed the key back in the middle of it. Closing my hand over it, he smiled. "Welcome home, babe."

I smiled back and let him pull me into a slow and tentative kiss. This was better.

We ate dinner sitting cross-legged on the inflatable bed, which proved more difficult than I'd thought. First on the list, get some chairs over here pronto.

After dinner we walked from room to room, talking about what might go here, and what might go there. We had a pretty good idea of where we wanted everything, but there was nothing like walking through it together and making plans. When he said he'd never lived with anyone before, he wasn't the only one. I'd had roommates, but never lived with a boyfriend.

Until now Simon and I had been very much together, but still very much our own entities. That had changed now. I was "living with someone." If someone asked, "Hey, is that Caroline seeing anyone?" the answer would be, "Oh yeah, she and her boyfriend are living together," or, "Yep, she and her boyfriend just bought a house together." We were taking a very big step here, but a step I was glad we were taking.

And as we walked through our new home, room by room, I began to dream a little. I'd always seen myself in a big house like this someday, but never thought it would happen so quickly. I could always see past the things that needed to be changed, but now that I was in here, and the space was really and truly ours, I could *feel* the house. Feel what it had been, and what would be again for us.

A home. And isn't that exciting? And a little scary.

When we finally made it to the master bedroom, I asked why we weren't staying in there tonight.

"No lights; all the bulbs are burned out. I'll get some tomorrow," Simon answered, tugging me toward the window. The moonlight came through the glass, illuminating the room with the barest hint of blue. He sat on the window seat, pulling me onto his lap. "Where do you think we should put our bed?" he asked, nuzzling my neck.

"Our blow-up bed?"

"No, our new bed. You're getting us a new bed, right?"

"New house, new bed. That sounds fair. I was thinking right there." I pointed to the opposite wall. "Then when we wake up, we can see the bay. The light in the morning will be fantastic."

"We might even be able to see the city," he mused, resting his head on my shoulder.

"When it's not foggy, for sure." I sighed, finally feeling the weight of the day beginning to fall away.

"Did I tell you I had the cleaning crew pay extra-special attention to the claw-foot tub?" he asked.

The one thing he'd managed to do right that day was get a cleaning crew in to scour the place top to bottom as soon as the key was officially in his hands. We might be tearing half the stuff out of this house, but by God, it'd be clean stuff.

"Shut up."

"If I did, you wouldn't hear the best part," he teased.

"Hit me, Wallbanger."

"When I went out to get the bed? I also bought you some Mr. Bubble."

"Shut *up*."

"If I did, you'll never hear the bestest part."

"Bestest?"

"Yes. The bestest part is that I'm going to take a bubble bath with you. And not because I'm planning on seducing you, which I'll try. And not because you'll need help washing your back, which I'll offer to do. But for a very specific reason," he said, getting up and pulling me toward the bathroom.

"To see me naked?"

"That's just a bonus. The real reason is that the lightbulbs are burned out in here too, and I know you'd get totally spooked if you had to stay here by yourself in the dark." He grinned as we entered the bathroom.

"You do know me well," I agreed.

From a bag in the corner, he pulled out a package of tea lights and a box of matches. "Practical bathing with a side of romance."

I laughed out loud. And took a bath with Mr. Bubble and Mr. Parker in that very tub. Heaven. And I thought *I* was the practical romantic.

An hour later, I was camping on the floor of my new living

room on a blow-up bed with my new roomie. I was relaxed; my limbs were limp and noodley. And when Simon slid into me to christen this first of many rooms, I allowed myself to be swept away.

Except I wasn't. He tried everything he could to sweep me away, but there was no sweeping.

But it was still wonderful and warm and delicious, and the perfect way to end such an up-and-down day.

"No?" Simon asked as he panted into my ear, his body slick on top of me.

I stroked his back as I shook my head, feeling him finally relax into me. "I love you, Simon," I whispered. "So much."

He rolled us so I could lie in his nook, where the rise and fall of his chest lulled me. "Love you too, babe," he whispered back, holding me close.

And as I slipped toward sleep, listening to all the unfamiliar sounds of our new home, I took a quick inventory. O was still in there, just a little skittish tonight.

All was good in the new neighborhood.

chapter eighteen

I sat in my office, rearranging the piles of paper on my desk once more. Lining up the edges, positioning the folders so that they were at perfect right angles with the side of the desk. I inspected and removed three petals from the roses in the vase, goldenrod shot through with the palest of pink.

Jillian was due in any moment.

As Simon and I spent our first weekend in *our* new home, she and Benjamin spent it readjusting in *theirs* after their lengthy absence. She'd texted me to let me know they were home, and we agreed to meet at work on Monday. I was handing back the keys to the kingdom.

I'd loved playing Jillian for a few months. It'd been longer than I'd planned, but I'd gotten a taste of what life might be like a few years down the road. I had always seen myself as part of a larger team, and my normal role was exactly what I wanted. I'd handled the additional responsibility well, but was I at heart a manager? No. Did I want to run a business, or just create beautiful and enchanting places that a business or family might want to inhabit?

I was a designer. And I wanted to keep on being a designer. So the keys would be given back, she'd tell me what a brilliant job

I'd done, she wouldn't be able to resist busting my balls about the third-floor carpet *no matter* that she knew it wasn't my fault, and then everything would go back to normal.

Yes? Yes.

I heard her before I saw her. That voice that could make you quake or dance. I was hoping for dancing.

"Where is that girl? Where's that Caroline?" I heard as she came closer to my office door. I grinned, moving out from behind my desk and approaching the door.

She breezed in, suntanned, healthy, and radiant. She literally glowed.

"What's up, boss lady?" I asked, and she pulled me into a tight hug.

"Good to you see you, kiddo." She moved me back out to arm's length and looked me over. "You look tired. And I have just the cure." She handed me a huge bag.

"What's this?" I asked, setting it on the desk.

"Presents, of course. France, Switzerland—you name it, you got a trinket."

"Is this the part where I say, Oh, Jillian, you shouldn't have?" I said, spying a box at the top. It said . . . No. It surely didn't. *Hermès?*

"Oh, Jillian, you *really* shouldn't have," I breathed, opening it carefully. A silk scarf. Salmon pink and bloodred, swirled through with buttercup yellow. "But I am *so* freaking glad you did!" I squealed, jumping up and down.

"It's the least I could do," she said. "Now come show me the third floor. After we get that over with, we can go to lunch and you can bring me up to speed."

We sat in our favorite booth at our favorite restaurant in Chinatown, eating sizzling rice soup. I delighted in just having her here again. She told me stories from their trip abroad, and I drank them up as quickly as I did the green tea. Palaces, castles, yachts, grand restaurants, and tiny bistros. The romance, the adventure—all of it just sounded magical.

"And Nerja—oh my goodness, I can't even tell you! You know how enchanting it is; I never wanted to leave," she gushed.

"I know, it was like a little slice of heaven," I sighed, remembering the trip I'd taken with Simon. I went there already a little bit in love with him, and that trip solidified everything for me. Watching him work, discovering a new locale with him, experiencing everything this tiny corner of the globe had to offer, immersing ourselves completely in a moment. I'd fallen 100 percent in love with him there. It would always hold a special place in my heart.

"And the food! I can't believe I'm not as big as house, the way we ate," she exclaimed, and I looked her over from stem to stern.

"You look fantastic, as always. Who are you kidding?"

"Speaking of fantastic, when do I get to see this new house? I can't believe we're neighbors!" she asked.

"Oh, it's a wreck right now. But you know what that's like, you lived through it."

"Blech—worst thing ever is living through a renovation. But it's worth it in the end."

"I'm trying to keep that in mind."

"I was surprised when you told me. I thought Simon loved the city," she said, eyeing me carefully.

"Believe me, no one was more surprised than me when he came up with this crazy idea. But he took to Sausalito quicker than I thought he would; he really loves it over there," I answered. "I do too."

"And Benjamin told me he's taken some time off work?"

"A little; he canceled a few jobs. He really wants to be here when the renovation gets going. But when he sees how boring it can be, he'll hightail it for Bali or Madagascar." I laughed, paying special attention to the bottom of my soup bowl. And not at all to Jillian's knowing gaze. "So, after lunch you want to stop by the Claremont and see how it's coming along?"

"Holy Christ, this place is sick."

"Sick is right. How much did she pay for the baby-puke-green stove?"

"Obviously she's getting rid of those, and besides, she didn't pay for it. Simon did."

"No shit, must be nice to have Mr. Moneybags for a feller. Why such a big house, though?"

"Oh, use your imagination! There's two of them now, but down the road . . ."

"Just because you plan on being pregnant within the year doesn't mean anyone else wants to be."

"Don't be such a downer, you big stick-in-the-mud. Just look at that view!"

"All I see are weeds."

"Honestly, I can't even believe that you—"

"Now look, Pollyanna, I just call it like I see it, and I think that—"

I stood in the doorway, watching my two best friends with amusement. I cleared my throat, and they both broke off, midtiff.

"Sorry, Caroline, we were just saying that—" Mimi started, and I waved my hand.

"I heard what you were saying; you two carry on. Let me know when you want me to give you the full tour—or I can just leave and let you two make out. I'm familiar with your foreplay."

Sophia snorted and set her bag down on one of the sawhorses. "Okay, Reynolds, show us your new digs."

I did indeed give them the full tour of the new house. My new house. *Our* new house. Which was, at this point, a war zone.

Besides the aforementioned sawhorses, we also had ladders,

Sheetrock, buffing machines, paint cans, several tarps, and yes, baby-puke-green appliances. To be fair, when they were initially manufactured, they were called avocado. Which was just insulting to avocados.

Experience had taught me that no matter how much money a customer had, no matter how many workmen you had on the job, no matter how creative the architect or how skilled the designer (very), there were hiccups. Hiccups that I simply left at the end of the day.

Now I was living with the hiccups. Every single day. Along with Simon, who was taking it much more in stride. He'd never done anything like this before, but he was determined to help as much as he could. He even bought himself a tool belt, which he looked utterly fantastic wearing. Had I made him model it for me one night wearing nothing else? Maybe. A little.

The building inspection had turned up more issues than I thought possible. Under the surface, there was wood rot. And leaky pipes. And busted duct work. Floor joists needed to be replaced, a new concrete slab possibly poured in the basement—the hits just kept on coming. All of it was totally doable, just time consuming. And costly.

I hired an architect I'd worked with before, we worked up the plans, we brought in a contractor, and walls started coming down. We were reconfiguring the entire layout downstairs, letting in more light, opening up hallways, and creating a more open concept without sacrificing the original integrity of the house. There was nothing worse in my book than Victorian on the outside and ultramodern inside.

It was a pile of crazy at the moment, but I could see that it was going to be beautiful. And we were moving at a breakneck pace, using more workers than normal to get everything done more quickly.

It's amazing what you can get done when you have deep pockets and a sense of urgency. Which Simon really seemed to have lately when it came to the house. Getting back to his photography? Not so much. But we'll pause on that particular pickle, and focus on this gorgeous old house.

Although "we" bought it, use of the word *we* here is stretching it considerably. There was no way I could have afforded a house like this, run down or not. It was in a prime area with killer views and a huge footprint in an established neighborhood. I wasn't comfortable with Simon paying for everything, no matter how much money he had stashed away. So I'd insisted that the house would be in his name only, and I'd contribute to monthly household expenses. He gave me an enormous budget to work with for the design, and while I still felt a bit guilty when I saw the invoices, I had to admit I liked having a rich boyfriend.

There. I said it. Revoke my feminist card. Take away my— well, whatever you take away when a woman admits she likes nice things. I was getting the house of my dreams, with the man of my dreams. And I reminded myself of this each time I tripped over a bucket or brushed sawdust off my sammich or tensed up whenever I heard Simon turn a job down. . . . There's that pickle again.

In addition to my own house renovations I was in the home stretch on the Claremont, which filled my days. Jillian had toured each job site I'd been working on in her absence, pored over the books with a fine-tooth comb, grilled Monica so thoroughly that I was scared for her, and then said I'd done an amazing job. I told her she could show me that in my end-of-the-quarter bonus, which she pretended not to hear. But she totally would.

Now she was spending some time meeting with her lawyers and her accountants, which freed me up for putting the finishing touches on the hotel. The launch party was getting closer and closer, and we'd be ready to show it off to all of Sausalito.

I focused on all the things that were on my plate at the moment, and not on the pickle on the side that was staring at me.

Because that was a pickle I was silly to even entertain. Who cared that he wasn't working? He had plenty of money, he didn't need to work. So why did this pickle prick at me so?

Pffft. Forget it—I had a fifty-cent tour to give right now.

I led my two best chickens through the house, explaining in great detail each finish and fixture that had been selected, painting a picture how it would all come together when it was complete. They made no comment on the fact that there was a toilet sitting in my dining room, which I greatly appreciated. I saved the best for last, and when I opened the French doors to the master suite, *I* saw gleaming furniture and polished oak floors. Mounds of pillows and the blue bay peeking through puddled curtains. What *they* actually saw were pine studs and yellow electrical wiring hanging from the ceiling, and that damn blow-up bed. But when they saw the claw-foot tub, even Sophia looked a bit wistful.

"This is kickass, Caroline," she said, perching on the side. That's her version of wistful.

"You gotta get in this tub, see how deep it really is," I encouraged, sitting down in one end, and her eyes opened wider when she realized how luxurious it was. Wider still when I dangled my legs over one side, flashing my panties in the process.

"This is going to be so fantastic when it's finished. How much longer until it's all done?" Mimi asked.

"We're on track to finish ahead of schedule, but I hate to even say that out loud. Who knows what else we might find?" Like the original knob-and-tube wiring that had to be ripped out, and the rotten subfloor downstairs, and the ghost that was living in the basement. Technically the ghost was a family of raccoons that had been relocated to a nearby nature preserve, but that was neither here nor there.

"I admit it, I never thought you two would be the first to get the house out in the burbs. How's Simon doing with all this change?" asked Sophia, now in the tub with me.

"Oh, he's having a grand old time. Yesterday he spent an hour examining the difference using a sandpaper with a forty grit versus eighty grit would make on the kitchen banquette. And don't even get me started on how much fun he had with the chalk lines the crew used to ensure the sightlines were even on the new kitchen pass-through. There was blue chalk everywhere; I finally found him by following his blue footsteps," I said flatly.

I couldn't complain though, could I? Who wouldn't want a boyfriend who was determined to create the most perfect home imaginable? And besides, once I found him, he quickly made me forget about the footprints. He showed me his tool belt, you see.

However, even the tool belt wasn't enough to bring my O out of temporary hiding. It *was* temporary, right? Admittedly, it was hard to get down to the sexy times when there was a thin veil of drywall dust coating everything that would stand still, but still. Even the tool belt wasn't making a dent.

If I ever saw Cory Weinstein again, I'd castrate him.

But seriously, it was just temporary. Right? I'd avoided sex with Simon for days now, something I'd never done. He was getting suspicious. I was getting frustrated. Even right now, I could feel the tension building up in my body.

Why wasn't he booking jobs?

Wow, wrong tension.

This was why I needed to stop picking at this particular pickle.

"I'm glad we decided to wait until after we get married to look for a house. Too stressful while planning the wedding. Plus, I don't want to live in sin. You know you're hellbound, Caroline," Mimi said with a wicked glint in her eye.

"Where do you think you'll look for a house?" I asked, settling deeper into the tub while Mimi sat cross-legged on the window seat (a window seat in a bathroom? I can't even) and looked out at the view.

"I think we'll stay in the city for now, although I can really see the appeal of moving out here," she said. The lot was wooded on either side of the house, and some of the trees in back had been cleared to see the water down below. It felt secluded, even though we weren't far from our neighbors. Golden light streamed in, and it was so quiet. "I bet Sophia would never want to leave the city though, right?" she asked, turning back toward us.

Sophia didn't answer right away, and that was the first time we noticed the tears.

"Hey, what's going on?"

"It's nothing," she whispered, rolling her eyes as Mimi immediately crossed over to us in the tub.

"Don't give us that. What's going on?" I asked, struggling to sit back up and flashing her more thoroughly this time. This tub was really quite deep.

Sophia laughed, then two more tears fell. "I want a claw-foot tub, dammit!" she cried.

Mimi pushed her forward and slid in behind her, wrapping her tiny arms around her. "You sure it's just the tub you want?"

"Yes. No. Fuck. Do I have to say it?"

"You want Neil in the claw-foot tub with you?" I asked, pulling a tissue from my purse for her.

She blew her nose loudly. "I do. I hate myself for saying it, but I do." She looked around at the tub, then chuckled. "What's funny is he wouldn't even fit in here, the stupid lug. He's so tall." She blew her nose again. "I miss him so fucking much. Did I tell you he doesn't even call me anymore? He stopped."

She sniffed a great sniff, then looked up with determination. "I think—I think I need to call him. I'm going to call him," she said, reaching for her purse as I met Mimi's eyes.

"Sweetie, you sure you want to do that?" I asked, snatching up her purse and holding it just out of her reach. Impulse + Ex = Not Always a Good Thing.

"Why the hell not? You're the one who's been saying I should talk to him all this time." She sniffled.

"Yeah, Sophia! Go! Go! Go!" Mimi chanted, always the Disney princess.

I gave her the purse and crossed my fingers. Sophia rarely made concessions like this. If it didn't work, even after she'd put her butt on the line? I not only crossed my fingers, I crossed my toes too.

She took out her phone, then stopped. Started to dial, then stopped.

"Maybe you should think this through before you—" I started.

"Oh, stop it, Caroline, let her call him!" Mimi cried. "Do it," she cooed in Sophia's ear, like an angel perched on her shoulder. Or was she the devil?

Sophia took a deep breath, scrolled through her phone, and brought him up. The picture on her screen made her smile. Neil, covered in Gatorade at a 49ers game, when he'd gotten a little too caught up in a big game and the subsequent victory. That was the thing about Neil. People loved him. That's why he was the most popular sportscaster in the Bay Area, maybe even on the West Coast.

Maybe this *was* a good idea. He obviously still carried a torch for her, and based on the stories Sophia had told about him in the bedroom, he carried more than a torch.

As the phone rang out, amplified by the porcelain acoustics of my bathtub, the three of us huddled close together.

It rang three times, then someone answered. A woman, breathless; then we heard Neil say, "Hey now, come on, gimme the phone," and laugh.

Sophia hung up.

No one spoke.

"Wow," Sophia muttered, then leaned back against Mimi. "I waited too long, didn't I?"

"Maybe?" I allowed.

She gave a great sigh, then blew her nose again. No swearing. No screaming. No tantrums. That would have been preferable to this terrible quiet.

Her phone rang and Neil's face appeared. She threw it across the bathroom, and it shattered on impact.

Mimi squeezed her little arms around her, hugging her close.

"Caroline?" she asked, her voice muffled in the napkin.

"Yeah?"

"I hate your tub."

"I know, sweetie," I said, turning around and leaning back against her. We pressed her together like a panini. I passed her Kleenex while Mimi braided her hair, in my hundred-year-old claw-foot tub with the sun setting in the distance.

When Simon came home and found us, he wisely said not a word. Not even when Sophia slugged him, blamed for someone else's dick.

Before I went to bed that night, I overheard Simon on the phone with a travel magazine he'd worked with for years. He was offered a job in Greenland, highlighting the mineral pools and hot springs that drew thousands of tourists each year. He loved Greenland; it was one of his favorite places because of how beautiful it was.

He turned the job down.

I'll give you a nickel to do something about that pickle.

chapter nineteen

Turns out if you don't deal with a pickle, it just gets more and more sour. Ever seen someone who just bit into a really sour pickle? Yeah, that was my face. More and more often.

A week had gone by, and things were moving steadily along. The Claremont? Almost done. The launch party was in a few days and Max Camden had people flying in from all over to see his latest property. I'd worked with their marketing team to make sure the hotel was photographed for several design magazines, and it was being covered in both local and regional newspapers.

We'd integrated environmental concerns into the hard materials we used in construction, so we had that angle to promote as well. In the land of California, ecofriendliness is taken seriously. But what we were really generating a great buzz about were the ongoing sustainability practices central to our design concept, which had made us stand out to the Camden team. These included little things like barrels for the collection and storage of rainwater to be used in cleaning. The vegetable and herb gardens created for use not only in the on-site restaurant but for the community. The classroom space dedicated for elementary schoolchildren to learn about composting.

And my favorite? The rooftop garden that helped to reduce the heating and cooling costs and turned it into a gorgeous space at nighttime, where we'd planned to host Movies Under the Stars evening all yearlong. Weather permitting.

The community was responding well to what we had created already, and with the opening of the hotel, we hoped the buzz would continue.

With Jillian back at work, I was able to focus once more on taking on new projects and continuing to mentor Monica. Business was booming, and I was actually busier than before. I'd even volunteered to speak to the senior design students in the program at Berkeley, the one that I had graduated from not so many years ago.

I was sitting in Jillian's office, waiting for her. She'd scheduled a planning meeting with me to set up for the summer season. Which was great, because I wanted to make sure I could take some vacation time.

I badly needed some time away. I felt like I'd been underwater for months now, and was hoping to get out of town for at least a week. I hadn't talked to Simon yet; I thought I'd see where things stood with the house. Maybe we could put Rio back on the table?

Simon was ready to put *anything* on the table, especially me. Sexually, he was at critical mass. He needed it; hell, I needed it. But O? Fucking fuckity fucker.

Can't think about that now.

So, back to Jillian and planning. We usually tried to schedule three to five months at a time, allowing us to see spaces for smaller jobs. When we planned like this we usually bounced ideas back and forth, getting inspired and stretching budgets to accommodate the grander concepts we had. I always brought my sketchbook and a stack of colored pencils along; they came in handy.

"Sorry I'm late, got tied up at lunch with Benjamin," she announced as she sailed into the room. I raised an eyebrow, and she realized what she just said. "Oh my, imagine that," she mused, getting a faraway look in her eyes.

I wrote TMI on my sketchbook and held it up to her.

"Let's try this again. I went to lunch with Benjamin, and it was longer than I thought— Oh, I give up!" She threw up her hands. "Anyway, thanks for meeting with me today, Caroline. We've got some things to talk about—exciting things."

I sat up a little straighter. "Is it the Vandertootes? I heard they were thinking about making some updates to that freaking castle, but I never thought they'd actually go through with it. *Please* tell me it's the Vandertootes! I'd kill for that job!"

I got my own faraway look in my eyes, thinking of the huge turn-of-the-last-century mansion. It was the Holy Grail of design jobs in San Francisco. Owned by an incredibly wealthy, eccentric couple, the house took up almost an entire city block and allegedly hadn't been touched by a designer's hands since 1977. And I thought I had it bad with my mauve wallpaper?

My brain began to buckle with all the possibilities, and I almost didn't hear Jillian calling my name.

"Caroline. Come back, Caroline; come back from wherever you are."

"Sorry, got lost in a shag carpet daydream. Anyway, are we pitching the Vandertootes?"

"No, we're not talking about the Vandertootes. I'm making some changes around here. Big changes." She sat back in her chair. "I'm semiretiring."

"Semi . . . retiring?" It felt like the floor had just opened and was threatening to swallow me whole. I pulled out a colored pencil and began to chew.

"Yep." She grinned. Why the hell was she smiling?

"Okay, I totally don't get what's going on here. Do I need to get my résumé together?"

"Why, you planning on leaving me?" she asked, still grinning.

"What the hell is going *on,* Jillian?" I half shouted, my voice sounding more than a little crazy.

She swung her laptop around to face me and started scrolling through pictures. Her and Benjamin under the Eiffel Tower. Her and Benjamin in an alpine meadow. In front of Prague Castle. On a gondola in Venice.

She stopped at a photo of a tall, thin, five-story house in what looked like Amsterdam. "See that house?" she asked.

"Yeah," I said slowly.

"We bought it."

"You're *moving*?"

"Semimoving. Hence, the semiretirement."

"I'm fully confused." I sat back in my chair. "I still have no idea what's going on."

"Though I love what I do, I want more than work. This trip was a totally different way of living, one that I want. We're young, Benjamin's been very lucky financially, and we don't want to be tied down any longer."

"This is being tied down?" I asked incredulously, looking around her fabulous office in her fabulous design firm.

"We'd rather spend our time living our life now than waiting to live it tomorrow."

"You sound like a commercial for fiber bars," I grumbled, getting up and starting to pace.

"This world is too big to not try and see it all."

"And now it's a bladder control commercial," I muttered. "So what *exactly* does semiretired mean?" I asked, turning and heading for the other end of the office.

"We'll be here half the year, and in Europe the other half. We'll have this great base in Amsterdam to travel from wherever we want, have friends come to visit, whatever we want to do. Who knows? I might even start up a little design consulting business over there."

"And what happens here?" Pace. Pivot. Pace.

"I talked to my lawyer and my accountant, and we've come up with a plan that will enable me to keep my hand in the business and oversee things, but let me start stepping back."

"Oversee things? That'll never work!" Pace. Pivot. Pace. "Before you went on this honeymoon you were here all the time, all hours of the day!" Pace. Pivot. Pace. "You're the *Jillian* of *Jillian Designs,* for Christ's sake—how in the world do you think this place is going to run without you half of the year?"

"I'm making you my partner, Caroline."

"You're making me your—whuh?" Pivot, trip, face plant.

Thank Christ I was no longer chewing on that colored pencil.

"**Y**ou face planted? Right in her office?"

"Totally. I ate carpet."

"I knew you weren't just experimenting in college!" Mimi yelled. I was on the phone with her as I drove home that night, still stunned over what had transpired.

"Funny," I muttered, making the final turn and heading down my street. "Then she helped me up, and then she proceeded to make me an offer I felt like I couldn't refuse." And I could kiss Rio good-bye.

"Why in the world would you refuse to be a partner? You're not even thirty, for God's sake; that's incredible to get an offer like that! Although we're getting close to the big three oh, can you imagine? Thank God I'm getting married before then, I can't imagine being over thirty and not being married—"

"Hey! Focus up—we're talking about *my* day. And what the hell, I didn't say I was going to refuse. And what the hell, Mimi, who gets married before they're thirty anymore? Besides, I'm three years away from being thirty! And what the hell is in my *driveway?*"

I yelled, swinging wide before I plowed right into . . ."Let me call you back."

I hung up the phone. Because in my driveway was a white Mercedes convertible. With a red bow on it. What the actual fuck?

I parked the van, hurried up the walkway, opened the door, hurdled over a sawhorse like an Olympian, and dashed into the kitchen. Where I found Simon, on a ladder. Faded jeans. No shirt. Tool belt.

"Um, what's that in our driveway?" I asked. He turned in slow motion, it seemed, and I noticed for the millionth time just how stunning he was. Sculpted arms, broad shoulders, dipping down to that sweet spot just above his bum. And a six-pack that, when he was really worked up, gave up a seven and eight as well. And then that V on either side that just seemed to slip into those jeans.

"Well, it was the funniest thing," he started, climbing down off the ladder and setting down his belt sander. He gave great sander. "I was watching you drive off today in that ridiculous van and I thought, my girl needs some wheels."

"So you bought me a car?" I asked, confused. Brain was not liking some of these words, but every other part of me was liking the walking sex coming right at me.

I couldn't let him just buy me a car, could I? Oooh, he's walking.

He crossed to me, slowly, and I walked backward as he advanced. Before I knew it, I was up against the wall. With a shirtless Wallbanger inches from me.

Now, for the record, when I went vaulting into the house, I was pretty sure what was going on. And what he'd obviously done. And I was pretty sure I was pissed.

Remember that.

Now think about how good he must have looked to make me forget how pissed I was.

"If you don't like the color, we can go down and pick out another one," he said, now only one inch from me. I could feel the heat from his body begin to penetrate mine. Penetrate? Yes, please.

But wait, he can't just buy me a car!

"Yeah, you can't just, just buy me a, ummm," I breathed, my words getting fuzzy as he leaned into me. There was so much tension in my body I was starting to vibrate like a tuning fork.

"Yes, I *can* just buy you a car. It's a gift—get over it," he replied, his brow furrowing as if he couldn't understand why I was giving him shit about this. And at that very moment, I couldn't tell you why either.

I'd never gone this long without having sex with Simon, not when he was in town. It was starting to get to me. And he smelled so good!

"But a car, Simon? I . . . uh . . . what is that cologne?"

"It's polyurethane."

"They should bottle that shit," I breathed, my voice going husky.

"It comes in a can."

"It's really working for you," I moaned as he dipped his head down and dragged his tongue right up my neck.

"I'll keep that in mind," he murmured, burying one hand in my hair.

"Did you do this on purpose? This whole handyman fantasy? The tool belt? The abs? The—holy fuck." I gasped when he took my hand and pressed it against his . . . drill bit.

"You came home early," he explained, thrusting into my hand. "I like early."

"Lucky me." I sighed and dropped my head back against the wall. He took this to be a green light, because within seconds my shirt was ripped, my skirt was pushed up, and he'd wrapped my legs around his tool belt. "I liked that shirt," I protested.

"You really care?" he asked, slipping his fingers underneath the lace of my panties. Slippery already, and he moaned at the first touch.

"Not really." I marveled at his strength; I always had. The idea of being actually wall banged always seemed impossible to me. Until Simon. He was strong without being beefcake. And he could carry my body around like I weighed next to nothing, when that wasn't the case at all.

"How much do you care about these?" he asked, tugging on the waistband.

"One guess." I smirked.

Off.

And then we were off.

We were half naked on the stairs, where he made me walk in front of him. We were lying on the floor, half in and half out of the bedroom. We were on the window seat, highlighted against the bay window.

We were hanging off the edge of the blow-up bed when a particularly powerful thrust made the bed blow up and poof to bits all around us.

And when I rose above him, sliding him inside deep and thick and heavy and oh so deep, my orgasm rocketed through me, bursting behind my eyelids and tingling through my skin, and every single part of me cried out as he grinned from underneath me, saying, "There's my sweet girl."

I exploded again and again, our bodies soaked with sweat and gleaming as I rode him hard and fast, his voice now bellowing his own release. I slumped down across him, panting heavily. He lifted his face to mine, kissed me deeply, and before he coaxed my head back down into the nook, he looked me straight in the eyes and said, "Don't ever shut me out again like that, you hear me?"

He knew.

I kissed him back. "I promise."

He was still wearing the tool belt.

• • •

An hour later we were in the kitchen, heating up yet another microwave dinner. The avocado appliances had been removed, but the new ones not yet delivered. So every meal was prepared in the microwave, then usually eaten on a tarp-covered box.

"Potpie or Salisbury steak?"

"Salisbury steak? Is this 1979?" I asked as he held up two boxes.

"Don't mock the steak, this is the best! My mom used to make these the nights I had soccer practice. Dad complained, but he secretly loved these frozen dinners," he said, plugging in the microwave. It moved daily.

"Potpie for me, then. I don't want to come between you and your steak," I replied, pouring a glass of wine into a plastic cup. I watched him as he moved around the kitchen, thinking how much more freely he mentioned his mom and dad and his childhood these days. That reunion had really changed things. He'd finally created a Facebook account, and was in touch with the apostles almost daily.

Though I'd released a lot of tension upstairs only a short while ago, I could feel it beginning to creep back in.

"So, something a little epic happened at work today," I offered, examining my toes.

"A little epic?" He laughed, peeling back the plastic and popping in our dinners. I dug through our silverware drawer (read, the plastic bag) for forks.

"Well, a lot epic. Did you know Jillian and Benjamin bought a house in Amsterdam?" I eyed him carefully.

"They did? That's great. He mentioned something about that, but I didn't know for sure."

"Benjamin mentioned something as huge as buying a house in mother-flipping Amsterdam, and you didn't tell me?" I asked, incredulous.

"What's the problem?"

"The problem is Jillian is 'semiretiring,'" I snapped, air quoting so angrily I almost got a finger cramp. "And she offered to make me a partner."

"Whoa, what does that mean?"

"I don't know yet. We just talked about it for the first time today and I don't know all the details." I filled him in on the details I did know: the six months she'd be gone, what I'd likely be doing in her absence.

We settled across from each other with our dinners.

"Well, it's obviously a tremendous opportunity for you. Congratulations," he said.

I couldn't figure out what he *wasn't* saying.

"Thanks?" I said, making it a question.

"It's a huge deal. I'm proud of you," he answered, stabbing at his Salisbury steak. He didn't look up at me.

"What's on your mind, Simon?"

"It's just—you've been working so hard. And so much. I thought things were going to slow down a bit for you now."

He only said everything I'd been thinking, but it bothered me to hear someone else say it. I balled up my napkin in my fist. "I can't turn down a huge opportunity like this. No one gets a chance like this at my age. And I love my job—how could I ever say no?" I chewed my potpie angrily. "And as far as us not seeing each other, that's kind of how we've always been, right? We're used to that. I mean, we used to be used to that—you used to be gone more often than you weren't," I said pointedly.

"I'm home now, though," he said back, just as pointedly.

I wanted to scream, *"But no one asked you to do that!"* And then I was horrified that I'd even think such a thought. Who the hell complains about that when a boyfriend's as incredible as Simon? Case in point: the tool belt and the multiple orgasms I just enjoyed not thirty minutes ago.

But I said nothing about that. No, I went right ahead and opened up another jar of pickles. "Plus the money is going to be incredible."

"We've got plenty of mon—"

"*You've* got plenty of money—not me. There's a difference." I pointed my fork at him. "Speaking of which, we need to talk about the car situation out there, while you don't have your hands in my panties."

"What's wrong with the car? Don't you like it?" he asked, truly not getting it.

"I love the car. How could I not? But you can't just buy me a car."

"I think I just did."

"I know, and it's incredibly sweet. And incredibly kind. And incredibly expensive, and I incredibly don't need it," I said, standing up to throw away my potpie.

"Caroline, come on. You loved driving Jillian's car. Don't tell me you didn't."

"This isn't about whether I love the car, Simon. It's about you *buying* me a car."

"Dammit, I wish I'd been outside when you pulled up. I had this whole thing planned out, and I think if you'd—"

"Simon, there's a brand new-car in the driveway with a red bow on it! I think I see what you were trying to do. And it's incredibly sweet, but it's just too much!" I sat back in my chair, at a loss. Was I out of line here?

"I don't get it." He sighed, standing up and throwing his dinner into the trash can. As he turned back to me, I saw total confusion in his eyes. "When I was thirteen, my dad bought my mom a new car. She came home from the grocery store one day, and bam—there it was. Red bow and everything. And she said all the same things you're saying. It's too much, you shouldn't have done this—everything. And my dad kissed her, handed her the keys, and said, 'Let's go for a drive.' And that was it. She gave in." He leaned against a sawhorse, dragging his hands through his hair. "You know why? Because she knew how much it meant to *him*. Everything *he* did was to make *her* happy." His voice deepened toward the end, sounding rough and a little choppy.

His blue eyes were huge, and I could see his jaw clenching. He cleared his throat. Twice. Then he swallowed hard. Shit.

"So keep the car, don't keep the car, whatever. I just wanted to do something nice for you, because I could." His voice wobbled a bit, and I couldn't take it anymore. I was in front of him, pulling him close and wrapping his strong arms around me. I held him tight. A minute later, I felt him hang on. Sweet boy.

What the hell was wrong with me? Picking a fight with my favorite person on the entire planet.

I pulled away just a smidge, placing my hands on either side of his face. I kissed one cheek, then the other, then his eyelids. My lips came away just the tiniest bit damp. I cringed inside, but all he saw was my smile.

I backed away and started pulling on my jacket. "You're leaving?" he asked.

"Yep, and you are too," I said, handing him his coat. "Let's go for a drive."

There is nothing like a Wallbanger grin. It gets me every time.

Just before we left, I heard the telltale rattle of glass. Racing, Simon beat me to the dining room and snatched up Clive, who was halfway through the rusty old casement window again. I checked Clive over, then slammed the window shut.

"I'll keep the car if you fix that damn window," I said, pointing my finger at Simon. He nodded and I turned my finger on Clive. "And if you do that again, you go on catnip detox. Permanently." He rolled his eyes at me.

Then Simon and I went out for a joyride in my new effing convertible, which I admit, was totally sweet. The things you do for love.

• • •

It was late, well after three in the morning. We'd been lying in the dark talking for what seemed like hours. It was as if once I started, I couldn't stop telling him everything.

"And now this thing at work—I mean, how in the world could I ever say no to this? It's such a great thing. If I had to do this on my own, do you have any idea how long it would take to try and build my own business? It's not enough to just be a great designer; there are very talented people who try to go it alone all the time, and it just doesn't work for whatever reason."

He nodded, rolling over to be closer to me as I talked it out. It helped.

"But now, to be offered the chance to basically help run things? Permanently? It feels amazing. That Jillian has that kind of faith in me, you can't know what that feels like. It's a lot more work, sure, but I can do it. I'd have to be crazy not to, right?"

He just showed me his teeth. He knew better than to answer that one.

"And then this house—it's literally a dream come true. Well, it will be when all the work is done. But holy shit, it's overwhelming! Living through a renovation like this is a pain in the ass! And I know it's been tough on you too, being stuck here all day while it's going on. It'll be worth it, though; this place is going to be amazing." I sighed, laying back and curling closer.

I wanted to say the other things, the bigger pickle things, but I couldn't. It was as if I said them out loud, especially in this house, then I was admitting I had a problem. Not "the first step is admitting you have a problem" kind of thing, but—

Actually. Maybe that's exactly what I needed to say. Maybe I needed to give voice to the bigger issue here—the one that was so terrifying that I was even avoiding it in my own head. What *was* my problem?

We met under very unconventional circumstances. We fell in love in the most unconventional way possible. The first time we made love? Conventional. Didn't work. The first time we fucked? Definitely unconventional, what with all the flour puffing and the raisins. Fucking fireworks, baby.

And for a year we lived unconventionally. He was gone, I was here. We traveled together when we could, seeing places and doing things I'd never imagined were in the cards for me. I didn't need spooning every single night; I liked having a bed to myself every now and again. We laughed, we loved, we nooked. And it worked.

Now we were moving closer and closer to a more conventional relationship, which was packed with awesome, no doubt about it. But it was almost . . . too . . . shit. I didn't know what it was. I just knew I needed to say it out loud.

I was once herded—very delicately, but herded nonetheless—toward a conventional relationship. I didn't want that. So at some point I was going to have to share this pickle.

"Keep this between us, okay, mister?" I said, scratching under his chin.

Clive gave a soft meow, and nodded his head toward the stairs. I picked him up and took him back to bed, where Simon was sound asleep in the remains of the blow-up bed.

chapter twenty

I drove my new car into the city the next morning. It generated quite a stir in the office, something I quickly tried to defuse.

I spent the morning with Jillian going over her proposal privately. She didn't want to worry anyone, and of course she didn't want our clients to know until she was ready to announce her semiretirement.

As we went through everything and I saw how it looked on paper, I admit it was a pretty heady thing. I'd continue to run things as I'd done before, essentially taking over the day-to-day operations. And since I made it clear that I still wanted to keep up with my clients and be able to bring in new business, it was also clear that we would need to hire another full-time designer.

She told me to think it over, to talk to Simon about it, but more and more, I realized that this wasn't something I could say no to. I mean, I could, but why would I ever want to?

So before we broke for lunch, I accepted her offer. I was now a partner in Jillian Designs! We shook hands, popped a bottle of champagne, and did everything but throw our hats into the air like Mary Tyler Moore.

Feeling a little on edge, from all the excitement, of course, I left work early and celebrated on my own that afternoon at World of Tile—favorite store ever. It was time to select the all-important backsplash for my kitchen.

Oh my *goodness,* my kitchen. Now here was something I could get excited about. Let me tell you about my kitchen.

White custom cabinets. Glass front on some, a few with open shelving. Deep gray soapstone countertops. Sub-Zero fridge. Two wall ovens—count them, two. And the best part of all?

Viking.

Stove.

Angels.

Sing!

And it gets better. A custom island with an inlaid sink, covered in white Carrara marble with veins of the barest gray and blue. Seating for six on one side, with custom cooling drawers on the other. *Just for dough.*

Deciding how tall to make the island was an exercise in ridiculous. Simon carried me around the house, setting me down on different heights to see what was the most comfortable. I'm sure the entire crew knew exactly what he was up to, and I didn't care. I was getting the kitchen of my dreams, and if my boyfriend wanted to make sure that the counter was a perfect height for sexy times? That kitchen just got dreamier.

It made me smile as I walked up and down the aisles, looking for exactly the right tile. Would it be subway? Would it be a glass design? I didn't know exactly what I wanted until I saw it. And then I turned the final corner and saw it.

Or him, rather.

James Brown was shopping World of Tile. And he was heading right for me.

"Caroline, what a surprise," he called out. Damn, he looked good. He always looked good.

"Hey, James." I smiled as I walked toward him. I hadn't seen him since I finished his design job last year. His apartment was young lawyer chic with an urban flair. "What are you doing here?" I asked as he leaned in to give me a kiss on the cheek.

"Tile, what else?" He laughed.

"Are you remodeling already? That's going to get expensive. I charged you an arm and a leg last year, as I recall."

"I do and you did. And you did a great job. I always tell everyone who my decorator was."

"Not a decora— That's great, James; thanks for helping get the word out," I said. Wasn't going to give him the satisfaction. Not worth the breath it would take me to explain it again. "So, where's the new tile going?"

"Marin, actually. I just bought a house there." He grinned.

"Really, wow, that's great."

"Yep, settling down, just got married. Hey, honey! C'mere, want you to meet someone." He waved toward a woman in the next aisle.

Wife?

"There she is. Come here, sweetie pie, and say hello to Caroline."

"Hello, Caroline," the prettiest girl in the world said to me. Blinking, I looked at Mrs. James Brown. Tall, blonde, young. Beyond pretty. She looked really sweet. "I'm Krissy."

"Of course you are," I said, then coughed to cover it. "It's wonderful to meet you. When did you get married?" I asked James. I felt like I was reeling.

"Just a few months ago. We're newlyweds." He grinned and tucked her into his side as she giggled. "We met at the club. Her father is a client of mine, and the rest was history."

"It happened so quickly, it was just like we were supposed to be together, you know? He proposed just three weeks later. Can you believe it?" She giggled again, showing her ring. It looked like a skating rink.

"I really can't." I smiled, trying to keep my eyebrows from flying right up into my hairline. Too late.

"Well, when it's right, it's right. Right?" James said, and Krissy's answering laughter was like tiny silver bells. He grinned at her and reached over and patted her belly. Which I now noticed was noticeably round. She laced her fingers through his and they held her perfect little round belly together. Krissy was on the nest. James smiled smugly at me.

"How do you know Jimmy?" she asked.

"Jimmy?" I asked. Eyebrows were officially a lost cause; they were on the back of my head at this point.

"Caroline and I used to date when I was in law school, and then we reconnected when she decorated my apartment last year. How's that going, by the way?"

"Fine, Jimmy. Great actually," I said through my teeth.

"Oh, you're a decorator! I love decorating. I took a class last year all about it. I love that tile you've got there. Are you decorating something for a client?" Krissy asked, referring to the black and neon-green geoprint tile I'd inadvertently picked up and was clutching so tightly my knuckles were turning white.

"This? No, just browsing. Actually, I'm looking for myself today. Just bought a house over in Sausalito, so yep. Tile. For my new house."

"Oh, I love Sausalito! Jimmy and I go there all the time. He takes me over for pancakes sometimes on Sunday mornings." Krissy giggled.

James looked at me more closely. "You bought a house? In Sausalito? With who?"

I love that he just assumed that it would have to be *with* someone, that I couldn't have bought something on my own. The fact that I was years away from being able to afford a house in Sausalito on my own was my own damn business.

"Yes, I bought a house. With Simon, actually. You remember him, don't you, Jimmy?"

"That neighbor guy?"

"Yes, that neighbor guy."

"Wow. That's great, Caroline, really great."

"Yes." I nodded firmly. "It is."

"I'm surprised, though. Not what I expected."

"What? Why?"

Krissy had stepped away by now; she'd found a shiny tile.

"You used to tell me no way were you going to live in the suburbs. Never going to settle down," he said.

"I'm not settling down, and for God's sake, Sausalito isn't the suburbs," I snapped, and his eyes danced. He always liked to stir me up. "I'll have you know I'm not settling at all—it's an amazing house. I love it; it's exactly what I always wanted."

"I didn't say settling; *you* did. I said settling down. And really, all I'm saying is you used to say you never wanted—"

"James, shut up!" I said, my face boiling hot at this point. Krissy was prancing back over, and I needed to get out of here. "Congratulations on getting married and everything, and good luck with your tile." I whirled around and ran right into a sales guy.

Throwing back my shoulders, I apologized, then said in a clear voice, "My boyfriend likes to fuck my brains out on our kitchen island. Which tile would you recommend for that?"

God bless him, the guy actually showed me some.

Turns out I was glad for the convertible, because the trail I blazed back over the bridge to non-fucking-suburban Sausalito was infinitely better in a high-performance automobile. Barreling across the bay in a clunky delivery van wouldn't have cut nearly as dramatic a silhouette on the Golden Gate Bridge. Revving the engine as I cut down the tiny streets, I whizzed up onto our street and peeled into the driveway. I got out and slammed the door.

"Caroline?" Simon called out, and I turned. He was standing at the edge of the yard, chatting with Ruth from next door. The neighbor who gave us the keys when we first saw the house.

"Oh, hey there, Simon. Evening, Ruth," I called out in my most neighborly voice. I click-clacked across the driveway, dodging saw-horses and plastic sheeting.

Simon said, "Ruth, you'll be amazed when you see how much progress we've made in that upstairs bedroom. The one you said used to be the sewing room?" He reached out for me and tucked me into his side. "Hey, babe, how was your day?"

"Oh, tip-top." My voice must have sounded off, because he looked down at me questioningly. "Sewing room?" I asked.

"Oh my, yes. Simon was showing me around last week; I can't believe how different it looks already!" Ruth exclaimed.

"It's amazing what you can do when you have a big work crew. So, sewing room?"

"Well, he was showing me the upstairs, and I was marveling over that sweet little room on the second floor—the one that's tucked under the eaves? I told your Simon that even though Evelyn used it as her sewing room, I always thought it would be perfect as a nursery. Don't you think?"

My grin froze as I looked back and forth between them. Simon was sheepishly looking down at the ground. But he was also blush-ing. And smiling. Big.

"Nursery?" I asked through the frozen grin.

"Of course! A cute young couple like you two, I'm sure it's something you're thinking about. I know you career girls these days like to wait, but you can't wait too long, you know. I know it's not for me to say, and heaven knows I sometimes stick my nose in where it doesn't belong, but I—"

I must have made the sucking-on-a-sour-pickle face, because somewhere around "heaven knows" and "stick my nose in," Ruth began to look at me strangely.

I turned without a word and walked toward the house, hearing Simon apologizing to Ruth over the noise that was filling my ears. A chain saw? Tile saw? Tiles—ha!

Inside, I looked around at the chaos. At the three painters on ladders on the first floor. At the two carpenters carpenting in the kitchen. And at the random guy who was sitting on my window seat with his feet up on my dining room table (tarp-covered box), reading a newspaper.

"Excuse me? Can I help you?" I asked over the din.

"You Caroline?"

"I am."

Just then I heard the front door slam and an angry Simon stood in the doorway. "I can't believe how rude you just were to Ruth!"

"You've got to be kidding."

"What the hell, Caroline. Have you lost your mind?"

"You seriously want to do this now?" I asked, gesturing to the obviously listening workmen and the guy with his feet up. "Who are you, anyway?" I asked.

"I'm Fred, here to do your closets."

"Okay, Fred. Let's start in the den." I gestured for him to follow me, holding up my other hand toward Simon to tell him to do exactly the opposite. As I started to open the door, Simon shouted, "Not the den! Clive's in there!"

Too late. Like a feline torpedo, he darted out and ran for the kitchen. I grabbed for him as he sped by, but he wiggled through my fingertips and continued on.

We'd been trying to keep him away from the commotion during the day, letting him out only at night. Usually he stayed in the "sewing room" upstairs, as that room wasn't getting much work done.

"Why the hell was he in the den?" I yelled, trying to follow Clive. He was startled by all the strange men in the house, and was doing his best dodgeball around all of them.

"They were working on the floors upstairs today, so I brought him down. That's why the door was closed," Simon yelled back, diving for him and crashing into a painter. "Everybody fan out," he said, and just like that, Clive now had six strange men chasing him.

"Stop it! Everyone stop, you're scaring him!" I shouted over everyone else shouting at Clive.

Fred made a grab for him, and Clive spun out *Tokyo Drift* style, ran up a ladder, down a ladder, and made for the dining room.

Toward the window seat.

Toward the rusty casement window that never shut tightly.

And went

right

through it.

He was there, and then he was gone.

I got there just in time to see his tail disappearing through the garden wall, into the twilight.

chapter twenty-one

I walked the streets of Sausalito until 2:00 a.m. that night. Jillian and Benjamin came over, so did Mimi and Ryan. Sophia was there. And if Neil hadn't been out of town covering a big game, he'd have been there too.

Armed with flashlights, catnip, and Pounce, we scoured the neighborhood. I went through every backyard I could, crashed through bushes, climbed the secret stairs, and scurried down every pathway in the hills above the seaside town. I could hear my friends calling for him all around, shaking their Pounce cans.

Clive was long gone.

I knew everyone would have stayed out there all night, but when the fog got too thick to see through, and everyone's teeth were chattering, we called off the search. Mimi had stayed back at the house in case he returned, and while she waited she created a Lost flyer with a picture of Clive and my phone number. We'd print them in the morning and hang them up all over town.

I said good night to everyone, thanked them again for their help, and closed the door. And turned to Simon.

"I'm exhausted, so I'm going to head up to bed. I'll be up early tomorrow; I want to get a jump start on getting those flyers up."

"I'll come up with you," he said, starting to turn out the lights.

"Leave that one on," I said when he reached for the dining room light. I could hear the plastic sheeting blowing back and forth over the hole in the window. I'd slammed it shut so hard earlier that I'd broken a loose pane. He nodded and I went upstairs.

My head hurt, my eyes were red and stinging with the tears I'd refused to shed. I plodded up the stairs and stopped at the end of the hall, looking down toward the tiny room at the end of the hall. Under the eaves.

When Simon got to the top of the steps, he stopped behind me. "Caroline?"

I felt him, warm and solid and so close to me. "A *nursery*?" I asked.

"Hmm?"

"You and Ruth were talking about that room becoming a nursery?"

"Babe, it's late. Let's go to bed," he replied, his tone icing a bit. He moved past me and into our bedroom. I followed him, my steps falling harder on the newly refinished floors.

"It is late, but answer my question," I said as he sank onto the new inflatable bed and started taking off his shoes.

"Look. She said something to me about it being a nice room for a nursery, and I agreed. That's it. End of story."

"Wrong. Beginning of story. You want a nursery?"

"Caroline, come on. It's late," he said, starting for the bathroom and yanking his shirt off.

"Hey, come back here," I insisted, following him. "We're not done talking about this."

"I think we are. You're exhausted, I'm exhausted, and you're making a bigger deal out of this than it needs to be," he snapped, kicking off his shoes.

"This is a *huge* deal. Are you kidding me?" I shouted. "You want a nursery and you don't even tell me about it? Yet you're talking with *Ruth* about it? Who seems to have all kinds of things to say on the topic?"

"I *didn't* say I wanted a nursery. Dammit, Caroline, that's not how it happened at all."

"Well, do you? Want a nursery?"

"Sure. Yeah. Of course I do."

The world exploded.

"Don't you?" he asked.

The world exploded twice.

"I don't know! I have no idea! Why in the world do I have to know that right *now*? Tonight?" I asked, my voice beginning to break. It was all too much—the house, the job, the car, the chaos—and Clive.

Brain and Backbone took a deep breath and steeled themselves. Heart couldn't be anywhere near this. "Why the *hell* didn't you fix that fucking window, Simon?"

Silence. The kind of silence where you can hear the words you just said ringing back to you.

We stared at each other across our master bedroom. How the hell did I get a master bedroom? Master bedrooms were something to aspire to, to grow into. Grown-ups had master bedrooms, and I didn't know that I wanted to be a grown-up anymore. I just wanted my cat back.

"Jesus, Caroline, I'm so sorry," he said.

I couldn't look at him. I just couldn't, because I knew I'd cave. And I was too angry to cave; too confused to cave.

I walked away, went downstairs, got my keys, and left.

I went to a diner. It was the only place that was open, and I didn't want to just drive around all night. And also, I wanted pie.

Was it fair to blame Simon for what happened with Clive? Two schools of thought on this one.

Technically, yes, I could blame him. He didn't fix the window that I'd specifically asked him to fix. Had he fixed the window, Clive wouldn't have run away. And right now? It felt good to blame him.

The other school of thought, the mature-adult school, said that there's no way I should even dream of blaming Simon for this. He loved Clive almost as much as I did, and he already felt terrible for what happened. So the right thing to do would be to call him, invite him down for pie, apologize for blaming him, and then band together to find our boy.

I was pissed. And scared to death that I'd never see Clive again.

When it was nearly dawn and there was no more pie, I decided to head home. When I walked out to the parking lot, there was Simon, getting out of his Range Rover and heading straight for me. Turns out I wasn't the only one who was pissed.

"What the hell, Caroline? I've been driving around for an hour looking for you!"

"Get back in the car, Simon. I can't talk about this right now."

"You wanna bet?" he warned, standing in front of my car door.

"I really don't want to do this right now."

"I really don't care," he said, angling his body as I tried to push past him.

"Let me *in*." I could feel the tears beginning, and if I started I wouldn't be able to stop. "It's starting to rain." Dammit, Clive was out in this rain.

"Then we'll stand here in the rain until you tell me what the hell is going on," he said, crossing his arms and planting his feet. Then the sky really opened up, and big fat drops began to splatter everywhere. Yeah, those were raindrops on my cheeks.

"Come on, Simon, let me in," I protested, trying to slip past him again.

"That's funny. I was going to say the same thing," he said, staring down at me.

And that did it. The dam broke.

"It's too much, okay? It's all just too! Fucking! Much!" It was all coming out; I was going full pickle.

"What's too much?" he asked, confused. "And what the hell does a pickle have to do with it?"

I was officially losing my mind. "*Ahhhh!*" I screamed, stamping my feet and punching one hand with the other. "Simon, I can't *do* it all. I literally *can't do* it all."

"Who said you have to? And what exactly is all?"

"I'm not fucking ready to be a full-on grown-up! You want a nursery? Christ, I just want to get laid on a beach in Brazil! You want to stop being a photographer? I just got offered a partnership, and *I can't turn it down*! Because that would be ludicrous." I stalked in a tiny circle, firing every pickle in my arsenal. "You went to one reunion and partied with the apostles, and suddenly, poof! You quit your job. And we bought this incredible house. And now you and Ruth are making plans. And fucking James Brown called me a decorator! Again! And his wife's name is Krissy, and she's got a bun in the oven and I bet their fucking nursery is just precious, so I told him you fuck me on the counter and—"

"Stop. Just stop." Simon grabbed my hands in his and held them down at my sides.

"How in hell can I *ever* be enough? How can I ever be the wife and the mother that your mother was? How can I ever make a home for you as wonderful as the one that you grew up in? How can I be designer of the century and still have time to bake pies?" I wailed, letting out the sheer terror that had been bottled up for months. "And my cat's gone, and I want him back," I sobbed.

"I know, babe," Simon said, crushing me to his chest as I cried it out in the rain. "I know."

Five minutes later we were stuffed into a booth, sitting across from one another. We each had coffee, and I had a wad of snotty paper napkins in front of me. Simon had a face full of questions, but he was still here. So that was good.

"Okay, so . . . wow." He dragged his hands through his hair. "You've got some things that you've been thinking about for a while, it sounds like."

"Yep." I sighed, stirring my coffee.

"I've got some thoughts now, if I may?" he asked.

"Yep," I said, steeling myself for the worst.

"I realize that I might not have had many traditional relationships—but is what happened out there normal?"

I looked up from my fingernail study in surprise, to see the tiniest bit of a smile on his face.

"Caroline, I love the shit out of you. So calm down and just tell me what you need. No more holding back. And then I'll tell you what I need, and we'll figure out how to work it out." He looked down, doubt now crowding out the tiny smile. "At least, I'm hoping we can work it out. If you want to."

"I want to," I said quietly.

"So let's talk about it," he answered.

And so we did.

I let every pickle fly, but without the yelling. It's so much easier to talk when there's no yelling.

It's also easier to talk when you're being brutally honest. And he was too, which I appreciated.

"I can't believe you thought I was quitting my job. I could never stop doing what I do," he said.

"But you canceled all those trips."

"Yeah. But I was always going to head back out on the road."

"But after the reunion, you—"

"You need to understand something. Going back east clarified some things for me, in a good way. I want a home again, and I want a family someday. That's not going to change. And for the record, I'd never have a discussion with Ruth about something like that without first talking about it with you," he said, taking my hand. "There's a lot of things we probably should have discussed before we jumped into this house thing. I just got excited, I suppose. It's something I've missed for a long time."

"I got excited too. And I love the house, don't get me wrong. There are just all these expectations that come with a step like this, and I guess I just got overwhelmed. I knew how much this meant to you, how big a deal this was for you. I just didn't know if I could measure up to what you wanted."

"I ran away from my past for years because it was too hard for me to deal with. Now I'm letting some of the good stuff back in. But the *really* good stuff is all with you, babe. The rest of it is just a pile of bricks. You want to get rid of the house? Done. You want to live in a hut on the beach in Bali? Done."

"I think I said get laid on a beach in Brazil —"

"Done," he breathed, his eyes dancing.

I looked at him, my dream boyfriend.

"I love that house. We're not getting rid of the house," I said, and leaned in. "And I do want a nursery—just not now. Is that okay?" I asked, suddenly very very serious. Jesus, this was big-time stuff.

"It's more than okay. Who said anything about now, anyway?"

When I started to answer, he squeezed my hand and whispered, "Please don't drag poor Ruth back into this."

"I owe her an apology."

"Probably."

"And I owe you an apology."

"For what?"

"For not trusting you enough to tell you what was going on. I should have. I just didn't want to ruin things. Who could complain when things look so perfect?"

"Better to complain than have a fight in a parking lot in the rain, don't you think?"

He had me there.

"I owe you an apology," he said, his brow wrinkling. "You were right, I should have fixed that window."

"Simon, no. I was mad and I never should have said—"

"No, it's my fault. But I'm going to find him, I promise." I nodded, my eyes full again. "C'mere."

I went around to his side of the booth and let him pull me onto his lap. He held me tight, and I kissed him. And then we left to go find our cat.

The next morning we called the Humane Society, the ASPCA, our vet in the city, and even the pet hotel. The word was out. My cat was lost.

Team Clive was out in force all day, traipsing all over the town. We talked to neighbors, made sure everyone knew whom to call if they caught sight of him.

Simon and I walked together as we searched on until dark, holding hands and flashlights and calling his name until we were hoarse. It wasn't the only reason my voice was hoarse; I couldn't stop crying. I tried not to let Simon see, because never had a man felt more terrible about forgetting to fix a window. And when he saw my sadness, it made it worse for him. So I limited my tears to gas station bathrooms and kneeling down to pretend to tie a shoelace over and over again. Stolen moments of panic to keep a strong face. We'd find him. Of course we'd find him.

But then it was the second day. And the third day. Then a week. I spent my nights lying awake listening for the *click click click* of that stupid hangnail, which would mean this was all just a silly nightmare and I'd wake up with Clive curled into my side. I'd listen for an angry caterwaul by the back door that was saying, "Hey, lady, you weren't dreaming. I really did run away, but I'm home now, so let me the hell in—it's freezing out here!"

I watched as the flyers got weatherworn and tattered. We put up new ones. And they got old too.

The worst part was that I kept imagining the worst possible outcomes; it was like my brain was trying to decide what it could handle by showing me phantom glimpses of what might have happened. To see if I could handle it, I suppose.

Clive cold and wet and trying to figure out how to get into a trash can to find something to eat.

Clive approaching a stranger and being chased away with a broom.

Clive flattened out underneath a tree while being circled by two or three other cats. He had no front claws to defend himself with; he was a pampered house cat that slept on a pillow and was served catnip on demand.

I was back at work; I had to. Because being busy helped; because I loved my job; and because the Claremont was finally ready to launch.

The house was really starting to take shape, and things with Simon and me were as well. We talked more than we had before—not just about the silly day-to-day things that made us laugh, but about the real things too. We cleared off more and more of our mental shelving, talking about what really matters and what kind of a life we wanted for ourselves. Don't get me wrong, there was plenty of the laughing and the sexy, because that's who we were. But we were evolving. Imagine that.

I told him I wanted to be the kind of couple that spent *some* of their holidays in some far-off fairy tale. He told me he wanted to be the kind of couple that had all their family and friends over for Christmas—*some* years. I told him I wanted to be the kind of girl who bought her own car. He told me he wanted to be the kind of man who bought his girlfriend a car.

For the record, I won this one. We took the car back and I bought myself a used Mercedes convertible. Silver this time. It was old enough that I could afford the monthly payments, but new enough that Simon was excited to drive it.

We were dipping our toes into Grown-Up Lake, rather than barreling into it like a giant cannonball. I wasn't giving up on Clive, but a resignation began to sink in after two weeks had passed, one that I had to acknowledge. I had to be practical here. In the grand scheme of things, I hadn't suffered an actual tragedy. Only little girls cry themselves to sleep because their favorite pet is gone.

Sure.

chapter twenty-two

I stood in the lobby of the Claremont, my eyes taking in every detail: the check-in desk created entirely of reclaimed wood. The original marble floor restored, polished, and gleaming. The replacement art installation. And the view of the bay as the sun cast its last bit of light over the water, making everything sparkle and shine.

There was a flurry of last-minute activity, with waiters hurrying this way and that, champagne towers beginning to flow, and the earliest of guests starting to arrive. I took a final look around, pronounced it good, and tried to turn my brain from Plan This to Enjoy This. It was time to kick up my heels a bit and dance them across the marble floor.

This entire project had been overwhelming, stressful, gray-hair inducing even, but it had also been the most rewarding, the most fruitful, and the best example of what I could do. And I did it on my own. That's saying something.

And what it was saying now was get a glass of bubbly, toast your damn self, and—holy shit, Max Camden was here! He was early!

I smoothed my dress, took a deep breath, and hurried down the steps to greet him.

"Mr. Camden, good evening."

"Evening, Caroline. Are you ready to show off our little hotel?" he asked, shaking my hand. "I thought I'd come by early and walk the space again, before everything gets too hectic."

"A wonderful idea, sir. Would you like some company?"

"No, thank you. I always do this alone right before we open a new property. It lets me breathe it in a bit."

"Of course," I said, watching as he walked past the reception area and down one of the corridors. It was always a bit tough, turning over a space once it was complete. But this job was done. What would be next?

"Caroline," I heard from behind me, and turned to see Jillian, accompanied by Benjamin.

I greeted her with a kiss on each cheek. "I'm going to vomit. That's normal, right?"

"Perfectly. I'd worry about you if you *didn't* feel like that. Remind me to tell you about the first time I hosted a launch party like this. I'll just say I never used a chafing dish again."

I stifled a laugh, then turned to Benjamin. "Hi, Benjamin," I said, blushing as he leaned in for his cheek kisses. He was just too fantastic looking.

"Caroline, you look lovely as always."

"Hey, babe, why are you so pink?"

I turned and admired Simon. Charcoal gray suit, black tie, clean shaven, wonderful jaw and cheekbones. And a smirk—don't forget the smirk. He knew I'd been school-girling over Benjamin.

"Oh, be quiet," I shushed, letting his strong arms catch me up tightly against him. I kissed his nose and his eyes danced.

"So, do I get a private tour?"

"Semiprivate. I thought I'd wait until the girls and Ryan get here, then I'll walk you around, show the place off a bit."

"It looks amazing so far; I can't wait." He took my hand and squeezed. "So proud of you."

I glowed.

And then I hosted. Guests were starting to arrive more quickly, photographers were milling about, and I needed to make sure that everything went smoothly. I waved to Mimi and Ryan when they arrived, and when Sophia sailed in a few moments later, I took a quick moment for a sip of champagne and an ass slap. I couldn't help it, she looked amazing.

All my friends were there, and when Max Camden proposed a toast to Jillian Designs and more specifically little ol' me, I was glad to have them all here to celebrate with me. It was big-time, baby, and in the big times, you want the people you love around you.

The evening was perfect and lovely, and in between talking with the various newspapers and posing for photographers, I mingled with many of the local business owners, who were delighted to discover that I was now a resident. It was a good feeling, beginning to belong to a community as close-knit as Sausalito. I adored this seaside town, and I could see myself settling in here for years to come.

Settling *in*. Not settling. Big difference.

I laughed with my friends, indulged in more than a glass of champagne, and was almost ready to pronounce the night a success. But while chatting with the mayor about how beautiful the hotel was, and how high expectations were for the new business it would be generating, I saw a certain sportscaster enter the lobby, scan for leggy redheads, and zero in the hottest cellist on the West Coast. Continuing to make small talk while channeling Mimi telepathically (it could work), I watched as Sophia and Neil met in the middle of the lobby. And began to argue. Loudly.

I excused myself from the mayor and swiftly made my way through the crowded lobby, where a production of *Take Me to Petty Town* was taking place.

"I still can't believe you. It's like talking to a brick wall."

"I still can't believe you don't understand that you will never be up against this brick wall again."

"It's like arguing with a child."

"The same child who called you and had to listen to some woman answer the phone? Giggling?"

"My mother doesn't giggle."

"Oh please, you expect me to believe that was your mom?"

"Why do you think I tried to call you back?"

"I don't care. I hate you."

"*Enough!*" I hissed, and grabbed them both by the elbows. Steering them behind the petit fours, I turned them both around and let fly. "That's enough. I'm tired of listening to you two fight; it's just ridiculous. Not here, not now, and not *ever* again. We're all friends, and we're going to continue to be friends, and I'm sick of you two dickheads making it miserable for everyone else! So knock it off—both of you," I snapped.

As I turned to stomp away I heard Neil say, "Jeez, she didn't have to yell at us," which was quickly followed by, "I know, right?" from Sophia.

I caught Mimi trying to muscle her way over to the petit fours, and I told her to leave it alone—no more meddling. She huffed a little, but quickly abandoned her plan when Ryan asked her to dance.

Everyone was dancing. We'd hired a big band to play for the party, old meets new. And as I sipped my champagne in the middle of the gorgeous hotel that I'd designed, I felt a tap on my shoulder. I knew it was him. My skin told me.

"Glen Miller?" I asked, turning around.

"I might have requested it." He grinned. "Moonlight Serenade" spilled over the dance floor, and I let myself be spirited away by my Wallbanger. He held me close, and as moonlight beamed down through the open windows, I sighed in his arms. Content.

Until Monica tapped me on the shoulder and told me we had a problem.

Excusing myself from Simon, I followed her toward the back of the reception area. Her face was beet red and full of apology as she sputtered and stuttered and tried to tell me what was going on. All I could get out of her was "coat closet."

"What's the problem? Is it full? We can use one of the guest rooms on this floor. Just ask housekeeping to bring up— Oh!"

I'd opened the door to the coat closet and saw something I can never un-see. Burned into my retinas forever was the image of Neil and Sophia, on a pile of minks. Going at it like—well, you guessed it.

"*Yes! Yes! Yes!*" Sophia was shouting. She should: Neil was . . . Hmm, how shall I put this?

Ever seen a Clydesdale?

As I say, I can never un-see.

As luck would have it, they "finished" while I stood there, my jaw on the floor next to his jacket and her undergarments. I backed out, slammed the door, and as they afterglowed on the other side, I instructed Monica to keep everyone away for at least five minutes.

And that any cleaning bills should be sent directly to Neil at NBC.

Two weeks later, Simon was back out on the road. Cambodia. He was doing a series on secret cities and hidden temples, buried by centuries of the jungle taking back the land. The photos he was sending back to me were haunting, riveting, and beautiful.

I still had my hands full. After the Claremont opened I finished up the last few projects I had going over there, worked with Jillian on some new office protocols, and then decided to take a few personal days to rest and relax. What I was really doing was putting the finishing touches on the house. I wanted to surprise

Simon when he came home and have it totally ready. Jillian had stopped by to help.

Initially I'd balked at ordering so much new furniture, but Simon kept insisting, "Make it how you want it, and I'll love it. It's just money, Caroline."

Anytime anyone says something like that, you know they've got wads of it. I'd seen a few figures on some of the banking reports when Simon bought this house, and Mother of God, it was a big wad.

Big Wad—what a great name for a band.

So order I did. I aimed to marry my style and his, while honoring the original beauty of the house. Taking my cue from the natural landscape all around, I let the surrounding hillside inspire the palette throughout, especially in the living room. Buttery creams, burnished bronzes, soft muted greens, and splashes of goldenrod made the house cozy. It was made even cozier by the tall stone fireplace where a fire crackled merrily, framed by refinished built-in bookcases stacked high with our collection of books behind the leaded glass doors. And by the bay window perched the customary telescope through which I could see San Francisco.

Windblown Girl on a Cliff with an Orange hung over the original wooden mantel, which now gleamed golden after being rubbed rich with oil. Simon loved this photograph of me, cringing in embarrassment at having my picture taken, orange juice clear on my lips and chin, hair blown out wildly by the Spanish wind. It was his favorite, and he'd insisted that it be displayed somewhere downstairs.

A long, thin custom shelf filled with the bottles of sand Simon had collected was positioned on one wall, with a smaller shelf just below with bottles from our trips together. *Tahoe, Nerja, Halong Bay,* they clustered together to tell the beginning of our story, with plenty of room for the next chapter.

In the kitchen, where marble shone and the counters were

of a very specific height, pots of rosemary, parsley, and thyme sat happily on the windowsill, catching the morning sun. My double ovens stood majestically, ready to bake cookies and pies and zucchini bread until Simon said uncle. So . . . forever.

In a place of honor on its own marble round was my KitchenAid mixer. Stainless steel. Cool to the touch and crafted to perfection. Was there an undermounted lighting fixture directly above it, to make it a beacon of hope and goodness throughout the land? You bet your sweet bippy.

And on a solitary shelf built in the exact center of the wall, a collection of Barefoot Contessa cookbooks were arranged— chronologically, of course. And in a windfall of good fortune, the title page of each one was inscribed *To Caroline. Love, Ina.*

Simon's friend Trevor's wife Megan's friend Ashley's boss Paul at the Food Network had them signed for me. And no one could touch them but me.

Jillian and I walked through the home, adjusting things here and there. Fluffing a pillow. Adjusting a vase. In the living room, I paused to display the final piece. I threw Simon's afghan—which we'd once spent a monumental night under, trying to keep the horror of *The Exorcist* at bay—over the plush chocolate couch. Jillian looked at it quizzically, no doubt wondering why a retro orange and pea-green afghan was the focal point in a room such as this. I looked around at the palette that I'd created, the afghan bringing it all together, and told her, "It was his mom's."

She nodded, and we stood for a moment just taking it all in. It was done, and it was kind of perfect. "Looks great, kiddo. It's really lovely."

"Thanks." I sighed, letting myself really feel the house and all it had come to mean.

"When's Simon coming home?" she asked as we headed back into the kitchen.

"Friday night. I'm glad I could get all this done before. Coffee?"

She nodded and grabbed the cream from the fridge while I poured. "You two want to come over for dinner Sunday night?"

"That's funny, I was going to ask if you wanted to come over here! Be our first dinner guests?"

"We'll be here." She smiled.

We sat down across from each other at the island, and while she added sugar to her mug, I looked at her carefully. I needed to talk with her, and I was hoping she'd still want to come for dinner after I said what I needed to.

"So, Jillian, I need to talk to you about something."

"Hmm?" she asked.

"It's about the partnership," I began.

She smiled sadly. "You're not taking it, are you?"

"How in the world did you know that?" I asked, baffled.

"It was a hunch. So tell me why."

"I'm not turning it down, but I have a proposition for you."

"I'm listening."

And she did. I gave voice to everything I'd been feeling about my job and my work and my place within the firm. In my heart I was purely a designer. I'd enjoyed the business aspects I'd taken over while she was away, but for me it was more enjoyable just to know that I could do those things, and do them well.

I didn't actually want to *do* them. And while I knew I was turning down the Job of a Lifetime, I needed to be strong enough to say no. And here's the important part.

Turning down the job was honestly the only thing I could do. I liked my life, and more important, I liked my *quality* of life.

It wasn't that a man was telling me that I needed to have his dinner on the table at 6:00 p.m. five nights a week. It was that I wanted to cook dinner for Simon sometimes, and not have to work twelve hours the day before to make that time.

It wasn't that anyone was telling me that I couldn't have it all. It was me saying good Lord, no, *I* can't have it all—and why the hell would *I* want to?

I had the life I wanted. And I wasn't afraid to say no to something more.

But I did still want a bigger piece of the action.

So here was my proposal, and it was incredibly simple. I'd take on a supervisory position within the firm, especially when Jillian was abroad. I'd continue to mentor Monica, sponsor new interns, and be the point of contact for all new business. I'd retain my existing clients, take over for some of Jillian's, and be responsible for bringing in new clients. And if Jillian approved, we'd hire an office manager to execute the day-to-day operations. Sure, there'd be long days when there were projects on a deadline, but no more working Sundays. No more leaving the office after 9:00 p.m.

There'd be plenty of time for running my own show later on, if I changed my mind. For now, this was exactly what I wanted to do.

"Wow, you've really thought this out," she said, flipping through my proposal. Which I'd prepared with graphs and charts, and bound in a colored folder. And hidden behind the cookie jar, until I was ready to bite this bullet. "You sure about this?"

"Yes. It's what I want, as long as you're okay with it." I held my breath.

She paused for so long I had to let it out and take another. Had there always been tiny little stars in the kitchen?

"Okay, Caroline—I think we can work with this. Let me show this to my accountant, but I see no reason it can't work," she said at last.

I finally breathed deeply. No more tiny stars.

Friday night, eight fifty-seven. I busied about the kitchen, getting things ready. Simon had texted me when his plane touched down, and he was on his way home from SFO. He'd been flying for hours and I knew how wiped out he'd be. But I still wanted his homecoming to be something special.

As I took one more pass through the first floor, making sure everything was in its place and looking spick-and-span, I paused by the dining room. Specifically, the window that was cemented shut. I winced every time I saw it and the deep windowsills that Clive barely got to enjoy before he ran away.

The sound of Simon's key in the front door brought me back from my thoughts and I sprinted into the kitchen.

"Babe? I'm back. Hey, when did you— Whoa!" I heard him say as he became aware of his surroundings.

When he left ten days ago, there was still chaos. The end was in sight, but it was still rough. But now it was complete. And tranquil. And filled with the smell of homemade chicken soup.

I listened to his steps through the house toward the kitchen, where I turned from the stove to meet his eye. Wearing his favorite apron, over clothes this time, mind you, I smiled at my sweet Simon. Worn out and travel weary, he was still the most gorgeous man I'd ever seen. Three days' worth of lovely scruff roughed up his face, accenting the most chiseled jaw this side of Mount Rushmore. Piercing blue eyes sparkled at me—he did love me in an apron.

"Everything looks . . . I mean, it's all so—" Shrugging his shoulders, he laughed. "I'm speechless. It's perfect, babe."

"Just wait till you get my bill. You hungry?" I asked, then ladled him a bowlful of chicken soup made with rich broth, eggy noodles, and packed with vegetables. I could see him sniffing the air and I smothered a laugh as he walked toward the breakfast nook where I'd set a table for two.

He sat down, and as soon as I'd set the bowl in front of him he pulled me onto his lap. "You've been busy," he murmured.

I felt that sandpaper jaw on the side of my neck and my skin immediately pebbled. "I wanted to make it nice for you," I replied, then leaned close to his ear. "Welcome home, Mr. Parker."

His hold on me tightened. He ate his soup and drank his milk with one hand, not wanting to let go of me with the other. As he ate, we talked comfortably about everything and nothing at all. Afterward, he showered off the travel while I cleaned up.

After he explored all the rooms that I'd put my finishing touches on, we found ourselves in our master bedroom. We chatted about weekend plans as he towel dried his hair, and I watched him walk around the room in his pajama bottoms. Best thing ever.

"We're having Jillian and Benjamin over for dinner Sunday night, if that's cool with you?" I asked.

He pulled down his side of the duvet. "Sure that's fine. Is everyone else coming too?"

"Mimi and Ryan are with her parents in Mendocino, and Sophia and Neil haven't come up for air yet." I smirked as we fluffed the comforter at the foot of the bed. Those two were back together like nobody's business. They'd barely left their bed.

We flipped pillows, turned down blankets, and I sighed when I saw the sheets. Egyptian cotton, thread count in the millions, and gleaming white.

"Hey, speaking of Mendocino, you'll never guess who called me the other day. Remember Viv Franklin?"

"Fishnets and tattoos? From your reunion?"

"Yep. She might be moving out here—to Mendocino."

"Really? Wow, that's great. I thought she was pretty set up back there with her . . . security guard company?" I asked, gesturing for the throw pillows. I had a special way I stacked them in the armchair at night.

"Security software, babe. She designs security software for companies. I'm not sure what she'll do; she's still thinking about it. Some great-aunt died, a big house on the shore was willed to her—I don't know all the details. But she might move out here and take over the house."

"That could be amazing!" The pretty brunette was a fun mix of badass and sweet; she'd kept Simon on his toes. I'd liked that about her.

"I told her to let us know when she made a decision. She doesn't know anyone out here, and we could go help her out," he said, throwing me the last pillow.

"Oops, don't throw that one!" I set it delicately on top of the others. "Yes, for sure. Just let me know when she knows for sure."

"Um, it's a throw pillow, right?" he asked.

"Hey, mister, if you knew how much of your money I spent on that pillow, you wouldn't be so quick to throw it."

"So I really don't want to know how much this set me back, do I?" he asked, nodding his head toward our new bed. A bed of our very own that had no history of past others. The California king was large enough to accommodate both his snoring and my flailing, and it was simple and elegant, with a massive, well-padded headboard.

"It's better if you just let me do my thing and not ask questions," I sassed, now crawling across the bed on all fours, making sure my pink nightie swished in all the right places.

"I like it when you do your own thing. Especially when you let me watch you do it," he breathed, raising an eyebrow when I turned to show him my ruffles. He pressed his body against mine, his shower-warm skin heating me as much as his words.

"Tonight I'd much prefer you touching me. With your hands. And that mouth," I instructed as I perched on top of him. I'd positioned the bed so that when we cuddled up, we could see the lights twinkling over the bay.

"Look at that view," I whispered.

"I'll say," he muttered from below, peeking up my nightie. The next thing I knew, he'd wiggled me right out of my coordinating panties.

And with the ruffled bottoms abandoned, the pink nightie pushed up around my shin, Simon brought it on home.

And goddamn it if he *still* didn't find a way to bang that headboard.

Thump.

"Be careful . . . Oh, God . . . That's new paint . . . Oh, God."

"You want me . . . to be . . . Christ, Caroline . . . Careful?"

Thump thump.

"Well . . . maybe . . . a little . . . Oh, God . . . Simon!"

"There's my Nightie Girl."

Thump thump thump.

"Simon?"

"Hmm?"

"You awake?"

"Huh-uh."

"Just wanted to tell you I love you."

"Mmm."

"Caroline?"

"Hmm?"

"I love you too."

"Mmm."

"Caroline?"

"Mmm?'

"You wanna fool around?"

"If I said no, what would happen?"

"I'd lie here next to you, thinking dirty thoughts."

"Would they be about me?"

"They're always about you."

"Really?"

"You're literally my fantasy girl."

"Okay, it's getting a little thick in here."

"Speaking of getting thick . . ."

"Oh, kiss me, you big Wallbanger."

I sat straight up in bed, body tense and hyperaware. Why had I suddenly awakened? At . . . 2:37 a.m.?

Simon was curled up on his side of the bed and snoring.

The hair on the back of my neck prickled, my skin pebbled into gooseflesh. Something was up, but I couldn't put my finger on . . . Wait, what was that?

I ran to the window, peering out into the darkness. Nothing. Nothing out of the ordinary. I crept back into bed, not able to shake the feeling that— Oh my God.

"Simon!" I ran out the door and down the hallway. The tiniest hint of a thought took hold on a corner of my heart as I raced downstairs, hearing Simon call out to me as his feet hit the floor. I flew down the stairs, across the living room, and into the dining room. I plastered myself against the window, searching, not wanting to let this feeling take hold, because I couldn't bear it if it wasn't . . .

Meow.

It can't be. He doesn't know where—

Meow.

"Simon!" I screeched, and he ran around the corner, brandishing a bat.

"Is someone in the house?" he asked, whirling about.

I burst through the patio doors with Simon right behind me, hope now blooming fully and out of control.

There, on the grass right below the dining room window, was Clive. Licking his paws like it was no big thing.

"No way," Simon breathed behind me as I sank to the ground and opened my arms.

Clive washed his ears like he had all the time in the world, then slow-trotted over to me with the biggest kitty grin I've ever seen. He tried to play it cool, but I could hear his rusty purr from four feet away. Tears ran unabashedly down my cheeks as I sobbed on the ground, holding my cat. Who purred and purred and purred. He was skinny, he was muddy, he was cold, and he was back.

Simon crouched next to me, running his hand down Clive's back as I held him tightly. "There's a good boy," he said over and over again as he stroked him and scratched between his ears. When Simon's eyes met mine, they were shining brightly.

I stood finally, clutching my Clive. I cooed and coddled him, telling him that he could never do that again or I'd kill him, and he could eat steak all day, every day. Simon just smiled as Clive head butted him, eager for more boy-on-boy lovin'.

As I turned to take him into the house, he suddenly dug in with his hind legs and jumped from my arms, running back into the bushes he'd disappeared into weeks ago.

"No! Clive, no!" I yelled.

But before I was even two steps across the lawn, he poked his head back through. He came out, and seemed to shrug his left shoulder. And there, materializing almost out of nowhere, was another cat. A tiny calico, round and plump, with the sweetest face I'd ever seen. She rubbed against Clive, then sat companionably next to him.

"Who's your friend, Clive?" I asked, kneeling down once more, not wanting to spook them.

Simon crouched next to me and whispered in my ear, "Looks like our boy's got himself a girlfriend."

Clive nodded at Simon wisely, and I smothered a laugh.

"I always thought it might be fun to have another cat. Think she belongs to anyone?" Simon asked.

"How do you know she's a she?"

"Oh, she's a she, all right," he responded, and Clive once more nodded at him. If they were closer, a paw bump would have occurred.

Then Clive seemed to shrug his right shoulder, and there before us was a third cat. Beautifully adorned with the most gorgeous long, dark silver fur, she had gleaming green eyes and delicate features. She nuzzled against Clive, who was now flanked with stunning pussy.

"I can't believe it," I breathed as Simon chuckled.

"I suppose having three cats isn't that different from having two, right?" he asked.

"Simon, come on. We can't have three cats. I mean, can—"

Clive cleared his throat as if to say *ahem*.

And then, pushing her way in between the plump calico and a grinning Clive, there was a third newcomer. She was playful, bumping into the other cats and throwing herself on the grass in front of Clive, rolling on her back and letting out the funniest little sounds. If I didn't know better, I'd swear she was giggling.

"Fuck me—he's got himself a harem," I swore, and Simon could no longer contain his laughter. As I shook my head, Clive tended to his ladies. Herding them together with a bap and a nip, he paraded them across the lawn and, one by one, into the house. Just as Clive crossed the threshold, he turned back to us. Leaning against the door frame, he regarded us with all the love in his eyes a cat can muster. Which is a lot. And when the catcalls started inside, he winked.

"Oh for God's sake," I said through a face-splitting grin. Still laughing, Simon extended his hand to me.

Linking my fingers through his, we walked across the lawn and into our home, where Clive and his ladies were waiting.

epilogue

The Last Word

I set off on patrol, keeping track of all the new smells in this new territory. It was different from the last time I'd been here. Shinier in some ways, baubles scattered here and there for me to play with. Two shelves filled with curious bottles for me to knock off. Thoughtful. I'd investigate that further tomorrow. Tonight I had other things on my mind.

For weeks I'd roamed the wilderness of this strange city, boxed in by mountains on one side and water on the other. Water I'd learned the hard way not to trust, fast moving and not drinkable. *Saltwater,* the captain of the Highsteppers called it. The Highsteppers were the wisest gang of street cats I'd come across in my travels, tough but fair. Not at all like the Whisker Sours, who were just mean.

I'd been offered membership in the Highsteppers, which was a great honor that I appreciated. But I knew which side my Pounce was buttered on and I knew the Feeder must be looking for me. I scoured the hillsides, searching for the home I'd accidentally run from.

Here's the truth, which no cat wants to admit. We long to be

outdoors; we long to run and jump and prance and play. But . . .
and here's the secret . . . *you can't let us out.*

Because we can't always find our way back.

I was one of the lucky ones. I never gave up. I knew how much
the Feeder must be missing me, and I couldn't have that. But then?
I found the ladies. Or rather, they found me . . . But that's a story
for a different day.

I knew my people would be so happy to see me, they'd not
deprive me of my new lady friends. Now those ladies were safely
tucked into a pallet constructed of blankets underneath the coffee table. The Tall One had originally put the bed right out in the
open, but I tugged it under the table, knowing my ladies were used
to sleeping under more cover. That's the difference between being
smart and being street-smart. The mean streets of Sossa Leeto had
taught me that.

I continued to check the perimeter, monitoring a tree branch
that was making an unpleasant scratching sound against a window on the east side. Not an immediate threat, but I'd keep my
eye on it. I made my way into the dining room, facing down the
window that had led to my greatest and most harrowing adventure
of my nine lives. I tested the repair; it seemed solid. I gazed at the
outside, which had always seemed so big and beautiful and full of
excitement. It was.

But now, as I turned to look out over this quiet space, *inside,*
full of nooks and crannies to nap and bathe and run and play, I
realized that this was a great adventure as well.

I truly was wise beyond my ears.

Chuckling at my own joke, I left the window and made my way
upstairs. As I passed my ladies, I could hear their deep breathing;
they were sound asleep. I'd tuck myself in with them soon. I had
a spot on the back of my neck that needed cleaning, and it was so
much easier to group bathe.

Entering the room of the Feeder and the Tall One, I regarded their sleeping forms. Nothing had changed while I'd been gone, I was pleased to see. The Tall One was curled into a ball on one side, the Feeder sprawled out like a starfish. I'd seen one of those in the *saltwater*.

Jumping onto our bed, I sat on the pillow between them, wanting a moment with my people. Stretching out so that my front paws rested on the Feeder's forehead, my back paws touching the Tall One's chin, I at last relaxed.

I was home.

Caroline didn't hear things "go bump in the night"—
she heard things go *thump* in the night.
And it was always her neighbor's headboard . . .

Read an excerpt from Alice Clayton's
USA Today bestselling novel

wallbanger!

chapter one

"Oh, God."

Thump.

"Oh, God."

Thump thump.

What the . . .

"Oh, God, that's so good!"

I scrambled up out of sleep, confused as I looked around the strange room. Boxes on the floor. Pictures propped against the wall.

My new bedroom, in my new apartment, I reminded myself, placing both hands on the duvet, grounding myself with the luxurious thread count. Even half asleep, I was aware of my thread count.

"Mmmm. . . . Yeah, baby. Right there. Just like that. . . . Don't stop, don't stop!"

Oh boy . . .

I sat up, rubbed my eyes, and turned to look at the wall behind me, beginning to understand what had woken me up. My hands still stroked the duvet absently, catching the attention of Clive, my wonder cat. Butting his head under my hand, Clive demanded to be soothed. I stroked him as I looked around and oriented myself in my new space.

I'd moved in earlier that day. It was a gorgeous apartment: spacious rooms, wood floors, arched doorways—it even had a fireplace! I had no clue how to actually build a fire, but that was neither here nor there. I was aching to put things on the mantel. As an interior designer, I had a habit of mentally placing things in almost every space, whether it belonged to me or not. It drove my friends a wee bit mad at times, as I was constantly restaging their knickknacks.

I'd spent the day moving in, and after soaking in the incredibly deep, claw-foot tub until well past prune, I settled myself into bed and enjoyed the creaks and squeaks of a new home: light traffic outside, some quiet music, and the comforting click-click of Clive exploring. The click-click came from his hangnail, you see . . .

At 2:37 I suddenly found myself gazing stupidly at the ceiling, trying to figure out what had awakened me, and I was startled as my headboard moved—banged into the wall was more like it.

Are you kidding me? Then I heard, very distinctly:

"Oh, Simon, that's so good! Mmm. . . ."

Aw, jeez.

Blinking, I felt more awake now and a little fascinated by what was clearly going on next door. I looked at Clive, he looked at me, and if I wasn't so tired I'd have been pretty sure he winked. *I guess someone should be getting some.*

I'd been in a bit of a dry spell for a while. A very long while. Bad, rapid-fire sex and an ill-timed one-night stand had robbed me of my orgasm. She'd been on vacation for six months now. Six long months.

The beginnings of carpal tunnel were threatening to set in as I tried desperately to get myself off. But O was on seemingly permanent hiatus. And I don't mean Oprah.

I pushed the thoughts of my missing O away and curled up on

my side. All seemed quiet now, and I began to drift back to sleep, Clive purring contentedly beside me. Then all hell broke loose.

"Yes! Yes! Oh, God. . . . *Oh, God!*"

A painting I'd propped on the shelf above my bed fell off and rapped me soundly on the head. That'll teach me to live in San Francisco and not make sure everything is securely mounted. *Speaking of mounted* . . .

Rubbing my head and cursing enough to make Clive blush—if cats could blush—I looked back at the wall behind me again. My headboard was literally banging against it as the ruckus continued next door.

"Mmm . . . yes, baby, yes, yes, yes!" the loudmouth chanted . . . and concluded with a contented sigh.

Then I heard, for the love of all that's holy, *spanking.* You can't misinterpret the sound of a good spanking, and someone was receiving one next door.

"Oh, God, Simon. *Yes.* I've been a bad girl. Yes, *yes!*"

Unreal. . . . More spanking and then the unmistakable sound of a male voice, groaning and sighing.

I got up, moved the entire bed a few inches away from the wall, and huffed back under the duvet, glaring at the wall the whole time.

I fell asleep that night after swearing I would bang back if I heard one more peep. Or groan. Or spank.

Welcome to the neighborhood, Caroline.

chapter two

The next morning, my first official morning in my new place, found me sipping a cup of coffee and munching a leftover doughnut from yesterday's moving-in party.

I wasn't quite as awake as I'd hoped to be during unpacking-palooza, and I silently cursed last night's antics next door. The girl was plowed; she was spanked; she came; she slept. The same for Simon. I assumed his name was Simon, as that was what the girl who liked to be spanked kept calling him. And really, if she was making up a name, there were hotter ones than Simon to be screaming out in the throes.

The throes . . . *God, I missed the throes.*

"Still nothing, huh, O?" I sighed, looking down. During month four of the Missing O, I'd started to talk to my O as though she were an actual entity. She felt real enough when she was rocking my world back in the day, but sadly, now that O had abandoned me, I wasn't sure I'd recognize her. *'Tis a sad, sad day when a girl doesn't even know her own orgasm*, I thought, looking wistfully out the window at the San Francisco skyline.

I unfolded my legs and padded to the sink to rinse out my coffee mug. Placing it on the rack to dry, I pushed my light blond hair back into a sloppy ponytail and surveyed the chaos that surrounded me. No matter how well I planned, no matter how well I labeled those boxes, *no matter how often I told that idiot moving guy that if it said* KITCHEN *it did not belong in the* BATHROOM, it still was a mess. Luckily I had the foresight to set aside my favorite coffee mug the night before.

"What do you think, Clive? Should we start in here or the living room?" He was curled up on one of the deep windowsills. Admittedly, when I was scouting new places to live, I always looked at the windowsills. Clive was fond of looking out on the world, and it was nice seeing him waiting for me when I came home.

Right now he looked at me and then seemed to nod toward the living room.

"Okay, living room it is," I said, realizing I'd spoken only three times since waking up this morning, and every word uttered had been directed at a pussy. Ahem. . . .

About twenty minutes later Clive had started a stare-off with a pigeon and I was sorting DVDs when I heard voices in the hallway. My noisy neighbors! I ran to the door, almost tripping over a box, and pressed an eye to the peephole only to see the doorway across the hall. *What a pervert I am, honestly.* But I made no attempt to stop peeping.

I couldn't see very clearly, but I could hear their conversation: the man's voice low and soothing, followed by unmistakable sighing from his companion.

"Mmm, Simon, last night was fantastic."

"I thought this *morning* was fantastic too," he said, planting what sounded like one helluva kiss on her.

Huh. They must have been in another room this morning. I hadn't heard a thing. I pressed my eye back to the peephole. *Dirty pervert.*

"Yes, it was. Call me soon?" she asked, leaning in for another kiss.

"Of course. I'll call you when I'm back in town," he promised, swatting her on her bottom as she giggled again and turned away.

It seemed she was on the short side. *Bye-bye, Spanks.* The angle was wrong for me to see this Simon, and he was back in his apartment before I could get any sort of sense of him. *Interesting. So this girl does not live with him.*

I hadn't heard any "I love you"s when she left, but they did seem very comfortable. I chewed absently on my ponytail. They'd have to be, what with the spanking and all.

Pushing thoughts of spanking and Simon from my mind, I went back to my DVDs. *Spanking Simon. What a great name for a band.* . . . I moved on to the Hs.

An hour later I was just placing *The Wizard of Oz* after *Willy Wonka & the Chocolate Factory* when I heard a knock. There was scuffling in the hallway as I approached the door, and I stifled a grin.

"Don't drop it, you idiot," a sultry voice chided.

"Oh, shut up. Don't be so damn bossy," a second voice snapped back.

Rolling my eyes, I opened the door to find my two best friends, Sophia and Mimi, holding a large box. "No fighting, ladies. You're both pretty." I laughed, raising an eyebrow at them.

"Ha-ha. Funny," Mimi answered, staggering inside.

"What the hell is that? I can't believe you guys carried it up four flights of stairs!" My girls did not do manual labor when they could get someone else to do it.

"Believe me, we waited outside in the cab for someone to walk by, but no luck. So we schlepped it ourselves. Happy housewarming!" Sophia said. They set it down, and she fell into the easy chair by the fireplace.

"Yeah, quit moving so much. We're tired of buying you stuff." Mimi laughed, lying down on the couch and placing her arms over her face dramatically.

I poked at the box with my toe and asked, "So what is it? And I never said you had to buy me anything. The Jack LaLanne juicer was not necessary last year, truly."

"Don't be ungrateful. Just open it," Sophia instructed, pointing at the box with her middle finger, which she then turned upright and displayed in my general direction.

I sighed and sat on the floor in front of the box. I knew it was from Williams-Sonoma, as it had the telltale ribbon with the tiny pineapple tied to it. The box was heavy, whatever it was.

"Oh no. What did you two do?" I asked, catching a wink from Mimi to Sophia. Pulling at the ribbon and opening the box, I was pleased as punch with what I found. "You guys, this is too much!"

"We know how much you miss your old one." Mimi laughed, smiling at me.

Years before, I'd been given a great-aunt's old KitchenAid mixer after she passed away. It was more than forty years old but still worked great. Those things were built to last, by God, and it had lasted until just a few months ago, when it finally bit it in a big way. It smoked and went wonky one afternoon while mixing a batch of zucchini bread, and as much as I hated to do it, I tossed it out.

Now, as I stared into the box, a shiny, new, stainless-steel KitchenAid stand mixer staring back at me, visions of cookies and pies began dancing in my head.

"You guys, it's beautiful," I breathed, gazing with delight at my new baby. I lifted it out to admire. Running my hands over it, splaying my fingers to feel the smooth lines, I delighted in the cold metal against my skin. I sighed gently and actually hugged it.

"Do you two want to be alone?" Sophia asked.

"No, it's okay. I want you to be here to witness our love. Besides, this is the only mechanical instrument that will likely bring me any pleasure in the near future. Thanks, guys. It's too expensive, but I really appreciate it," I said.

Clive came over, sniffed the mixer, and promptly jumped into the empty box.

"Just promise to bring us yummy treats, and it's all worth it, dear." Mimi sat up, looking at me expectantly.

"What?" I asked warily.

"Caroline, can I please start on your drawers now?" she asked, stutter-stepping her way toward the bedroom.

"Can you start doing what to my drawers?" I answered, pulling my drawstring a little tighter around my waist.

"Your kitchen! I'm *dying* to start placing everything!" she exclaimed, running in place now.

"Oh, hell yes. Have at it! Merry Christmas, freak show," I called as Mimi ran triumphantly into the other room.

Mimi was a professional organizer. She'd driven us crazy when we were all at Berkeley together—with her OCD tendencies and her insane attention to detail. One day Sophia suggested Mimi become a professional organizer, and after graduation, she did just that. She now worked all over the Bay Area, helping families get their shit together. The design firm I worked for sometimes had her consult, and she'd even appeared on a few HGTV shows filming in the city. The job suited her to perfection.

So I just let Mimi do her thing, knowing my stuff would be so perfectly arranged, I'd be astounded. Sophia and I continued to putz around the living room while Sophia admired my DVD collection, laughing over DVDs we'd watched throughout the years. We paused over each and every Brat Pack movie from the eighties, debating whether Bender ended up with Claire once they all went back to school on Monday. I voted no, and I further bet she never got that earring back. . . .

Later that night, after my friends left, I settled on the couch in the living room with Clive to watch reruns of *Barefoot Contessa* on the Food Network. While dreaming of the creations I'd be whipping up with my new mixer—and how one day I wanted a kitchen like Ina Garten's—I heard footsteps on the landing outside my door, and two voices. I narrowed my eyes at Clive. Spanks must be back.

Springing from the couch, I pressed my eye against the peephole once more, trying to get a look at my neighbor. I missed him again, only seeing his back as he entered his apartment behind a very tall woman with long brown hair.

Interesting. Two different women in as many days. Manwhore.

I saw the door swing shut and felt Clive curl around my legs, purring.

"No, you can't go out there, silly boy," I cooed, bending down and scooping him up. I rubbed his silky fur against my cheek, smiling as he lay back in my arms. Clive was the manwhore around here. He would lie down for anyone who rubbed his belly.

Returning to the couch, I watched as Barefoot Contessa taught us all how to host a dinner party in the Hamptons with simple elegance—and a Hamptons-size bank account.

A few hours later, with the imprint of the couch cushion pressed firmly into my cheek, I made my way back to my bedroom to go to sleep. Mimi had organized my closet so efficiently that all I had left to do was to hang pictures and arrange a few odds and ends. I quite deliberately removed the rest of the pictures from the shelf above my bed. I was taking no chances tonight. I stood in the center of the room, listening for sounds from next door. All quiet on the western front. So far, so good. Maybe last night was a one-time thing.

As I got ready for bed, I looked at the framed pictures of my family and friends: My parents and me skiing in Tahoe. My girls and me at Coit Tower. Sophia loved to take pictures next to anything phallic. She played the cello with the San Francisco Symphony, and even though she'd been around musical instruments all her life, she could never pass up a joke when she saw a flute. She was twisted.

All three of us were unattached at the moment, something rare. Usually at least one of us was dating someone, but since Sophia had broken up with her last boyfriend a few months ago, we'd all been in a dry spell. Luckily for my friends, their spells weren't quite as dry as mine. As far as I knew, they were still on speaking terms with their Os.

I thought back with a shudder to the night when O and I had parted ways. I'd had a series of bad first dates and was so sexually frustrated that I allowed myself to go back to the apartment of a guy I had no intention of ever seeing again. Not that I was averse to the one-night stand. I'd made the walk of shame many a morning. But this guy? I should have known better. Cory Weinstein, blah blah blah. His family owned a chain of pizza parlors up and down the West Coast. Great on paper, right? Only on paper. He was nice enough, but boring. And I hadn't been with a man in a while, and after several martinis and a pep talk in the car on the way, I relented and let Cory "have his way with me."

Now, up until this point in my life, I'd shared that old theory that sex was like pizza. Even when it's bad, it's still pretty good. I now hated pizza. For several reasons.

This was the worst kind of sex. This was machine-gun style: fast, fast, fast. This was thirty seconds on the tits, sixty seconds on something that was about an inch above where he should have been, and then in. And out. And in. And out. And in. And out.

At least it was over quick, right? Hell no. This horrible went on for months. Well, no. But for almost thirty minutes. Of in. And out. And in. And out. My poor hoohah felt like it had been sandblasted.

By the time it was over, and he yelled, "So good!" before collapsing on top of me, I had mentally rearranged all my spices and was starting on the cleaning supplies under the sink. I dressed, which didn't take that long as I was still almost fully clothed, and departed.

The next night, after letting Lower Caroline recover, I decided to treat her to a nice long session of self-love, accented by everyone's favorite fantasy lover, George Clooney, aka Dr. Ross. But to my great regret, O had left the building. I shrugged it off, thinking maybe she just needed a night away, still experiencing a little PTSD from Pizza Parlor Cory.

But the next night? No O. No sign of her that week, or the next. As the weeks became a month, and the months stretched on and on, I developed a deep, seething hatred for Cory Weinstein. That machine-gun fucker. . . .

I shook my head, clearing my O thoughts as I crawled into bed. Clive waited until I was situated before snuggling into the space behind my knees. He let out one last purr as I turned out the lights.

"'Night, Mr. Clive," I whispered, and fell right to sleep.

Thump.

"Oh, God."

Thump thump.

"Oh, God."

Unbelievable. . . .

I woke up faster this time, because I knew what I was hearing. I sat up in bed, glaring behind me. The bed was still pulled safely away from the wall, so I felt no movement, but there was sure as hell something moving over there.

Then I heard . . . hissing?

I looked down at Clive, whose tail was at full puff. He arched his back and paced back and forth at the foot of the bed.

"Hey, mister. It's cool. We just got a noisy neighbor, that's all," I soothed, stretching my hand out to him. That's when I heard it.

"Meow."

I cocked my head sideways, listening more intently. I studied Clive, who looked back as if to say, "T'weren't me."

"Meow! Oh, God. Me-yow!"

The girl next door was meowing. What in the world was my neighbor packing to make that happen?

Clive, at this point, went utterly bonkers and launched himself at the wall. He was literally climbing it, trying to get to where the noise was coming from and adding his own meows to the chorus.

"Oooh yes, just like that, Simon. . . . Mmmm . . . meow, meow, *meow!*"

Sweet Lord, there were out-of-control pussies on both sides of this wall tonight. The woman had an accent, although I couldn't quite place it. Eastern European for sure. Czech? Polish? Was I seriously awake at, let's see, 1:16 a.m. and attempting to discern the national origin of the woman getting plowed next door?

I tried to get ahold of Clive and calm him down. No luck. He was neutered, but he was still a boy, and he wanted what was on the other side of that wall. He continued to caterwaul, his meows mixing with hers until it was all I could do to not cry at the hilarity of this moment. My life had become a theater of the absurd with a cat chorus.

I pulled myself together, because I could now hear *Simon* moaning. His voice was low and thick, and while the woman and Clive continued to call to each other, I listened solely to him. He groaned, and the wall banging began. He was bringing it home.

The woman meowed louder and louder as she undoubtedly climbed toward her climax. Her meows turned into nonsensical screaming, and she finally yelled out, "*Da! Da! Da!*"

Ah. She was Russian. For the love of St. Petersburg.

One last thump, one last groan—and one last meow. Then all was blessedly silent. Except for Clive. He continued to pine for his lost love until four in the mother-loving morning.

The cold war was back on. . . .

Can feisty redhead Grace Sheridan deal with dating
Hollywood's hottest leading man?

Find out in

the unidentified redhead

seven

Gladstones is one of my favorite restaurants, and although it's a little touristy, it is perfectly so. It's an indoor/outdoor restaurant, with a worn plank floor and concrete benches to sit on outside. We chose to do just that and had the entire Pacific Ocean as our back-drop. I ordered a beer immediately, which Jack joined me in as we continued to smile at each other. I know I must have looked like I had fallen asleep with a hanger in my mouth. I could still feel his hand on my arm, as if it had burned an impression there.

Our server came back with our beers and we ordered our lunch. As it was a seafood restaurant, I always got the she-crab soup and the coconut shrimp. I'd been ordering the exact same meal for years. Even when I came back to visit, I'd always made Holly bring me here.

After the waitress finished taking our order, Jack raised his glass of Killian's Irish Red to me and said, "To Van Morrison, and the sexiest version of 'Into the Mystic' I've ever heard."

I blushed a little. "Well, thank you, sir. But you're really in for it if a U2 song ever comes on the radio. I *really* lose control when I'm subjected to the Edge," I admitted.

"Then here's to me finding more ways to make you lose con-trol," he said with a wink.

Before I had a chance to respond to that little nugget, I saw his eyes flick up behind me. I turned and noticed two women, a little older than I was.

They wore the same expression Sara had had on that morning. They began to approach us, both giggling, neither wanting to be the first to say something. Finally the bolder of the two stepped forward and said, "Hi, are you Joshua—I mean, Jack Hamilton?"

Jack began to blush. "Yes, how are you? What's your name?"

"Wow, I'm Claudia and this is Michelle. Can we take your picture?" she said, the words rushing out.

"Sure, of course." He smiled as they clicked away merrily.

The two women paid no attention to me. They were caught up with their Super-Sexy Scientist Guy.

He chatted with them for a moment and then the forward one said, "Okay, enough. We'll let you eat your lunch now. Thank you so much. You don't know how much we, uh, I mean, uh, bye!" she said, turning quickly and then marching them away. They had barely made it twenty feet before the screaming started.

"Oh, man, you really are a hit with the womenfolk, huh?" I said teasingly, taking a sip of my beer. When it was just us, it was easy to forget that all signs were pointing toward his becoming a major Hollywood player by the end of the year.

"Yeah, yeah. The ladies, they love me. What can I say?" He shrugged.

"Ass," I stated as the server brought our lunch. Then we slipped back into our comfortable conversation; the fans had broken the tension that had been building all day.

After sitting and watching the waves for a while, we decided to take a walk before heading back into town. Malibu was always beautiful, and this day was no exception. I held my sneakers in my hand as we walked along the water.

"This is really a Hallmark moment, Hamilton. Walking on the beach, sunshine, seagulls. It's freaking perfect," I said, glancing at him sideways. He was silhouetted against the horizon, the sun highlighting the exquisite planes of his face.

"If it was perfect, we'd be rolling around on the sand together, kissing like mad."

I stopped walking and looked him straight in the eye. Then I lay down on the sand and began to roll myself back and forth.

He closed his eyes and tilted his face to the sky. "Fucking nuts girl." He sighed.

"Come on, big boy, get down here and roll with me. I can't do this alone. Someone will call *Baywatch* and tell them there's a girl on the beach having some kind of fit." I snickered, getting covered in sand.

He laughed and joined me, wordlessly rolling back and forth, making me laugh harder. It was so easy, so authentic, being with him. We both stopped and lay on our backs next to each other, looking up at the sky. The sun was out over the ocean, and I raised my legs. Pointing my toes, I covered up the sun with my feet and then moved them apart to reveal it again. I did this several times; then I noticed that Jack was staring at my legs. My yoga pants had slid down toward my thighs, revealing the skin above my knees.

Thank you, God, for the shaving reminder this morning.

He rolled onto his side, propping his head up on his arm. I looked at him but kept my legs in the air, toes pointed toward the sky.

"See something you like, Hamilton?" I retorted, waiting for his witty response.

"You have no idea," he answered softly, his tone making my legs stop in midair. I brought them back down and rolled onto my side as well, facing him.

"I have some idea," I said, dragging my fingers through the soft sand between us. His hand began to creep toward mine. My heart stopped, then started up again, crazy fast.

"I was wondering about something," he said.

"Yes?"

"Did you know that U2 is one of my favorite bands? I mean, like, my absolute favorite band?" His hand was dangerously close to mine.

"How would I know that? I just met you." I picked up a shell to examine it, then put it down, my hand landing closer to his.

"There's all kinds of stuff on the Internet about me lately. You could've Googled it." He moved his hand closer still. I could feel the energy between us begin to hum again.

"I think that you should go Google your*self*, Brit boy. I'm not interested in Googling you." I frowned, moving my hand back toward me slightly.

"Are you intrigued by film stars?"

"Not particularly," I lied. *Only one . . .*

"Are you intrigued by romantic beachside gestures?" he asked, moving his fingers an inch away from mine.

"Nope," I said, barely breathing. His eyes were actually smoldering as they looked deeply into mine. A lock of hair had fallen over his forehead, and I was aching to sweep it back.

"Would you be intrigued by a film star who wanted to kiss you?" he breathed, his fingers finally touching mine.

I paused as I looked back at him, almost panting. "Mm-hmm," I whispered.

Holy shit. Holy shit. Holy shit.

His eyes were heavy as he gazed into mine. He closed the distance between us and his hand came up to my cheek. I could feel the sand clinging to his fingers graze my skin, and it was cool. I was not.

As he cupped my face gently all I could focus on were the perfect, soft-looking lips that were about to touch mine. I moved in to meet him and then closed my eyes. I knew if I had to look at him right now, I would lose my nerve.

I felt him even before I felt his lips. The energy between us shifted, and I knew exactly where he was. The instant before his lips met mine, I could tell that he was about to deliver a kiss that would stun me stupid.

It was soft and sweet. It was tentative and deliberate all at the same time. He kissed me once, then again, and then a third time, with a little more *grrr* behind it. His scent, which up until now I had somehow overlooked, filled my nostrils. He smelled like sand and sun and sweat, mixed with chocolate and smoke. Not icky cigarette smoke, but warm pipe tobacco and chimney smoke all rolled into one.

Sweet Jesus, he's like your own personal s'more.

The combination was seriously messing with my head, as well as making my pants feel excessively confining. We broke apart and just looked at each other. I inclined my forehead to rest against his. Frankly, I needed the prop—I was spinning.

He smiled first, and I answered back with my own.

"Did you feel that?" he asked, concern crossing his face.

"Yeah, I felt it. You too?" I answered, flirting back.

"No. I mean, yes, obviously I felt that—but didn't you feel *that* hit your head?" He began to grin broadly.

"What are you talking about?" I asked, raising my hand up to my hair.

"Grace, a seagull just shit on your head," he stated, beginning to shake.

"*What?*" I shouted, springing up to run in circles.

Of course *a seagull shit on my head.*

His laughter rang out down the beach.